BLUE-COLLAR
ROMANCES

Crew's Ship Affairs:
Merging Cultures and
Romance Aboard Ship

BOB OJALA

CREW'S SHIP AFFAIRS
Copyright © 2021 Bob Ojala

Library of Congress Control Number: 2021922085
Paperback ISBN: 978-1-955090-20-9
E-book ISBN: 978-1-955090-21-6

Published by The Unapologetic Voice House
www.theunapologeticvoicehouse.com
Scottsdale, Arizona
Edited by: Amma Twum-Baah

Cover Design and Interior Format

DEDICATION

To the working men I have known and worked with, particularly those in the maritime industry.

They are hard-working and dedicated to their jobs and are also great role models for their children. On the Great Lakes, they have spouses who put up with their long absences and understand their sailor's dedication. The sailors on Cruise Ships have an unbelievable dedication to their duties, and you need to thank them for keeping you safe when you take a cruise vacation.

Together, they keep the marine industry moving, and our country's heavy industry and infrastructure alive and healthy, or the cruise industry safe.

They are a diverse group of men and women, of all races, creeds and sexual lifestyles, who cooperate and take care of one another. They work together to feed their families, and when needed, they "have your back" as well as their co-worker's welfare.

ACKNOWLEDGEMENTS

In my previous novels, I explained how important an Editor can be to an author, and I know it may have sounded overly dramatic. I gave a lot of credit to my Editor, Nicole Amma Twum-Baah!

This third novel had a much more complicated story to tell, because of the mixture of Great Lakes and ocean cruise ship stories. The stories in my mind appeared on the written page, but may not have been real well organized. Amma again performed her magic, and the stories began to flow properly with her help, and were vastly improved.

Once again, Amma, I cannot thank you enough!

PROLOGUE

—

BILL HEARD THE shower running and looked at his watch. It was six-thirty the next morning. He threw off the covers and gasped. He was naked. It had obviously been a wild night, but he could not remember the details. His genitals ached. He looked on the floor, there were three used condoms there. He only remembered using one.

Just then, Vicky came out of the shower, naked. A bit lacking in the chest department, Bill thought. Otherwise, a nice body.

"Good morning sunshine," Vicky said, greeting him. "About time you wake up. You were great, by the way."

"Well, if we do this again, I'd rather not drink so much so I can remember how good a time I had," Bill responded, looking at Vicky, at his naked body, at the floor, then back at Vicky.

"I have another free night on Thursday. If you're better without the drinks, I'm all for that," Vicky chided.

"I'd better get back to my cabin," Bill said. "I have to meet the others for breakfast at eight. By the way, what's with all the condoms?"

"Don't worry. I'll explain on Thursday. Keep you curious, so you come back."

He quickly threw on his clothes but couldn't find his underwear.

"I'll find them later and let you know," Vicky told him.

As Bill left the room, Vicky caressed Bill's groin, saying, "Can't wait until Thursday, Billy boy."

Bill noticed no one had switched the coffee pot on the night before. He had never had an experience like this in his life. He wasn't sure if he enjoyed it, and at this point, it was scaring the hell out of him.

As Bill sobered up, he started thinking about the evening, or as much of it as he could remember. Maybe if he stayed sober, this could be a really great experience. He never thought he would learn about sex from a young girl like Vicky, but he was willing to let her teach him.

On the way down the crew hallway, Bill reached for his wallet; everything seemed to be there. Hans was wrong, he thought.

CURT

MEETING BOB EVERS

MY JOB WITH Strauss Marine Construction had started just over two years ago. My experience with ship-handling, which I had gained from twelve years in the Coast Guard, led me to a job with the uncle of my old high school sweetheart, Lois Strauss. Although it wasn't part of my plan, I could see that Bill Strauss was using me as part of his management team, because he had no family to help him with the business. I didn't mind because I appreciated how Bill was treating me. Bill's philosophy was to treat his employees like family, and this resulted in extremely high employee retention, compared to most similar marine construction companies. And now, married to his niece, Bill considered me to be family.

Originally, I had only wanted to be a tugboat captain and had reached that goal, but management duties were becoming a constant happening. I liked people, and this gave me a way to meet many new and interesting characters, other than just the crews I worked with.

Once Lois and I married, and I adopted Lois's 10-year-old son, I could tell that Bill was depending on me to help him find new captains and crane operators, and to look at tugs, crane barges, and stone scows, which Bill wanted to purchase, expanding his growing business.

Rising water levels on the Great Lakes had created a demand for shoreline protection, which Bill's operation was well suited for.

Back at our Toledo job site earlier that spring, Bill Strauss had told me that I would spend a couple months on the big tug, the 118-foot Samantha B, so I could sit for my 300-ton master's license. After several rotations on the *Samantha B*, Bill then sent me to Chicago, where he had purchased another smaller tug, a 75-footer, plus two more stone scows.

In Chicago, I was meeting Bob Evers so that he could do a condition and valuation survey of the tug and the two barges for our insurance underwriters. Bob was a naval architect and marine surveyor; he had started his own business inspecting ships all over the world. I first met Bob in Tampa, Florida, while inspecting a new tug that Bill Strauss was buying. He met us again in Norfolk, during our delivery of that tug back to the Great Lakes. Bob told me he had worked in nearly sixty countries, doing everything from simple pre-purchase inspections, like he was doing for Bill, but also investigating tanker explosions, accidental deaths, and one of the most amazing jobs he had was making environmental audits during over 160 cruises on large passenger cruise ships.

Every time Bob was with us at a shipyard or during a tug ride up the lake, the crew would ask Bob to relate one of the many amazing stories he shared with the tug crews. Bob said he had written down many of his cruise ship stories, which he emphasized, were not sea stories. Sea stories are based on true events, but the storyteller occasionally embellishes them, at least a little, to keep the listener's attention. Bob swears that his stories are true, only changing some names. I had met Bob's current wife, Jody, as well as his ex-wife, Chris, who were both very good friends, and Jody vouches for the validity of Bob's tales because she was a participant in most of them. Bob had even mentioned to me that he and Chris's youngest son was born after he and Jody were married. He said he'd explain how that occurred, at a later time and kept saying, "But that's a story for another time."

"And the two wives are still good friends?" I asked him that time.

Again, Bob just said, "Later. You won't believe that story."

I asked Bob if he wanted to make the trip up Lake Michigan with me, to deliver these new vessels. I knew that despite all of Bob's ship-riding time, he was not wild about being on the water, because he was prone to motion sickness. However, maybe due to all the wine he had drunk that night, Bob agreed to make the trip, as long as he could be back in Chicago by the following weekend. Seeing this was only a two-day trip up to the Soo from Chicago, I told Bob that shouldn't be a problem.

The evening before I was to leave with my tug and two barges, I was sitting outside a South Chicago restaurant near Chicago Drydock, with Bob, Lonnie Willis, my Toledo work-mate captain, two of my deckhands, and a new captain we had just hired out of Chicago when Bob asked if we wanted to hear one of his stories. We were in Chicago inspecting a new tug in need of minor repairs. None of the others had heard any of Bob's stories.

"Sure. Why not?" I said, responding to Bob's question. "We have all day tomorrow to recover before our run up the lake. No use going back to the tug early tonight."

"Okay then. But just so you know, most people I've told this to think I made it up," Bob said. "But ask my wife. She saw it happen."

"I'll remember to ask Jody," I answered, smiling, knowing this was going to be another good one. I was getting to like his stories. I'd never traveled outside the

United States and never been on a cruise ship, so Bob's experiences working in over fifty countries and having audited cruise ships on over 160 weeks aboard them, made for some rather amazing stories. I was learning about people and places I might never otherwise experience in my life.

Because Bob got to know the various cruise ship crews after many repeat visits, they started to open up to him about their personal lives. You can imagine that life for crew members creates some very unusual social circumstances upon occasion. It comes from spending about four to eight months on a ship, away from their homes and families. Life on those ships, below the passenger decks, does not fit the mold of what landlubbers consider normal. Even though Bob said he'd spent a lot of his life aboard tugs and ships, he never spent anything close to those four or eight-month contracts aboard, and he wasn't surrounded by all those women from all over the world, while on tugs, cargo ships and tankers. That created a vastly different atmosphere.

However, Bob said some of the craziest events involved the non-crew members. The crew may be having unusual relationships with other crew members, but they were more civilized in their dealings with one another. Every cruise ship has a brig, the marine term for a jail, and the brig is seldom used for the crew. The crew has rules, both written by the company, and unwritten amongst themselves, but not the same can be said for passengers.

"Just listen to the news for crazy cruise ship problems," Bob began. "Everything from throwing their wife overboard, to suicide! I had landed a contract with an environmental contracting company, which was auditing the pollution prevention equipment and record-keeping for a fleet of large, passenger cruise ships. I was hired because of my familiarity with the engine room equipment and records, such as Oily Water Separators and the Oil Record Books, which the Coast Guard keeps a close eye on.

I had met the other team members at a couple planning meetings, but this story started on our first cruise, from Miami to Aruba and back. We were then flying back to Curacao for a second cruise. The story ends on our third cruise which started in Los Angeles. That may seem confusing, but it will make sense as the story progresses.

And by the way, these cruise ships were medium-sized, with 2500-3000 passengers, with about 450 crew. They weren't small, but they also weren't the newer, 5500 passenger mega-ships, which have as many as 1000 crew members.

This story happened on one of our cruise ship auditing assignments. Bill Taggart was one of our fellow auditors. None of us had much cruise ship experience at that time, having just started the project. There was Bill, me, Sam, and Jody, we were a crew, a team. Some of us were having marital problems, due to our nomadic lifestyles, but we were still married and trying to work on our relationships. None of us fooled around while on these cruises. But Bill, Bill was single, around thirty-five, and he liked to head off on his own after dinner. He didn't feel any social connection to Jody, Sam, or me. He told others that he liked working with us, but we otherwise seemed old and beyond our ages. That sorta' hurt my feelings a little when I heard what he said about being old. And by the way, Samantha, whom we all called Sam for short, was divorced, so we had two women and two men on the audit team, including me.

Bill first started hanging out in the ship bars after dinner but found that most people were older, and he found no single women to talk to, other than 60-year-old widows. So, one night he decided to attend a show in the ship's theater. He hadn't realized that the shows included a team of men and women dancers, all of whom were young and good-looking. Remember, none of us were experienced cruisers.

One afternoon, during a break between crew interviews, Bill was walking near the theater when he heard singing. Surprised and curious, he entered the theater and sat in the back row. He watched and listened intently to the rehearsal, quite amazed by their talent. Not too long after, he heard a feminine voice behind him.

"Passengers aren't allowed to be in the theater during rehearsals," the voice said.

"Well, I'm not really a passenger," Bill answered, turning around to see who she was.

"Are you a crew member?" she then asked.

"No, I'm actually a contractor."

"In the shops?" she continued.

"No, I'm sorry. I'll explain. We're auditing records and conditions in the engine room, garbage room, and places like that." Bill explained.

"Oh, I see. No wonder. I've seen you around, and you never seem to have a lady with you. You also seemed too young to be cruising on this ship," she said with a slight laugh.

"You got that right," said Bill. "Even the people I'm working with are boring. I don't know what to do with myself at night."

"Well, seeing as you're a contractor, maybe we can invite you to hang with us when we have a night with no show. What's your name? I'm Veronica, but here they call me Vicky. It sounds better for the shows. My mother would hate them doing that."

"My name's Bill."

"Okay, Bill. Let me ask the group and see what they think."

Vicky ran up on stage, waited for a break in the

rehearsal, and then spoke to the other performers while pointing toward Bill. She then "literally" bounced back to Bill.

"Bill, you're in, if you want to be. The others would love to meet you. We have no show tonight, so can you meet me in the main crew hallway, down on deck one. About six-thirty? Let's meet around the main embarkation door. The passengers will all be aboard by then."

"Fantastic," said Bill. "I'm really looking forward to some energetic company for a change."

That afternoon, after the crew interviews were done, Jody said they would meet for the early seating dinner, as usual, to discuss the day's findings.

Bill then asked, "Would you mind if I skip dinner tonight? I have some things to attend to. I can catch up on any changes or problems at breakfast."

"No problem, Bill," said Jody.

As Bill walked away, Jody looked at Sam and me, and said, "That's strange. I wonder what he's up to?"

I answered, "Bill just doesn't click with us socially. That's okay. Let him have a break."

Bill went to his cabin, showered, and changed into something more casual, and was waiting in the crew hallway fifteen minutes early, not wanting to miss Vicky. Hans Nilsen was walking down the hallway, and seeing Bill, walked up behind him.

"Are you lost, Bill? I thought you three had a dinner meeting every night."

"Oh, Hi Hans. I begged off tonight. I needed some younger companionship, and one of the showgirls invited me to hang with them tonight."

"I see," said Hans. "Can I warn you about the showgirls, though? The crew calls them, young trouble. They're not like the crew; being contractors. Many of them are fresh out of school, still trying to break away from over-protective mothers, and some are looking for a quick husband. They don't make much money on these contracts, so they're always looking for a sugar daddy."

"Warning registered, Hans. Thanks. I'll be careful."

Just then, Vicky came bouncing down the hallway. She walked up to the two men, threw her arm around Bill's arm, and started to walk away.

Bill turned to Hans, with a smile on his face, and said, "See you tomorrow, Hans."

"How do you know that guy, Bill? We all think he is a stick in the mud."

Bill explained how he worked with Hans on this contract, but quickly changed the subject.

"So, how many performers are on board? Are you a dancer or a singer?" Bill asked.

"Our troupe is just eight, but there are some special artists in the show, like tonight. We don't count them because they're older and don't hang with us much. The magician guy is weird. The trapeze act is a man and wife from Brazil, so they don't even talk with us."

"And what about you?" Bill reminded her.

"Oh, yeah. We all dance and sing, but only the better singers get a solo. I'm rehearsing a solo, so maybe I can sing it in the show by the end of my contract. I'm really excited."

"And how long have you been performing?" asked Bill.

"This is my first contract. I spent two years studying dance and voice in college when one of our graduates came to school recruiting for this troupe. It sounded exciting to perform on a cruise ship, and when she chose me to be in her group, I left school. My Mom was not happy."

Bill was about to ask more questions, but Vicky pulled him through a doorway and into a space he had not seen before. It was a small lounge, with a wet bar on one end and several leather sofas along the walls. The middle of the floor was open, and two couples were dancing. One of the couples was two guys.

A tall thin man, about thirty, said, "Welcome to the performer's lounge. The crew doesn't like us hanging with them, so we put this place together ourselves. Make yourself at home. If you want something to drink, just leave a few bucks. It's the honor system."

Vicky went straight to the bar and asked Bill what he was drinking.

Bill saw a bottle of vodka, and a bowl of half-melted ice, so he poured a half-glass. Vicky poured herself nearly a full glass, turned to Bill, and said, "I think three bucks should cover it."

Bill smiled and dropped three dollars into the jar. Then he went over and tried to talk to the other members of the troupe, but Vicky came over a few seconds later, obviously wanting his attention. They finished their drink together and Vicky wanted to dance. Bill was starting to enjoy her company.

They danced to two songs and Vicky went back to the bar and poured two full glasses of vodka.

"I think we'd better leave four bucks for this round," she said to Bill.

Before the night was over, Bill was totally sloshed. He told Vicky he needed to get some coffee before he left, or he'd never find his cabin.

"Tess and I have a coffee pot in our room," Vicky said. "Come on. I'll make a pot."

Bill started for the door as Vicky said goodbye to the others. Then she led him down the hall to her room. There were two single beds, one on each side of the room, and the room was strewn with clothing. Vicky started a pot of coffee and told Bill to have a seat. The only chair in the room was covered in clothes, so Bill sat on the edge of the bed.

Vicky walked over to Bill, faced him, and sat on his lap, wrapping her dancer's legs around his waist. Then she began kissing Bill's neck and caressing his back, pulling his shirt up. Before long, his shirt had been pulled over his head. Vicky unwrapped her legs, pushed Bill backwards onto the bed, and started to take off his pants.

"Won't your roommate be back soon?" Bill said.

"I told Tess to get lost," Vicky said. "I do the same for her."

THAT Thursday, the auditors had been invited to eat dinner with the chief engineer, and after dinner was over, we all stood around talking to the chief, who was a great guy, living in Denmark.

As soon as the chief started shaking hands, Bill got in front of him, shook his hand, thanked him, and said he was sorry and needed to leave.

"No problem," the chief said.

Then Bill headed to the crew's main hallway where Vicky was waiting.

"Got worried you weren't coming, Billy boy. What happened?"

"Had dinner with the chief and the other auditors. Boring evening. So, what is the plan for tonight?"

"Maybe a couple drinks in our lounge, but I don't want you drunk tonight. You said you'd be amazing if you weren't drunk."

"Well, actually, I said I might remember what a good time I had if I wasn't sloshed. You were the one who hoped I could do a better job."

They both laughed, so Bill expected this was going to be a great night. They went to the entertainer's lounge, and Bill saw the same people he'd seen earlier in the week. Everyone greeted him like they did the last time, but several seemed even friendlier than they had been during his previous visit.

After a couple of quick vodkas, which Bill purposely spilled, Vicky grabbed Bill by the arm and led him to the door, and down the labyrinth of corridors to her room.

As soon as Vicky had Bill inside, she started disrobing him. Bill was getting excited fast. He let Vicky pull off his pants and undershorts, and she pushed him back onto the bed. Then Vicky slowly took off her clothes, as she danced in front of him and straddled him on the bed.

At that moment, there was a knock on the door. "Come in!" Vicky yelled.

Bill was shocked when two guys and another young girl walked into the room.

"What's with this?" Bill asked.

"Oh, don't worry," Vicky said. "They were here last time, but you just don't remember. Toby and Josh get excited watching us, and they do their boy-stuff on the other bed. Lindsey here, she'll join you and me later, if you have anything left. Are you okay with that? No rough stuff. Just group sex. Okay?"

Now Bill began to understand where the other condoms from the last time had come from, though he wasn't sure who had used them.

"Okay. As long as there's no rough stuff, and I don't want to be part of the boy-stuff. I'm not into that."

"Promise," said Vicky.

"I'll watch them, but I'm not into that either," Lindsey said. "I just want you after Vicky warms you up."

Bill knew it was going to be a night to remember!

"I'm leaving the details to your imagination," Bob Evers said. "I think you get the picture."

SHIP CHANGES

LOS ANGELES

———◆———

W E LEFT THAT ship after our audit, and a few
weeks later, we were boarding another ship in Los
Angeles. This was after my trip to New Zealand," Bob
continued. "The audit company was introducing several
new personnel into the audits, to be sure that they had
a sufficient number of trained personnel to cover the
ship audits, especially seeing their people also had other
projects they needed to cover.

Being the outsider, I had learned to watch for reactions from the other three auditors, and I noticed a very
disappointed look on Bill's face when Jody informed us
that two new auditors, Leslie Bowles and Amber Cole,
would be joining us in LA. Funny, I thought, especially
because Jody had told me that Bill and Amber had a
developing relationship, which Jody thought was getting serious.

I arrived at the hotel where we were meeting the evening before the cruise. Jody was in the lounge waiting
for the rest of us to arrive when I walked in.

I had already met Amber at a training session in Miami
before the first audit, but that was just socially. Just like
Jody and Sam, I was impressed by Amber's knowledge
and professional attitude. But I had not heard about Leslie Bowles before.

"So, tell me a little about Leslie," I said to Jody after settling on a stool next to her.

"Leslie Bowles is from our Seattle Office. The company management is attempting to have personnel available on both the East Coast and West Coast, not only to save expenses but to have trained personnel for this project, located only a few hours away from either Miami or Los Angeles. Leslie has been with us for about three years and has a waste disposal background, like Sam. She is well-liked in the company, and I'm happy she was available. I recommended her to the main office, and they freed up her schedule to make this audit. Leslie can take some of the West Coast audits, and Amber can cover the cruises from Miami."

Before Jody could give me more info on Leslie, Bill and Amber arrived. Bill had picked Amber up from LAX and seemed happy to have Amber with us, I thought. Maybe I had misread his disappointed look when he first heard that she would be joining us on the next cruise.

A few minutes after we all got reacquainted with each other, Leslie walked into the lounge. She was an attractive, young black woman, and I guessed her age to be around thirty-five. She had that same, confident attitude I had come to appreciate in these auditors. When she entered the hotel lounge, all heads turned, because her presence took over the room.

Leslie walked up to the team and greeted them. She had met none of them before, but she said, "This sure looks like a group of auditors. I assume you're my colleagues? Hi! I'm Leslie Bowles."

As the men started to rise from their chairs, Leslie said, "Oh, just stay seated. We're working together, and I'm the new guy. No formalities needed here."

I was immediately impressed. How does this company keep finding these strong, professional women? Working in the maritime industry, where women seldom had such roles, I was enjoying these ladies, and it sure was nice to work with people who weren't swearing constantly, like the sailors I was used to.

"So, what's the plan?" Leslie asked. "Sorry I'm a little late. Traffic from LAX to San Pedro was terrible, and the taxi finally got off the 110 and took the Coast Highway down. That's slow, but a nice drive. I prefer flying into John Wayne when coming to the LA area, but nothing worked for our schedule."

"Gosh, no problem, Leslie. Most of us just got here, and we were just catching up. It's been a couple of weeks since the last audit, so we haven't moved beyond personal stuff yet."

"We haven't even spoken before, Leslie. With me out of Miami, I don't normally get out west. How long have you been with the company?" Amber asked Leslie.

"I moved over three years ago from a small, Seattle-based, waste disposal company. I wanted to get more into the consulting side of things. It's been a great move."

Bill then said, "If you remember, Leslie, we worked together at that Wilmington refinery job, just down the road from here."

Leslie responded, "Oh, sure Bill. I remember."

Jody and I looked at one another. We both noticed the change in tone when Leslie recognized Bill.

We held our meeting at the hotel that night and headed for the ship the next morning.

THE BACKGROUND STORY

—

A FTER OUR FIRST full day on the ship, we had our normal meeting over dinner, to compare notes and discuss plans for the next day. We met our wonderful environmental officer, named Bridget. Bridget was a good-looking, fiery redhead, Canadian Maritime Academy graduate with her 600-ton master's license. She was the type of redhead people tell you to watch out for because of their temper. Being just a hair over five-foot-three, she wasn't physically threatening, but when she got that look on her face, the crew knew she was upset, and something was going to happen. Bridget knew how to handle people, get their attention, and make them feel better about their jobs and their responsibilities on board the ship.

She had become bored with captaining small ships in Quebec and Ontario, even running a fireboat for a while, and later went back to college to pursue a bachelor's degree in environmental science. She had her act together, and we enjoyed working with her. She had been a captain on a Canadian flag, Great Lakes tanker, and then became a Great Lakes pilot, taking foreign flagships into the Great Lakes, through the Welland Canal, on the St. Lawrence Seaway.

As the group left dinner, Jody saw Bill grab Amber by the arm and head toward the shops. This reminded her that she needed to talk with Leslie.

"Hey, Leslie. Would you have time for a chat?" Jody asked. "I need to talk with Bob first, but I'll call you when Bob and I are done. Where will you be a little later?"

"I'd love to talk," Leslie answered. "I have a bunch of questions after today. I'll be in my cabin. I want to look over those protocols before tomorrow. Just call my room, 412."

"Great. Would you mind coming to my room? On the first night at sea, all the public spaces are jammed with passengers. I'm just down the hall, in cabin 418."

"Works for me," Leslie answered. "Call me when you're ready."

After dinner, I saw Jody talking with Leslie, but then Leslie left.

"I guess you saw Leslie's reaction to Bill yesterday?" I said to Jody when I had her attention. "Was that why you looked over at me?"

"Oh, I sure did," said Jody. "Something is going on there. I'd forgotten they worked together, almost three years ago, just after Leslie started with us. She did a great job, and Bill told the company she'd worked out great. I also remember asking her to work with Bill on another project down in the Gulf, but she had an excuse not to take the job. Her excuse was reasonable, and I never questioned it."

"Have you personally ever had any trouble with Bill?" I asked.

"Not really. He seemed like a flirt when we first hired him, making comments about my new hairstyle, new clothes, and that sort of thing. I thought he was just blowing smoke, trying to get on my good side. I thought it was a little inappropriate, but then he stopped. Why do you ask?"

I answered, "Well after you told me Bill and Amber

had a relationship, I noticed Bill's reaction after the last cruise when you said Amber and Leslie were joining the team. Bill looked disappointed; maybe even worried. He certainly did not seem happy about one, or both, of them being here.

"Am I starting to see a pattern here?" Jody asked. "Did you also see the attention Bill was paying to Bridget on the way to lunch? That did not seem appropriate, and particularly if Bill is trying to impress Amber."

Jody sat silent for a minute, but I could see she was deep in thought. Finally, Jody said, "I like Amber. The last thing she needs in her life is someone just wanting to use her. I wouldn't normally say anything about this, but Amber has a young daughter. The father deserted her when he found out she was pregnant. Amber has had enough problems in her life, and I see her as being vulnerable. Bill has seniority over her, and maybe he thinks he can use that if things go wrong. I think we need to do something, but I don't know what. Until this cruise, I have only known Leslie through phone conversations. But maybe she will be willing to talk to me privately about Bill. I asked her to come and see me, so hopefully, I'll find out what she knows."

I respected Jody for her honest concern about Amber. Jody was a great auditor, and very competent, but her sincere concern for Amber impressed me. This was the same concern I saw when she worked with the ship's crew members. I must admit, I was very attracted to Jody.

Jody called Leslie's cabin and said she was ready, and that Leslie could come over to her cabin. In Jody's room, she asked Leslie for reactions to her first day on the ship and could see the interest Leslie already had in the project.

After ten minutes of conversation, Jody finally said to Leslie, "Leslie, can I ask you a personal question?"

"Of course, Jody," Leslie replied. "What do you have for me?"

"I wouldn't normally ask this, but afterwards, you'll understand why."

"No problem, Jody."

"Yesterday at the hotel, both Bob and I noticed your reaction when you saw Bill with us. Can I ask why you reacted so coolly towards him?"

"Oh, man. I didn't realize it was so obvious. I'm sorry."

"Don't be sorry, Leslie. There may be something going on, which you could shed some light on."

"I don't want to talk about people I work with, Jody. I don't want to get people in trouble, and I like my job. I don't want to jeopardize my career either."

"Leslie, this may be important. So, I give you my word, this conversation is just between us, and I will never tell anyone about it."

"Okay, Jody. I'll take your word on that. I've never had reason to doubt you."

"You have my word. So, what happened between you two?"

"It was the refinery job in Wilmington. Bill mentioned it yesterday."

"Sure. I saw your reports. Everyone liked you. Even Bill."

"Well, the first day we worked together, Bill started complimenting me. First, it was work-related, then compliments on my looks, my nice complexion, and so on. I tried to ignore him, but he kept going at it. There were a couple guys at the refinery who saw that I was not happy with Bill's comments, one guy even pushed Bill and told him to leave me alone."

"Oh my! I wish I had heard about it back then. I wish

the men at the refinery had complained to us."

"Well, that's my fault. I thanked those guys but asked them not to say anything. Remember, I was only a few months in on a new job. I just made up my mind I'd have to avoid working with Bill in the future."

"Was that all that happened?" Jody asked.

"No, you haven't heard the worst part yet. One afternoon, we were working in the refinery office, and nobody else was there. Bill came up behind me, bent down, and whispered, 'We could have a good time at the hotel tonight,' and he accidentally put his hand on my breast. Accidentally is his word for it, not mine, by the way."

"Holy crap, Leslie. He's a scum bag!"

"Well, I turned and hit him in the face with my elbow. I gave him a nosebleed and he cut his lip on his teeth. That's when Bill said the touch was accidental, so I said his comment about a good time was inappropriate. He said I misunderstood, and he only meant a few drinks."

"I love the elbow in the face, Leslie. I need to remember that move. But you still didn't want to report this?"

"Remember, Jody. I was new, and although I hate to say this, I also think Bill thought he could get away with it because I'm black. I know our company better now, and I now know that behavior wouldn't have been and won't be tolerated."

"So, did that end it?" Jody asked.

"It ended his flirting and hitting on me. We just kept our distance until the job was done. But there's more."

"Oh, shit! More?"

"Yes, seeing as I'm finally spilling my guts, I want someone else to know about this sleaze bag!"

"Okay, what now?"

"We were staying at the same hotel, nothing fancy, being in Wilmington. We typically ate in the hotel diner, or at a place across the street. We never ate together, but I'd see him most nights. He always stayed at the bar, next to the restaurant, after I'd head back to my room. One night, I came back to the lobby to get a snack and heard Bill's voice, so I turned in the direction of the voice and noticed him talking to a woman at the bar. My first thought was that he had picked up a hooker. There are a number of them in that area."

"This is unbelievable! I need to hear the rest," said Jody.

"Just so you know, I'm not making any of this up," Leslie added.

"I believe you! I believe you! Go on," Jody replied.

"I sat in an easy chair outside the bar. The high back of the chair faced the bar entrance, so I hoped he wouldn't see me. He was talking smooth, and I could tell he was trying to seduce this chick with words. It seemed like he had convinced her to go to his room and they started to leave. As they walked away, I turned slightly, and I could tell this girl was maybe just twenty, certainly no more than twenty-five. Bill was patting her butt as they walked down the hall, and they were gone."

"He never quits, does he? "Jody inserted.

"Do you want more? I have more if you want," Leslie said.

"This has gone beyond the *need* to know. I *want* to hear everything, Leslie."

"Okay, so I decided to stay in the lounge for a while, just to be sure he wouldn't see me. As I was about to leave, five young girls walked into the lobby, all about the same age as the girl with Bill. They went into the bar and asked the bartender if he'd seen 'the stick'. The bartender laughed and said, 'Your skinny girlfriend just left with some guy.'"

"Keep going, please," said Jody

"As these girls came back into the lobby, I said hello. They were very friendly, so I asked them why they were in town. They told me they were from some small town in Nevada, and they were a dance troupe, trying out for parts in some stage show. I asked why they were staying in Wilmington, and they said it was the cheapest place they found near Long Beach. I then said, 'I'd heard you refer to your friend as Stick. I wondered why.' The girls all laughed and said, 'Because she has no boobs!'"

"And then what?" Jody asked.

"I was concerned for the girl Bill had seduced, so I told the girls that I hoped their friend was going to be okay with this guy. I couldn't believe their answer. 'We hope *he's* okay. Stick came here hoping to get laid. Sounds like she found her man-tool. He's the one gonna get used.'"

"Bill thought he was seducing the girl, but in fact, she seduced him. Splendid," Jody said. "So, that has to be all, isn't it?"

"Well, almost. Before the girls left for home, two days later, another one of that group also seduced Bill, even though Bill thought he was talking her into going with him. If they had stayed longer, they might all have had their turn with him."

"What's the male equivalent of a nymphomaniac?" Jody asked.

"If Bill was a nympho, I might understand. I don't think he is driven by sex. He is driven by conquest. He thinks he gets these women by sweet-talking them, and that makes him feel like he's in charge... like he won. I don't think he likes women that much. He just uses sex to control women. His sweet-talk is what turns me off. It's just so obvious, it made me sick. And I once looked up that word for guys, it's satyromaniac. Something to do with over-sexed goats, which I don't even want to know more about."

"That is funny, Leslie. I'll now see Bill as a sex-crazed goat. Gee, thanks."

"But Jody, you mentioned your question had something important involved. What was that? Can I help?"

"Not sure what will happen, but you may have noticed that Bill seems to be hitting on Amber. She's certainly not aware of Bill's intentions if they are sinister. And after what you've told me, I cannot imagine his intentions are sincere. Even if he intends to marry Amber, I don't think he will stop this conquest fetish of his. Amber has had a rough life for a young woman, and she doesn't need to get hurt again by someone like Bill."

"What do you think we should do? Shall we confront Bill or tell Amber about him?" asked Leslie.

"If Amber has not seen Bill's bad side yet, she will not believe us. If we confront Bill, he could turn it around and accuse us of smearing him, possibly ruining his career. I guess we just need to wait, keep an eye on Amber, and counsel her when the time is right."

"Amber seems like a sweet one. Probably a bit naïve. Bill's sweet-talk might work on her if she's not world-wise," Leslie said.

"Yes, our hands are sort of tied until something happens. I thank you for this frank discussion, Leslie. If it wasn't so serious, I'd say it was downright entertaining. I guess we'd better get to sleep. Meeting with Hans for breakfast in the dining room. See you at eight. Good night."

"Good night, Jody. Thanks for trusting me and believing me."

"Not a problem."

BILL GETS CAUGHT

———

A FTER THAT FIRST evening's dinner, Bill took Amber on a tour of the ship. He was familiar with the ship's general layout after a couple cruises and was enjoying the feeling of showing Amber the ropes.

While walking through the shops, Bill heard a familiar voice behind him saying, "Hi, Billy boy. Didn't expect to see you here. On another job?"

It was Vicky, the dancer from the first cruise.

"I guess I should ask the same," Bill said, turning around to face Vicky. "I thought you were still on the Prince." Bill was shocked to find himself face-to-face with Vicky.

"No, we only had another week left on that first contract. Our troupe took a couple of days off but got this new contract. We have this show on the Conquest for six weeks, but then we don't know what's next."

"Well, nice to see you again. Vicky, wasn't it?"

"Come on, Billy. You weren't that drunk the second night. You don't even remember my name?"

"Oh, yes. I remember. Sorry."

"Well, we have another night off tomorrow," Vicky continued, obviously unfazed by Bill's attempt to pretend he did not remember her. "No lounge on this ship, but I can clear my bed for a night. Still interested? I sure am."

Bill stood in total shock. Not only had a couple passengers heard Vicky, but Amber was standing just a few feet away and heard everything too.

"I'm pretty busy on this cruise, sorry," Bill said.

"Well, if you change your mind, stop by the theater tomorrow afternoon. We'll be rehearsing. I'd love to continue where we left off," Vicky said, and then turned and walked off.

Bill turned toward Amber and saw her already walking away. He caught up with her and grabbed her wrist.

"It's not what you think, Amber. We just had a couple drinks together. Nothing more."

"Bill, I know girl talk. You slept with her, and it's obvious. And at least twice because you weren't as drunk the second time. Remember? So, these are the boring cruise jobs you told me about, with nothing to do but read in your cabin. I thought we had something important going between us, but if this is your life, I want no part of it."

"It was just one stupid fling, Amber. I'm sorry. I got drunk and wasn't thinking straight."

"And the second night? Even she said you weren't so drunk. I think you'd better go see her rehearsal tomorrow because I'm done with you. You assholes are all alike!"

Bill went back to his cabin. He remembered Hans Nilsen's warning when he first met Vicky. He called the performers young trouble. Hans sure was right. Guess he had learned more than just hot sex from that experience.

INDIGNATION

———

THE ATMOSPHERE AMONGST the group was strange the next morning. Hans was his usual, congenial self, and Jody and I were deep in conversation, but Sam and Amber were sitting across from Bill with their stares eating holes into Bill's chest. Neither of them would look him in the face.

Bill had realized after last night that there was no going back, Amber was gone. He may as well forget about her and move on. It was going to be tough working with her though. They shared projects through her Miami office, and now through this cruise ship job. He wasn't quite sure what to do, but whatever!

Both Jody and Leslie noticed the icy stares aimed at Bill coming from Amber and Sam. Something had obviously happened, and Amber had gone to Sam for help. Although Jody or I might have helped, Sam was probably a good choice for Amber to have made.

Hans also seemed to have joined in on this cold staredown. At the time, I could not understand how Hans would be involved, but it was amazing to see how much you could read from people's faces alone.

"Well, how did the tour go yesterday?" Hans finally asked, breaking the silence. "Anything we need to discuss this morning?"

"The tour went well," Jody said. "Some of the same

issues we saw on the first audit, but it does appear like Bridget is already working on the improvements we recommended."

We had all gathered in the breakfast buffet, from where we would all be leaving to gather our notebooks from our rooms. And after breakfast, we all headed in the direction of our rooms.

"I'm going to the ladies' room," Jody said, as Amber and Sam started down the stairs. "Does anyone want to join me?"

Amber and Sam turned on their heels and followed Jody into the restroom.

"I wonder what that's about?" Bill said to me as we observed the women. "I'll never understand women," He added.

I had seen the cold stares and figured something must have happened between Amber and Bill. Because both Amber and Sam were doing the staring, I assumed Amber had sought counsel from Sam.

Sam was probably the best choice for her because I knew Sam had gotten divorced early in her marriage and had some experience with distasteful men. Sam was a talented woman, but also very feminine. Not just attractive, but she showed femininity which would attract any man. However, she also had a "dark side" to her personality. I assumed it had taken shape after her bad marriage experience. That deep, dark side was still a little frightening until you got to know her.

It appeared that Amber was getting good counsel in the ladies' room, so I decided to get my notebook and head to the engine control room, where I was going to review the oil record books.

Meanwhile, in the Ladies Room, it was quite busy, as I was told later. Amber quickly relayed the story with the dancer in the shop the prior evening. Sam told Jody and Leslie about Amber calling her and asking if they could talk. Jody then asked Leslie to briefly relate her experience with Bill, and the four of them agreed that Bill was a useless piece of human flesh. Jody thought it was good that Amber had discovered this now. Then they gave each other a big group hug and left the ladies' room.

"Men would never understand what just happened here. Even Bob!" Sam said.

"I'm so glad this happened with you ladies here. I'd have been a mess if I didn't have you to talk to," Amber said.

"We never checked the stalls. I sure hope nobody was in there listening to us," Jody said.

"They'd think it was all too weird to be true," Sam said. "Let's go to work. Interviews today."

BRIDGET

B RIDGET HAD SET up the interviews for the day using two meeting rooms outside the main deck bar. This woman was really in charge aboard this ship. As the environmental officer, she was well-respected among the crew, and they listened to her. When the paperwork was not done her way, she let the guilty person know about it, and she swore better than most sailors. The crew seemed to learn from her and respected her more than they feared her. Even the oil record book entries, which had been trouble on other cruise ship audits, seemed much better aboard this ship.

I asked Bridget if she was reviewing all of the oil record book entries aboard the ship, and she said, "Why the fuck wouldn't I? This is my ship!"

'This is the attitude needed by all the ships in the fleet,' I thought.

Hans and Bridget were responsible for sending in the crew members and because Jody was trying to train Leslie with the interview procedure, Bill was outside the rooms talking with Hans and Bridget.

Bill seemed quite interested in Bridget's sailing experience and was asking her a lot of questions. Questions that only showed his lack of maritime experience, by the way. Because Hans had known about Bill's experience with Vicky on the first ship and had sensed something might have happened with Amber, causing the cold stares at breakfast, he was not happy about the extra attention Bill was giving to Bridget.

Bill must have sensed Hans's opposition because he soon excused himself to find a men's room. Once he was out of earshot, Hans asked Bridget if she realized what was going on."

Bridget laughed. "I sure do. And you know my story, so I don't need to explain. It just happens, I was in the ladies' room this morning, and happened to overhear a conversation between Amber, Sam, Leslie, and Jody. Apparently, Bill was fooling around with a dancer on the last audit and Bill and Amber bumped into this dancer last night, while he was showing Amber around."

"Here on the Conquest?" Hans asked in surprise.

"Yes. Luckily for Amber, she heard enough from the dancer to figure out that Bill is a real tail-chaser if you catch my drift. He is out of control."

"So, what are you planning to do about it?" Hans asked her.

"I'll play along and let him hang himself. Do you mind, Hans? You're my boss, so you can tell me what you think I should do."

"As long as you don't embarrass the cruise line, I'll trust you. Eventually, I'd like you to let Jody in on what you may be planning. Can you do that?" Hans asked.

"No problem, Hans. If you'd heard what I did in the ladies' room, you'd know they'll be happy with my plan. I'll eventually tell them I heard their conversation."

"Okay then," Hans said.

Just then, Bill came back from the men's room. "Did I miss anything?" he asked.

"No, they're on their last crew members before we break for lunch," Bridget answered.

"So, where did we leave off?" Bill asked. "Oh yes. How did you decide to leave the tankers, and become a pilot? That sounds like a brilliant career move."

"I don't know about brilliant," Bridget replied. "I just wanted to get away from the constant smell of oil. And the guys in the crew smelled worse."

"So, your fellow pilot captains were more refined, I assume?" Bill said.

"Not so refined, but they respected my lifestyle, and we got along."

"I'd love to hear about your lifestyle. Maybe we can discuss that this evening," said Bill.

Just then, Jody and Leslie came out of their meeting room laughing with their last crew interviewee, one of the dining room waitresses. They had gotten along well with the young lady.

Soon after, Sam and Amber emerged from the other room and shook hands with the young man whom they had interviewed. He appeared to be one of the Bos'n crew, based upon his coveralls.

"So, things went well? Any problems?" Jody asked Sam.

"It was good to see the improvements made since the last two audits. Just as Hans had mentioned, the training methods are better here. The crew members all mentioned that they're getting hands-on training and they don't just sit in front of the computer like they had been doing just a month ago. Everyone seemed quite happy with the changes."

"I'm so happy to hear you say that," Bridget said. "We've worked hard to get these hands-on training sessions implemented, and we've seen the morale of the crew improve as a result."

"Great job, Bridget!" Bill said.

Amber and Sam looked at Bill. As an auditor, his comment seemed inappropriate. Jody made a mental note to speak with Bill about his obvious plays of complimenting Bridget over these first two days.

Bridget picked up on the reactions of the women auditors and figured she'd better speak to Jody sooner than she had planned.

"Are we ready for lunch?" Bridget asked.

Everyone said they were ready, and they all wanted to avoid the passenger dining areas again. It was a sea day, so all the passengers were on board.

I was still working in the engine control room, so Bridget asked Bill to come and find me since he knew his way around the crew area. We were to then meet her in the crew dining room where she would give us "those forms Jody had asked to see."

Everyone went their way, and Jody followed Bridget to the EO's office.

When they arrived at Bridget's office, Jody said, "I wasn't sure what forms you were talking about, Bridget," Jody said when the two of them were alone.

"Thanks for playing along," Bridget said, smiling. "I saw everyone's reaction to Bill's constant flattering remarks, so I wanted to talk to you later today. But when I saw Amber and Sam looking troubled by his latest comment, I decided to pull you aside sooner."

"Are you upset by his obvious flirting?" Jody asked Bridget. "I planned on talking to him and telling him it was not appropriate."

"I caught on to his compliments and attention yesterday as soon as he started. I was just going to ignore it, but I now have to tell you that I was in the ladies' room this morning and overheard your group's very interesting conversation about Bill."

"Oh my God. How mortifying! I had hoped nobody was in one of the stalls. I think it was Sam who said, nobody would believe it anyway."

"Oh, I've experienced more than my share of losers, but from what I heard you girls say, it looks like Bill is near the top of the list."

"Well, I'll talk to him and tell him to knock it off," Jody said.

"You can if you prefer, but first listen to my plan. And by the way, I spoke with Hans, and he said it was okay with him, so long as you agreed. Hans just doesn't want me to do anything embarrassing to the cruise line."

"Tell me your plan, Bridget. At this point, if it puts Bill in his place, I'm all for it."

"Well, Bill does not seem to have noticed the ring on my finger, yet he is obviously hitting on me. I wear it on my right ring finger, my partner prefers it that way since she's a Polish immigrant."

"I see you said partner, so you're not married?"

"Well, I hope you are open-minded. Al and I are a lesbian couple, and we have an adopted daughter who just turned three. Al, short for Aleksandra, and I have been together for over five years. Gay marriage is legal in Ontario, but we just never saw the need."

"Well, I'm familiar with the gay lifestyle," Jody said. "My eldest daughter, Alexa, is gay, and she has a serious relationship. They're both in college and are waiting to see how life goes after graduation. I love Alexa's partner and have learned a lot from them."

"Yes, tell them to wait until after college. Having a partner, hetero or gay is tough, and just like a hetero couple, you don't want to make a total commitment too early in life. Al and I were 28 and 27 when we met, and as I said, we've been together for five years. We didn't adopt Louisa until we knew we were a good match."

"Then what's the plan for Bill? I hope it's a good one."

"Well, apparently Bill has an eye for those dancers. Most of them are young and stupid. I had not met this Vicky until she came aboard last week. I have to give indoctrination meetings to all new contractors. She and her friend, Lindsey, are definitely Bill's type. Sex-crazed kids trying to break away from their over-protective mothers. There are also two gay men in that troupe, who give the lifestyle a bad name. But the Choreographer is a repeat crew member. Her name is Audrey, and she is a very nice lady, pretty as a picture, and I could easily see Bill hitting on her. But the thing is, Audrey is gay and has been married for about ten years. Al and I visited Audrey and her family last year."

"And the plan?" Jody asked.

"I'll take Audrey into my confidence and ask her to cooperate. I know she would like to put these girls in their place, and maybe teach a lesson to those two guys as well. Let's see what Audrey comes up with, and I'll keep you informed.

PAYBACK

———

DURING A MORNING coffee break, Bill went to
the theater to find Vicky, but this time he was con-
fronted by a lady about his own age, or maybe a few
years older. She was slender, and Bill thought she had a
great body.

"Passengers are not allowed to watch rehearsals,"
Audrey said.

Bill gave the same explanation he had given to Vicky
in the theatre of the cruise ship where they had first met.

"So, why are you interested in our rehearsal?" Audrey
asked Bill.

"I was looking for Vicky, as a matter of fact," he
answered.

"You're a little old to be toying with teeny-boppers,
aren't you?" Audrey quipped.

"I thought Vicky was 23. At least that's what she told
me."

Audrey chuckled. "She turns 20 next month, and her
friend, Lindsey, is even younger. I hope you didn't bed
them down because we all worry about what they might
be carrying. They're with someone new almost every
night."

"Oh, really!" said Bill. "They seemed like such nice
young ladies."

"Looks can be deceiving. And then there are those

two guys they hang around with. Be careful of them," Audrey added.

About then, Vicky and Lindsey came in through the back of the theater. When they saw Bill, they came over and said hi to Audrey.

"I see you've met Audrey," Vicky said to Bill. "She tries to be our surrogate mom, but otherwise she's okay. So, are you available to party tonight, Billy boy?"

"We're really busy on this cruise, Vicky. I think I'll have to pass."

"Okay, but if you change your mind, come to the crew hallway and find us. We have a new girl who wants to meet you. We can try to fit the three of us in bed together." And then Vicky and Lindsey skipped down to the stage.

Bill looked very humiliated. He looked at Audrey and saw the look on her face.

"Oh, Bill! So, you have slept with those two! I'm worried about you now. As I said, we all wonder what they might be infected with."

"Yeah, twice on The Prince, when I first met them a couple weeks back," Bill confessed.

"Did you at least use a condom?"

"I did the second time, but I was so drunk the first time, I'm not even sure who was in the bed with me."

"Oh, my goodness. I tell you what. I know the ship's doctor very well, and I can ask him to test you for STDs. If you're infected, you need to take care of it fast," Audrey said.

Bill looked worried. "Can you ask the doctor to see me?" he simply said.

"Of course," Audrey replied. "I'll see him later this morning. Why don't you meet me around lunchtime, at the infirmary? We'd better take care of this quickly."

"I'll be there," Bill said. "Thank you very much."

Audrey called Bridget to tell her what had happened,

and to let her know the rest of her plan. Bridget laughed and said she would let the others know. "This worked out great," she said to Audrey. "Bill will learn a big lesson, and there's no need for any public display that Hans might object to. Thanks, Audrey!"

Bill met Audrey at the infirmary, and Audrey brought him inside to meet the doctor.

"Doctor Alvarez, this is that contractor, Bill, I told you about. Bill, I never got your last name."

"Bill Taggart. Thank you, Doctor, for agreeing to see me."

"No problem, Bill. Audrey explained what happened. We'd hate to find you were infected by those girls, and then carry it home to your wife."

"Well, I'm not married, but I still don't want to think I might have an STD."

"This is a quick test, Bill. I can have the results in just one hour. Take this bottle into the toilet over there and give me a sample."

Bill did as the doctor asked and left Audrey with Doctor Alvarez. As soon as Bill closed the door, Audrey gave the doctor a high-five and a big smile.

Audrey whispered, "So, you can keep this out of the records? And what about charges?"

"I've got it covered, Audrey. I'll do the urine test for STDs, and that's not expensive. We use those tests frequently on board, so I won't even mention the cost. Therefore, there is no need to record anything. If he happens to have an STD, I'll put him on an antibiotic, for which we will need to be paid, but that is not very expensive. Otherwise, I plan to put him on a strong laxative. Either way, he will be spending a lot of time in the restroom for the next couple of weeks."

Bill came out of the toilet and handed the full bottle to the doctor.

Doctor Alvarez said, "That's fine, Bill. I'll have the

results after lunch. This test only finds gonorrhea and chlamydia, I don't have the test aboard for syphilis, so I suggest you see your doctor when you get home and ask for a full panel of tests for all STDs. Tell him you have been sexually active with some people of suspicious sexual habits."

"So, you'll know in an hour?" Bill asked.

"Sure will. Please come back around one o'clock. My nurse returns at one-thirty, and I'd rather she wasn't aware of this. Okay?"

"Thank you so much, Doctor. And thank you, Audrey," Bill said, turning from one to the other, a look of concern on his face.

"That's what I'm here for, Bill," Doctor Alvarez said. "And by the way, even if this test is not positive until you get an all-clear from your doctor back home, please do not have sex with anyone."

"That's for sure," Bill said.

"I'm very embarrassed, Audrey," Bill said as he left the infirmary with Audrey. "Thank you for helping me."

"No problem, Bill," Audrey replied, "but my goodness, you need to be more careful about who you sleep with. Not everyone in the world is as innocent as they first seem. You come back at one o'clock just like the doctor told you. I'll just back out of your life at this point." And with that, Audrey turned on her heels and walked away from an embarrassed and most likely, confused Bill.

As soon as Audrey got to her cabin, she paged Bridget to tell her what had happened.

Bridget said, "Thank you so much, Audrey. So, whether he tests positive or not, he'll still be making frequent trips to the restroom during this cruise?"

"That's right," Audrey said with a chuckle.

Bridget laughed.

"I'll be sure to let the girls know," Bridget continued.

"This way, Hans will not be upset with me when he finds out."

"As long as Bill makes it to the restroom in time, nothing embarrassing," Audrey chuckled again.

"What about those two girls, Audrey? Are they really that bad?"

"The word onboard is that they have a new partner at least several times a week. I'm going to suggest to them that they also need to be tested. For all I know, with what you told me about Bill, he could have infected them."

Meanwhile, Bill had grabbed a quick hamburger at the pool-side grill and anxiously returned to the infirmary. He knocked on the door and Doctor Alvarez let him in.

"I'm glad you came back, Bill. The test was positive. There is no way to tell how advanced the disease may be at this time, but I'll give you the treatment you need. When you get home, ask your doctor to give you a test for the full array of possible STDs. By the way, have you felt any itchiness in your groin area lately?"

"You know, maybe I have been a little itchy, but not sure. Why? Is that a symptom?"

"The reason I ask is because I found an organism in the sample bottle commonly known as crabs. We call it a pubic louse. It is very common with sexually active people who have multiple partners, and it appears you may have a bad case of pubic lice. I'll also give you a small bottle of strong anti-louse wash, like shampoo. It burns a little and smells pretty bad, but it will kill the lice quickly. However, the lice lay eggs in the pubic hair, so you may need to repeat the treatment when you get home."

"Oh my God, I had no idea."

"The repeated treatment is important," said Doctor Alvarez, "because pubic lice can migrate to the under-arms, the hair on your head, and even eyebrows. Be sure to buy a good magnifying mirror when you get home, so you can check out your hair and eyebrows. You will feel them start causing you to itch if they do spread."

"So, Doctor, what must I take for treatment, besides the treatment for the crabs?"

"I'm giving you fifteen pills today. Take two right now, one this evening, and then one at breakfast and one at dinner for the rest of the week. After that, please see your doctor at home. These pills will give you bad diarrhea, so don't be surprised. That is a normal side effect."

"Should I order more pills when I get home?"

"I'd rather have your doctor follow his own method of treatment. I'm giving you these pills in a plain envelope. This way, there will be no record onboard about your visit."

"Oh, I understand, and thanks for that. What do I owe you?" Bill asked.

"I did this as a favor for Audrey. No charge. But be sure to thank her," the doctor responded.

"I sure will thank her again."

"Okay then, here's the envelope of pills. Be sure to take two now, and then start the dinner and breakfast regimen until they're gone. Use the louse wash morning and evening with your showers."

"I'll follow those instructions, and thanks again," said Bill.

"Just be careful about sleeping around in the future," the doctor said, and then added, "It can get you into real trouble."

"Warning taken. I've learned my lesson," Bill said. Then he headed out in search of the rest of the audit team.

He found the team that night at dinner, discussing the day's work. I was excited about my warm reception in the engine room, and Amber had found Bridget's hazardous waste records to be in good order.

"So, what did you find in the garbage book records

so far?" Jody asked Bill when he joined the team at the table.

"Sorry," Bill said. "I didn't get very far with those."

"Why not?" Jody asked him.

"Well, I've been in and out to see Doctor Alvarez most of the day, I haven't been feeling very well," Bill replied.

"I'm sorry to hear that," Jody said, glancing slyly at Amber.

"Thank you," Bill said.

"But you'll need to step it up then, Bill," Jody continued. "Remember, this is only a five-day cruise, and tomorrow is filled with more interviews."

"Got it, Jody. If I have to, I'll work after dinner to catch up."

As Bill was getting up, I asked him, "You okay, Bill? You looked uncomfortable during dinner."

Bill didn't answer, but then Jody, Leslie, and Amber started chuckling amongst themselves. Sam just sat there with a big smile on her face.

"Am I missing something here?" I asked, looking around the table.

"Just don't ask, Bob. It's better if you don't know," Jody said.

I decided to let it be.

The next day was a full day of crew interviews. Between each interview, Bill was running to the restroom, which luckily was next to those small conference rooms. I later heard it was a good thing I was in the engine room because the women were actually breaking into occasional laughter and giving each other high-fives every time Bill ran out of the meeting room.

Hans noticed what was happening and decided to ask Bridget what was going on. It was then that Bridget reminded Hans about what she had told him about teaching Bill a lesson and asked if he wanted to know more.

"Will it be embarrassing to the cruise line?" Hans asked.

"Only if he doesn't make it to the toilet in time," she replied. She had liked Audrey's little joke!

"Well, okay. I guess I want to know," said Hans.

Bridget explained the whole set-up devised by Audrey, while out of earshot of the waiting interviewees. To Bridget's surprise, Hans simply said, "Serves the son-of-a-bitch right. I tried to warn him." Bridget wasn't aware that Hans had seen Bill and Vicky during their first encounter. But she had also seldom heard Hans swear.

"So, you like our payback?" she asked Hans.

"Yes, it worked out fine. But what about cost?"

"Luckily, the test was negative, so the doctor just gave Bill a double dose of laxatives."

Hans laughed. "So, that explains his frequent trips to the toilet. But are there any records?"

"Doctor Alvarez said there was no need for records. He was careful to use generic terms like treatment and pills and put them in a plain envelope. However, he *did* find that Bill has the crabs. So, he gave him that nasty, burning lotion, rather than the weaker shampoo type."

"Good job Bridget. But I don't want to know anything more. Okay?"

"Thanks, Hans. We girls needed to stick together, and Amber now feels better knowing that Bill has been punished. According to Audrey, the doctor laid it on thick and told him he needed to be tested again when he gets home."

"No more, please," said Hans.

I followed up on Bill's career several years after that incident. And, according to Jody, Bill is now vice-president of her company, even though most of his co-workers still consider him a jerk!

We had all worried about Amber, but Jody tells me that Amber fell in love with a young widower. They met at a single parent's group. He lost his wife in an auto accident and had a young son, and Amber decided to leave her professional career when they married. They now have a child of their own, in addition to her daughter and his son from his previous marriage. The last Jody heard about Amber, she and her new family were very happy.

BOB EVERS' STORY

B Y THE TIME Bob finished telling us the story of Bill Taggert and his unfortunate incident aboard the Conquest, it was getting late, so we called it a day and went to our rooms to get ready for the next day at the Chicago drydock. The next morning, we fueled up and stocked groceries and supplies for the trip and left. The weather was good, but after leaving the Calumet River, we put the two barges on our towline and headed north.

I was in the pilothouse, had the tug on autopilot, and was standing my own visual watch, with Bob sitting on the settee behind me. I then asked Bob if he wanted to explain his great, but unusual relationship with his current wife and ex-wife.

Bob asked, "Do we have a couple hours? This gets complicated."

I told him we had two days, so I was all ears.

So, then let me continue. I'd been traveling a lot, even before that cruise ship contract. My wife, Chris, and I had been married for eighteen years, and I considered us to be a very compatible and happily married couple. We had three children, a fantastic 17-year-old son who was getting ready for college, and two wonderful daughters, fifteen and thirteen, who both loved the ballet.

Chris was a great wife who took on all the family responsibilities when I traveled. She was a beautiful woman, and I truly loved her and I'm proud to say that I never cheated on her. It just wasn't in my nature to have any flings or affairs, and I bragged about this to my friends often saying to them: "I have more than I can handle at home. I don't need anything more on the side." And I truly meant it, despite my friends' disbelief. They figured that with all the traveling I was doing, that I would have a girl in every port.

When the other women auditors on our team, Jody and Sam, started working with me, I think they expected the worst out of me when it came to my marriage, because of the problems they were having in their own lives. During a training session we had in Miami before these cruise audits began, the spouses were invited to attend, so they all got to meet Chris. Both Jody and Sam liked Chris, and Chris got quite frisky during the two nights that we spent in Miami. She joked with Jody and Sam about giving me a workout before I went away on that cruise. She told them she was reminding me of what I had at home so I wouldn't be tempted on the ship. I blushed bright red, and Jody and Sam always chided me about blushing whenever sex was mentioned.

So, this background brings me to the meat of my story!

THE KEY

WE STARTED TO see that being an auditor on these cruise ships had some nice rewards. For instance, the captain on our first ship invited us to his table in the dining room one evening. It wasn't the big, fancy affair that occurs on Formal Night, but we were pleased to accept the invitation.

We were asked to meet in the lounge, outside the dining room entrance, and the four auditors, including Bill, the only other guy on the team besides me, were there well ahead of schedule, not knowing what to expect. None of us had ever taken a cruise before, and we had only heard about the experience from our cruising friends back home.

The social director entered the bar and saw us in the corner of the room, so she came over to us.

"We have an area set aside near the dining room entrance, where you can meet the other guests for the captain's table," she said to us. "Follow me over there and I will introduce you to the others."

So, we did.

Upon arriving in the waiting area, she introduced herself to all of us who were gathered there. She said her name was Rebecca and that the captain would be joining us shortly, at which time we would then go into the dining room. In the meantime, she went around the room and introduced all the guests. There was Mr. and Mrs. Althoff, who had sailed with them twenty-one times. Mr. and Mrs. Felling had sailed with them twenty-four times. Mr. Bruner, who was the port director for their "great destination of Curaçao," Miss Lister, who was on board with forty passengers from her tour company. And finally, she introduced our crew: Miss Cooper, Miss Hough, Mr. Evers, and Mr. Taggart, we were aboard auditing their marine operations.

Everyone shook hands and greeted one another, then started to make small talk. Rebecca asked each person for their drink preference and then directed us to several trays of hors d'oeuvres.

"I forgot to mention," Rebecca said as we headed towards the trays, "the table has been set with name cards, so you will know where to sit. I will lead us into the dining room, and when you reach the table, please find your name tag, and stand behind the chair until the captain arrives. He will enter last. When he arrives, the captain will request that everyone be seated, and then the ship's photographer will take a group photo. You will each receive a copy of that photo in your stateroom tomorrow."

Shortly after the drinks arrived, the captain walked into the bar, shook everyone's hand, and took a small glass of wine from Rebecca. He proposed a toast for good weather and a happy voyage. Quite frankly, the whole thing seemed overly orchestrated to me.

After the toast, Rebecca motioned for everyone to follow her into the dining room, and the captain followed behind the rest of the group. Everyone began to look for their name cards, and Jody and Sam were shocked to see that their cards were on each side of the captain's chair. I was placed on one end of the table, sitting next to Miss Lister, and Bill was on the other end of the table, next to Mr. Bruner. The two couples with over twenty cruises were sitting across from the captain, with the two women next to one another.

As soon as the captain directed everyone to take a seat, the photograph was taken, and the waiters went around the table taking drink orders. A glass of champagne was poured for each of us, but the waiters whispered to us that this was to be saved for the captain's toast during the dinner.

Conversations began, and Miss Lister immediately started quizzing me on my duties aboard the ship. I avoided talking to her about environmental issues and instead told her about my travels and ship inspections around the world. I also mentioned my upcoming trip to New Zealand with my wife. I was relieved when the waiters finally came to take our dinner orders, getting a break from her constant attention. However, as soon as the orders were taken, Miss Lister continued her onslaught of questions. Trying to change the subject, I asked Miss Lister about her tour business and how she was able to get forty passengers on this cruise. After a very short answer, Miss Lister continued asking me to describe my work and my travels.

I turned my attention to Mr. Felling, who was sitting on my other side, asking him about his career and his numerous cruises on the Stellaris Cruise Line. Before Mr. Felling could even answer, Miss Lister interrupted.

"Doesn't Bob's career just sound spectacular?" She said to Mr. Felling.

I noticed Jody's constant glances and smiles from across the table. In response, I grimaced at Jody, showing my displeasure with the constant chatter from Miss Lister.

A few minutes into our meal, the captain proposed another champagne toast. Miss Lister's glass was already empty by this time, she had probably drunk at least five glasses of wine during dinner as well.

When dinner was over, everyone got up to leave. Miss Lister looked at me with a disturbed look, as I rose and left the table. Perhaps, she had been expecting some kind of special attention.

As we were leaving the dining room, Jody and Sam motioned to me and led me out to a secluded area on the opposite side of the bar.

"Bob, why didn't you take her key?" Sam immediately began to tease me.

"What key?" I said, probably with a puzzled look on my face.

Jody said, "Bob, she set her room key on the table between you and pushed it towards you at least five times. Don't you know what that means?"

"Well, I thought I was a man of the world, but I must admit, I never saw it happening," I said. "Even if I did, I get more than I need at home, and I would not have taken the key."

Jody said, "I must say, I was impressed, Bob. I figured I knew your good relationship with your wife, and tonight, you sure proved it in my mind."

However, Sam was not nearly as complimentary, telling me, "I think you're just plain stupid, Bob! Lister didn't seem to be a bad person, and she sure was interested in you. You could've had a good time for one night. Chris would never know."

"Sorry, but I just don't think that way. I've never cheated on Chris and see no reason to start at this point in my life," I simply said.

"I like that, Bob! You don't have to apologize to me," said Jody.

———

The next morning, another sea-day had begun. The audit team met Hans, the fleet environmental officer, at the breakfast buffet. They were all curious about anything unusual which might have happened at the captain's table the night before.

Sam was about to speak when Jody interrupted her. "No, it was a non-event. Some nice people, but mostly boring conversation."

Sam got the hint to keep quiet.

"So, I think we know our plans for the day," I said to Jody. "I'm off to the engine room. I love the smell of diesel fuel in the morning!" Nobody laughed.

I then asked Hans if he was ready, and we headed for the engine control room together. When we arrived, the chief greeted us with a huge smile. "So, Bob, I understand you're a straight shooter," he said.

"Oh my God, does the whole damn ship know? That was just not my style," I replied.

"No, I understand. And despite Hans's description of my Viking ancestry, I'm not a womanizer. Besides, my wife would shoot me if she ever found out I had another woman on the side. Nevertheless, the word sure does spread about such things aboard a ship because I guess the waiters noticed what was happening. There are more positive things being said about your reaction than there are negative."

"Well, maybe I am a little naïve, but I didn't see her pushing that key toward me. If I had, I know I wouldn't have taken it, but I might have been very nervous about the situation. This way, when I got up and left, I would like to have seen the look on her face. She probably thought I would take the key at the last minute. To be honest, she was driving me crazy with her constant talking."

After this experience, Jody and Sam started to believe in me. I'm not saying this to brag or say that I'm a saint, but I was just raised to respect my wife and to be monogamous.

———

As I had told Miss Lister during her very one-sided dinner conversation, I was making a business trip to New Zealand between cruises. Over the last few years, I had been inspecting the fleet of tuna seiners that worked the South Pacific. Those trips had taken me to places like American Samoa, Fiji, Australia, and several trips to New Zealand.

I had been trying to convince my wife to make some trips with me because I could see she was very upset with me being gone so much. Chris knew I loved my work but, despite my love for my family, she had been accusing me of putting my job before her and our kids.

Chris had agreed to make this next New Zealand trip with me after that first cruise, and I had arranged for my mother to stay with the kids while we were gone. Chris trusted my mom, which voided her normal worry she would have had about leaving our children with friends for more than a day or two. I was looking forward to showing Chris a good time, and it sounds a little corny, but I was excited!

———

I arrived home late on Thursday night after a good non-stop flight from San Juan to Chicago O'Hare. I walked in the front door hoping Chris would still be awake, but found all the lights out, except for the porch light. Everyone was asleep, so I crept upstairs quietly, used the bathroom, disrobed, and crawled into bed. I had hoped to discuss the cruise ship experiences with Chris, and make plans for our trip to New Zealand, which was just a few days away.

Because my mind was racing, it took me over an hour to fall asleep, so the next morning, I awoke to find Chris already out of bed. I slipped on a robe and went downstairs. As I went into the kitchen, I saw it was already eight-thirty am.

"Darn, I over-slept. I guess the kids already left for school?" I said to Chris as I walked into the kitchen and kissed her.

"Yes, I knew you got home late, so I let you sleep," Chris said.

"Sleep is over-rated. I'd rather have had breakfast with the kids. Then we could have gone back upstairs. I missed you and need some lovin'. Are you in the mood? Maybe we can start where we left off in Miami."

"Sorry, but I have a raging bladder infection. I have an appointment with Doctor Travist at one o'clock," Chris responded.

"Oh, sorry," I said, trying to hide my disappointment. "I can drive you to the clinic, so we can talk about our trip."

Chris moved a little further away from me before responding.

"That's the other thing. I called your mother and told her not to come. I totally forgot that Lilah has a school trip that I promised to chaperone. I committed to it several months ago, and it slipped my mind until her teacher called to remind me. I can't go to New Zealand with you after all."

I felt like I'd been punched in the gut. It wasn't like Chris to forget such things, and I knew she could have tried to find a replacement for chaperoning.

"What school trip is this?" I asked instead. "I don't remember that being on the calendar."

"Some of her classmates are winter camping out at Starved Rock. The parents stay in the Lodge, not in tents. We're there for the hiking events to keep the kids safe on the trails. I know I told you about it."

"I thought Lilah didn't want to go on that trip," I said.

"She needed the extra credit to get an "A" in Biology.

Her grade slipped to a "B", and she needs this trip to raise her grade."

Feeling demoralized, I left the kitchen and went back upstairs to take a shower. When I came back to the kitchen, there was a note from Chris saying she was out shopping and would go directly to her doctor's appointment from there. The note said there was breakfast in the fridge for me to heat up. I also noticed the lack of the heart which she normally put on her notes to me. Suddenly, my mind began to wonder, what on earth was going on? The knot in my stomach tightened. Something was seriously wrong, I thought.

That evening, I had a tough time not showing my growing depression to my daughters, Melanie and Lilah. They quizzed me about my trip and the people I had met, but I could not concentrate.

Lilah seemed to notice. "Dad, are you okay?" she asked, "you seem sorta' in the dumps."

"Sorry girls. Just bummed because Mom can't go to New Zealand next week like we'd planned."

Lilah said, "Oh yeah, that dumb camping trip! I didn't want to go, but Mom said my teacher told her I needed the extra credit. I could have found something else. I hate camping!"

"Well, I'll have to find another trip we can take together. By the way, where's Todd?" I asked.

"Todd is staying with his friend Jeremy. He took a bag to school today, so he could head to Jeremy's house after school. He's staying there next week, while Mom and I are at Starved Rock."

"And what about you, Melanie? Where will you be?" I asked.

"Mom asked Mrs. Sullivan if I could stay with them. I need to be in the neighborhood for my babysitting jobs."

I excused myself and went to the study and called Todd's cell phone. I heard it ringing in the kitchen, so

I went into the kitchen and found Todd's phone still plugged into his charger. He must have forgotten it when he packed his bag for school that morning," I said to myself.

Just then, Chris came in through the garage. I went to the back door and asked if everything went okay at the doctor's office.

"Oh, sure. Just take pills for a week until it goes away," she responded casually.

I left for O'Hare around Noon on Sunday to catch my flight to LAX, where I'd board a Polynesian Airlines flight to Auckland. I'd flown Polynesian one time, getting out of American Samoa, having missed my 'only twice per week' United flight. Then, I was lucky to have sat next to the President of the company, which was then just flying local routes, and only small planes at that time. I had recognized the President from his picture in the airline's magazine. It was a great conversation, and after that, I flew Polynesian any chance I got.

Before this trip, I had been to Nelson, New Zealand four times, each time working insurance claims on damaged tuna seiners. This job was a follow-up to my previous visit to that shipyard in Nelson on the South Island. I had also worked a couple times in Whangarei, on the North Island.

Before departing for New Zealand, I could feel the tension at home. When I asked Chris what was going on, she just blamed it on not feeling well. I asked for Todd's friend's phone, so I could talk to Todd before leaving, but Chris always had an excuse for why she couldn't find it.

I talked to Melanie and Lilah, but I didn't want to overly concern them with my feelings. They already seemed upset, not knowing why their mom was acting so out of sorts.

As I was waiting for my flight, Chris called my cell phone, and I answered, saying. "Hi, honey. What's up?"

Chris responded, "Just wanted to wish you a safe flight. I'm sorry I was so down the last few days. Too much going on, I guess. So, when do you get back from New Zealand?"

"Well, I won't stay those extra days we were planning to, so I'll try to get home in a week if the shipyard repairs go as planned."

"Okay. I guess I thought you'd be gone longer. What's next, after you get back?"

"Another cruise, LA to Mexico, and return to LA. That one is just 5 days."

"More cruises after that?" Chris asked.

"I think I'll schedule John to take some, but I may have to go along on his first one, to train him. That'll be weird, me training John, the old-timer who has trained me in the past."

"Very weird," Chris said, "So, call me from New Zealand and let me know your schedule. Gotta' run, picking up the girls from school soon. They had a Sunday club meeting."

"One last thing," I said to Chris before she rushed off the phone, "ask Todd to call me when you get his phone back to him. My phone works in New Zealand. I feel bad I wasn't able to see or talk to him while I was home."

"Okay, Bob. Will do." And Chris hung up.

I had started to say "Love you" but she had already hung up. I noticed that Chris did not end her call with any similar goodbyes, and again, I felt very concerned.

This would have been a perfect trip for Chris because I only needed to check the progress of repairs two or three hours a day, and just Monday through Friday. The insurance claim did not allow overtime charges, and the ship owner didn't want to pay for weekend overtime, which was an even higher cost than weekday overtime. I'd planned to spend the weekend visiting friends, with Chris, on the North Island. Friends I'd known from a previous job at the shipyard in Whangarei.

The flight to LAX was boring. It was too early to sleep, and my head was full of nagging questions after my short trip home.

When the flight landed in Los Angeles, I turned on my cell phone and a strange "708" Chicago number showed as a missed call. I called the number back and was surprised to hear Todd answer.

"Hi, Dad. Sorry I missed you when you were home. I waited for you to call, but you didn't."

I was confused but caught myself.

"I did call. Your phone was on the charger in the kitchen, and my call rang on that phone. What number is this? Your friend's phone?"

"Didn't Mom give you this new number? I needed a new smartphone before I left for college, and I had intended to keep my old phone number, but Mom told me she needed a second phone, and wanted to keep my old phone because it was simpler to use. She told me I should just get a new phone with a new number."

"I see," I said, "but she didn't tell me you had a new number."

"Dad, the reason I wanted to talk to you while you were home, is because I'm worried about Mom. Ever since she came back from Miami, she's been acting very funny. She has had a lot of appointments but wouldn't say what was going on. Did things not go well in Miami?"

"Just the opposite, Todd. I thought she was very happy on the Miami trip. But while I was home the last few days, she has acted very strange."

"Another thing, Dad; she got mad at Lilah for asking

so many questions about how things went in Miami. Not sure if you know this, but it was Melanie and Lilah who told Mom she had to go with you to Miami. Lilah even told Mom, 'You're not treating Dad very nice lately,' before she decided to go with you on the Miami trip."

"I had no idea," I said. "I'm glad you told me, but don't get in trouble with your mom. I won't tell her you took me into your confidence. Mom is going through a tough time because I travel so much. I'm trying to work things out, but the last few days at home, she was not feeling well, so it was difficult."

"I'm worried too, Dad. I think I know more, but not sure you want to hear it."

"Todd, you shouldn't have to get in the middle, but I guess what happens to Mom and I will also affect you, so do what your conscience tells you."

"My conscience is the problem, Dad. That's why I called. You need to know. I heard Mom talking to her old boss, Libby, at Parkside Realty. Mom didn't know I'd gotten home from school early that day, so she was talking loudly in the office. She asked Libby, 'If I divorce Bob, would you take me back in my old job?' Libby must have said yes, because Mom then said, 'Thanks, that'll make things easier.' And then she hung up."

"Oh, my! I was afraid of that. Things were just not adding up while I was home this week. Todd, I'll keep this to myself, but thank you for telling me. I can't handle this with your mom over the phone, but I'll have a week to think everything over and try to prepare myself."

"Okay, Dad. I knew I just had to tell you."

"So, Todd, what else is happening? Any college decisions?"

"Still just narrowed down to the two U-of-M's, Minnesota and Michigan; Michigan's Naval Architecture program has me intrigued. I can follow in your footsteps, but hopefully in a stay-at-home job, like a shipyard or design office."

"Well, seeing what's happening with your parents, that may be a smart move. I'd better let you go. If you or the girls need anything, my phone will be on in New Zealand. Love you, Todd."

"Love you too, Dad. Sorry for this unsettling news. See you next week?"

"Yes, I have a couple days home next week before I head to a cruise in Los Angeles. Bye for now."

As you might figure, this had me very upset, and my LAX to Auckland flight was anything but pleasant as I spent the entire trip wondering what I was going to do when I got home.

NEW ZEALAND

I LOVED NEW ZEALAND, but I especially felt at home in Nelson, a small town on the north end of the South Island, on the strait between the two Islands. Nelson had a great shipyard called Northland Port, which serviced the Pacific fleet of tuna seiners, amongst other vessels. I had worked in this shipyard four times before and had come to like and trust it. My work always centered around damaged tuna seiners since I represented the vessel owner's insurance underwriters.

After changing planes in Auckland, I arrived at the airport in Nelson, rented a car, and went directly to the shipyard. I needed to check on the progress of repairs to the seiner, "Bonnie", which had been damaged and had nearly sunk. The damage investigation revealed some significant structural problems over and above the damage claim, and the underwriters wanted my assurance that the vessel was seaworthy before it could return to fishing.

I had been looking forward to introducing Chris to the shipyard managers, who had become good friends over the last two years. It was a disappointing first day when the managers asked me where I was hiding my wife, and I tried to explain to them what had happened. The managers seemed as disappointed as I was because they had hoped to invite me and Chris for dinner a couple times during our stay, so their wives could meet this American couple. Americans go to Australia a lot, but very few go to New Zealand, and those who go, stay in Auckland or Christchurch. They miss the best part, but that's okay with me!

The shipyard manager told me there was no need to get dirty on that first day. "Why don't you get settled in at the hotel, have a nice dinner, and start recovering from your jet lag," Brian McKenzie said. "We'll see you in the morning, but not too early. Tuesday is our staff meeting, remember?"

"I'd forgotten that," I replied. "Is ten o'clock, okay?

"Perfect," said Brian.

I went to check into my favorite hotel, a comfortable, yet rustic-looking building, just a short walk from the shipyard. I usually drove to the yard though, knowing I'd want to try different small take-away restaurants for lunch scattered around town. The food in Nelson was spectacular, and because of the local fishing fleet, the fish was always fresh and varied. And then there were the fresh, green-lipped mussels! Each of these memories made me feel more disappointed each time I thought of how I'd intended to show all these things to Chris.

At the front desk of the hotel, the owner saw me coming in and came out from behind the desk to give me a big bear hug.

"Bob, we've been looking forward to your arrival. When I saw your reservation, I told Margaret and Sylvia you were coming again. I see the reservation is for two persons, I assume your wife is along on this trip?"

"No, Herb. She couldn't make it. I planned on her coming, but the kids had school plans, and she had to cancel. I'm very disappointed."

"Well, Sylvia might be happy. She's always said if you were single, she'd snap you up."

"Yeah, your daughter is fantastic, but I keep telling

her, I'm not available," I said with a laugh.

"Well, Bob, let's get you checked in. How long will you be with us? Your reservation said eight nights."

"Those extra three nights were for some extra sight-seeing with my wife, Herb. So, I'll probably try to leave on Saturday, instead of Thursday."

"No problem Bob. We're not too busy now that fall has arrived. I hope your wife can make the next trip."

"Thanks, Herb. I'll get settled in my room and catch a nap before dinner. I didn't sleep much on the flight from Los Angeles to Auckland. When does the restaurant open?"

"The restaurant opens at 1800, but there are always snacks in the bar. Sylvia would love for you to stop by the bar to say hello, I'm sure."

"Oh, of course. I may need a couple drinks before and after dinner. I'm pretty bummed out that Chris didn't come."

With that, I found my room, took a quick shower, set the alarm for four-thirty, and laid down. Although I thought I wouldn't sleep, in just a few minutes, I was in a deep slumber. The alarm woke me during a crazy dream and, at first, I wasn't sure where I was. I hate that feeling, which I often experience when recovering from jetlag. I splashed my face with cold water and started to wake up, then I got dressed and went to the lobby.

This time, Herb's wife, Margaret, was behind the counter, and she also came out to receive her hug. It sometimes amazed me how close I'd become with this family in just a few visits. They were the type of family best described by the term, 'salt of the earth'.

Margaret said, "You'd better get into the bar. Sylvia has been waiting to see you."

"Oh, I figured that. I'm on my way," I replied.

SYLVIA

S YLVIA WAS TENDING to a patron on the far end of
the room when I entered the bar. I quietly found a
seat at the bar before saying, "What does a guy have to
do to get served in this place?"

Sylvia turned and saw me, and her face broke out in
the biggest smile. "I thought I recognized that strange
American accent," she said, and then she came running
across the room and hugged me. I could feel her hug
was a bit friendlier than her mother's hug had been.

Sylvia was thirty-four and looked like the true picture of a Scottish Lass. She had a shapely figure, and I
always thought she looked a lot like Chris, except that
Sylvia had reddish-auburn hair, almost purple. From our
previous conversations, I'd learned that Sylvia had been
married to a local fisherman, but his trawler had sunk
during a terrible typhoon. She'd been widowed for six
years and told me she never saw another man in Nelson good enough for her. She flirted with me constantly
when I stayed at the hotel and kept telling me she'd
attack me if I weren't married.

"Okay, Syl. Have you found the man of your dreams
in Nelson since I saw you last?"

"I sure have," she quickly replied. "He just sat down
at my bar."

Looking around the bar, I laughed, saying, "He must

be invisible."

"Oh, you devil. You darn well know who I mean."

"Quit playing with me, Syl. Tell me what's new in Nelson, and what's new with you."

"There's never anything new in Nelson. At least not for me. If it wasn't for Mom and Dad, I'd be out of here. But what's this I hear? Your wife was supposed to be here. What happened?"

I hadn't intended to discuss my problems with any-one, but I just couldn't hold it all inside any longer. The bar was now empty, so I told Sylvia about the events of the last month, and the conversation with Todd, who had overheard Chris mentioning divorce.

"I can hardly believe she would leave me after all these years," I lamented, "but it would certainly explain the way things have been going lately."

"Bob, I'm sorry you're going through this," Sylvia said sympathetically. "Just so you know, my flattery is not just in fun. I am attracted to you. This would be a bad time for me to act on my desires, but if you were available, and if you felt the same about me, I really would attack you. Seriously! Just let me know."

"Syl, right now that's actually tempting, but I would still consider it cheating, and I just can't do it."

"I understand, Bob. I like that true-blue streak in your personality. But for now, we can talk things out if you want. I'm available to talk all week while you're here."

"I really would like that," I said. "I know how you feel about me, but I also consider you a friend. And I need a friend to confide in right now. Okay with you?"

"I'd be honored," said Sylvia.

"Can I order dinner from the restaurant, and eat at the bar?" I asked.

"Not a problem. Let me get you a menu."

"And how about a pint of that wonderful amber from the local brewery?" I added.

Sylvia changed her demeanor to that of a friend while talking over my situation. I think she really would have liked me to look at her as a lover, but she understood that this was not a good time to act on it, and I was just happy to have a friend whom I could talk to.

Eating my dinner, with three pints of beer while we talked, I had forgotten how strong the New Zealand beer was. Deciding it was time to get a full night's sleep, to be ready for the shipyard in the morning, I got up to leave, but my legs were a bit shaky, and Sylvia laughed at me.

"Well, I guess I'm not much of a drinker, as you can see," I said.

"There's another thing I like about you," Sylvia responded. "See you tomorrow night?"

"Oh yes. I'll be here. And thank you for letting me talk. I know it was not what you wanted to hear."

FINALITY

———

THE WEEK AT the shipyard was busy, but I hurried my inspections, hoping to finish on Friday. On Thursday afternoon, the shipyard told me the final hull inspection would not happen until Monday morning, due to their no overtime policy from the insurance company.

"Sorry, Bob. I know you wanted to head home on Saturday," said Brian.

"I understand," I said. "I guess this is just proof of why my wife is jealous of my job. Can't leave until the job is done, even though I should be home."

"Truly sorry," Brian McKenzie said. "So, what have you been doing every night?"

"Pouring out my troubles to poor Sylvia, I'm afraid."

"You know, Bob, every available guy in Nelson has tried to catch that girl's attention, and even us married guys think she is a real beauty. Not just her looks, but that girl has a heart of gold. And since her husband died, she has not been with a man. I mean, she has been truly celibate. Truly, she does not fool around. In a town full of sailors, she has a lot of opportunities. We all wonder who she's waiting for."

Heading to the hotel, my cell phone rang, and I saw the call was coming from Chris.

"Hi, honey. I was going to call you after I left the

shipyard this afternoon. My departure has been delayed until Monday afternoon. Only a little to finish, but the Underwriter will not authorize overtime. So, what's up?" I asked.

"I wanted to call you before you got home," she said.

And by the sound of her voice, I could tell what was coming next.

"I hate doing this over the phone," she continued, "but I have some bad news. After the last few weeks, I've decided to get a divorce. I know you won't understand, and I struggled with how to break the news. I didn't want to hit you with this as soon as you came home, and I think this will give you time to think it over, during your flight home."

There was a long pause over the phone before I said, "I felt this was coming, but hoped I was reading you wrong. Why, Chris? Do you not love me anymore? I thought we were trying to work things out."

You can imagine what I was feeling during that phone call, but because my son had warned me that this was coming, I guess I was prepared for what Chris was going to do. I knew I wasn't going to be able to change her mind.

"Bob, I still think you were a good husband, and I still love you. It's just that I can't handle your job taking precedence over our family anymore. I just can't fight that feeling of being in second place. I know your job is important, and I know you're concerned about our family, but I needed you home every night, and as long as I have waited, I now know that's impossible."

"I get that, Chris. I've been thinking about this since I got here to New Zealand. And I wondered how I would argue this out, to tell you that it would be wrong for you to leave me. I actually concluded that I have no good argument. You know how miserable I was with that forty-hour job when we first moved to Chicago. Not only wouldn't I want to go back to that, but you didn't like my moods then either, or my depressed state of mind. I'm sorry I drove you to this, and if you can't be happy with me as I am, I have no argument to keep us together."

"Bob, I'm so sorry it has come to this. I didn't want to hurt you."

I took in her words as I unlocked my hotel room and slumped my frame on the bed. As much as I thought I had been mentally prepared for Chris's words, hearing them spoken out loud by her was tearing me up inside. I rubbed my temple and sighed before saying, "Do me one favor, Chris. Prepare the kids for this before I get home. I don't think it would be fair to them if I had to be the one to tell them."

"I've already told Todd. And Todd said he would help me talk to the girls. They'll know before you get home. And this may sound odd, but I love you for how you took this news. You're a great man, Bob."

"I love you too, Chris. See you late on Tuesday, or maybe Wednesday."

Hanging up, it was surprising how relieved I felt. The huge knot in my stomach was gone, but it was replaced by sadness. I was losing the woman I loved, but this was better than the constant tension we both had lived with for the last year and more.

I decided to head down to the bar, where I ordered a Brandy Manhattan.

"What? No amber beer tonight?" Sylvia said, looking at me with curiosity.

"No, I just got off the phone with Chris. She called to officially tell me she is filing for divorce."

"Goodness," said Sylvia. She couldn't wait until you got home?"

"She said she was doing it this way to give me time to think things over on my trip home. Of course, she wasn't aware of my talk with Todd, so she didn't know

I've already had some time to think."

"So, what are you feeling right now? Sylvia asked.

"You know what? That knot in my stomach has softened. I'm sad, and a little mad, but getting rid of the tension has been a relief. I'm not happy about it, but the pressure is gone."

"I'm glad you feel that way. I think I understand that. Knowing is a relief. I remember when my husband's trawler was missing, I felt terrible for the first two weeks when he was just listed as missing. Once they found the debris, and we all knew the ship was lost and that all hands had died, I felt the same type of relief. Then I finally allowed myself to cry."

"I'm sorry. I've been so wrapped up in my own problems all week, I never thought it may have re-opened your old feelings of loss."

"Don't be sorry, Bob. Other than my mom and dad, I've never mentioned my feelings about loss, so hearing about your loss has actually helped me this week."

"But a divorce is not the same as losing your husband to death," I said.

"I'm not so sure. Death is very final, but a divorce leaves lingering doubts in your mind, which you may never lose. I could see that from our conversations this week."

"I still feel like I've ruined your week by venting about all my problems," I said to Sylvia. "Can I repay you somehow? Is there something nice I can do for you?"

"Well, seeing that you asked, I've been looking for an excuse to go to Wellington. Have you ever been over there, Bob? They have a great Maritime Museum. Plus, I'd love to go to the ballet. Would you come along? We can catch the ferry on Saturday morning and return on Sunday. I have a friend who lives in Wellington, and we can stay at her apartment. You'd be back to get to the shipyard on time. I understand you're leaving on Monday afternoon for Auckland, right?"

"Right. That'd be great. I've never been to Wellington; I'd love to treat you to the ballet. My two daughters dance ballet and I have developed an appreciation for good ballet. We'll see about the Maritime Museum, but it all sounds great."

"Fantastic," Sylvia said, "I'll call my cousin and ask her to fill in for me tending bar over the weekend."

"Is that a problem? Will your dad mind you not working?"

"Heavens no. He always tells me I need to enjoy myself more."

"Okay. I'll be ready for the trip. What time is the ferry?"

"I think they run every two hours on Saturday out of Picton. Let's plan on leaving the hotel at nine in the morning. It's less than a two-hour drive to Picton, so we will try to catch the eleven o'clock ferry. The ferry ride is about three hours but is very scenic and beautiful. We'll have time to meet my friend, Anita, have a nice dinner, and make it to the ballet. I'll call her and have her arrange ballet tickets for us."

"This all sounds great. I'm looking forward to the trip," I said.

WELLINGTON

———

THE NEXT MORNING, I met Sylvia in the hotel lobby, and we drove my car to the ferry terminal but didn't bother to take the car on the ferry. The ferry terminal in Wellington is near the Royal Ballet, and Anita lived nearby as well, so Sylvia said it was just a short taxi ride between our destinations.

The Inter-islander, Cook-Strait Ferry trip through the islands was spectacular. The trip into Wellington Harbor was also very scenic, and Sylvia loved playing tour guide and describing everything to me.

Anita, Sylvia's friend, met us at the Wellington ferry terminal. She and Sylvia had met while in college, there in Wellington. Anita was from Whangarei, far north on the North Island, but she had remained in Wellington to study law and now worked for a Wellington law firm. She was not nearly as outgoing as Sylvia was, but I could see the two of them were great friends.

Anita had arranged dinner at a restaurant near the theater for us, and she had already purchased the ballet tickets. She said her apartment was not far from the theater, but a taxi would be a good idea late at night. Even though she had purchased the ballet tickets for us, Anita refused to take any money for tickets, so I insisted on buying dinner. At dinner, I ordered a lamb crown roast, but they both said they had enough lamb growing up and ordered a seafood platter of mussels, oysters, and a lobster instead.

The ballet was better than I had ever experienced, even though I'd been to several professional ballet performances in Chicago. I told my hosts I'd need to describe the performance to my daughters, so I purchased two souvenir books during the intermission.

After the performance, we found a taxi and Anita directed the driver to her apartment. She had a small apartment on the third floor of a modern building, with a good view of Wellington Harbor. Anita offered us coffee or a nightcap, saying she only had brandy. Sylvia and I both declined, saying we needed to be sharp for the next day's activities. Anita then showed us the bathroom and her spare room, which had a single bed and a sofa sleeper. We both thanked Anita and closed the door.

"It never occurred to me that we'll be sleeping pretty close together in here," I said to Sylvia as soon as we closed the bedroom door.

"I'm not asking you to sleep with me," Sylvia said, chuckling softly, "although I'd love it if you said yes."

"Oh boy. I'm so attracted to you right now, Syl. I don't know what to say. This week has made me see what kind of a person you really are, way beyond the flirting you'd done during my last few trips."

So, what do we do then?" Sylvia asked.

"I'm still married, Syl. I can't get that fact out of my head."

"But technically your marriage is over. After your divorce, do you plan to stay alone for the rest of your life?"

"No, I need the companionship of a woman. I'd eventually find someone."

"Then give me a chance to be the first person. Nothing permanent."

"But you live here, and I need to be near my children

back in Chicago."

"I'm not asking for a commitment, Bob. At this point, I can't say I love you, but I just need to know if we are compatible. Are you attracted to me as well?"

"Oh, yes. My hormones are surging right now. But I don't want this to be a one-night stand with the chance of hurting you."

"Bob, I'm only asking for a one-night stand, but with a great guy, who I've come to respect. If you leave on Monday and never come back, I'll understand. Really! I've thought about this moment all week, and if you want me as much as I want you, then I will only be hurt if you tell me no. If you're not attracted to me, then there's the sofa."

"Syl, this scares the hell out of me. Can we lead into this slowly? I need to see what my mind says."

"I'm really into slow. We can start with the old bundling custom from one hundred years ago. Let's just lay next to each other and see what happens. Okay? Underwear stays on. Sound fair to you?"

"Lights on or off?" I asked.

"Oh, definitely leave them on! I don't want to miss any of my senses tonight."

We undressed and laid side by side, on top of the bedding. Sylvia put her arm on my chest and leaned on me to kiss my neck. She then placed my hand on her breast and slid her leg between my legs.

"Am I feeling an attraction, or is that just an unconscious anatomical response?" Sylvia asked. "What's your mind saying to you now?"

I started to shudder, and Sylvia stopped abruptly. "Is something wrong?"

"It feels really wrong, I guess because I don't think I want to stop."

"So, what's next? Can I continue?" Sylvia asked.

"I guess I'm hoping you will," I said. "I haven't felt

this turned on in a long time."

"I thought you told me Chris was fantastic that night in Miami."

"Oh yeah, I forgot," I said, a bit sheepishly.

"Then hold on, because my goal tonight will be to make you forget Chris, at least for one night, seeing as she has apparently forgotten you."

We spent most of the night trying to please one another. This wasn't just sex, it was a means for both of us, very frustrated people, to relieve the tension we'd had in our lives. We occasionally awoke during the night, gently fondled one another, and then fell back asleep. It was wonderful and gentle!

We were both awake when the sun came up.

"You have my mind messed up, young lady!"

"So, is that a good thing?" Sylvia asked.

"It feels right, as of this moment," I answered. "But I'm afraid of what happens on Monday."

"I told you, don't worry about Monday. I expected a one-night stand. However, I wouldn't mind an extension to two nights if you will have me again tonight? And by the way, don't just lie there now. You still have a very horny lady here next to you. Anything left in your tank this morning?"

"I always thought mirrors on people's ceilings were stupid," Sylvia said staring at the ceiling, as we laid in the bed next to each other. "But right now, I wish we had one. I'd like to imprint the image of the two of us on my brain, to remember this."

We finally came out of the spare bedroom and found the coffee already on, and Anita in the shower. When she eventually came out, she looked at us mischievously and said, "Are you two showering together or alone? You guys were quite entertaining last night. I should have warned you about the thin walls."

"Oh my God," I said. "I'm sorry."

"On the contrary, Bob, I'm so pleased to finally have Syl open up to someone."

"And just so you know, this was a one-night stand," said Sylvia. "Well, maybe two nights, if I can convince him."

I sat there, blushing red. Sylvia was so very open about our relationship or lack thereof. It reminded me of Chris, and it brought about a tinge of guilt for what had happened.

"Let me use the bathroom quickly, but I think you'd better shower alone, Syl," I said, standing up and fleeing the room.

"Kill-joy!" Syl quipped as I retreated.

While Sylvia was showering, Anita and I drank coffee in the kitchen.

"Bob, just so you know, Syl has talked about you since she first met you two years ago. She was mainly impressed because you never hit on her. You always talked about your wife and kids, and never once flirted with her. Although she said she always flirted with you, testing you. She knew she couldn't have you, and she is not the home-breaker type. But she called me every night last week, asking for advice. She told me about your impending divorce, and then on Friday, she said the divorce was official."

"So, she was asking you for advice? What advice?"

"She didn't want to make you think badly of her, but she knew this could be the last time she ever saw you. She didn't want to let you go once she knew that the divorce had been announced by your wife."

"But I'm leaving on Monday. I don't know if I'm ready for any commitment so soon."

"She knows that. That's why she keeps joking about the one-night stand. She was aware of that possibility going into this, but she needed to experience a good man, even if it was just for one night. Her marriage wasn't that great. Her husband was a sailor and quite a rough guy. I doubt Syl ever experienced a night like last night, ever before in her life."

I started to blush again!

Anita continued, "And she told me about that blush of yours. That says wonders about a guy who blushes when sex is mentioned."

"So, what do I do now?" I asked.

"If you want to, spend one more night with Syl. Then go home and do what you need to do. I'm hoping you stay in touch via email or something. Tell her how your life turns out. If you find another good woman, just tell her. I don't think she wants to move to Chicago, and she knows your business will not allow many visits to New Zealand. She might hope she could keep you, but she knows better. You have opened her still heart, and now maybe she can move on to a better life."

"I just don't want to see her hurting," I said.

"Syl was hurting before. Trust me, you're leaving her in a much better state than she was before she met you."

Sylvia came out of the bathroom looking radiant. Her face was glowing, and Anita was happy for her.

"So, what are you two up to doing today?" Anita asked.

"Well, we were going to take in the Maritime Museum before we head to the ferry, but I think we may need to skip that. I need to get this guy back to Nelson so he can get to work in the morning. He seems a bit tired, for some reason. Must have been a lumpy mattress," Sylvia quipped.

"Then why don't I drive you to the terminal, after I whip up a quick breakfast. Nothing fancy; just some bacon and eggs, I'm afraid," answered Anita.

"Good idea," I said. "That curvy road from Picton back to Nelson is something I don't want to drive on in the dark. I'm a good driver on the left side but using a stick shift with my left hand is confusing, and then with the rotaries, curves, and hills, just to make it interesting."

"I agree," said Syl. "Can I help you with breakfast? And Bob, it's your turn in the shower."

After a quick breakfast, Anita dropped us off at the ferry, just ten minutes before departure. Anita got out of the car and came around to the passenger side. She hugged and kissed Sylvia, and then came to me. She hugged me and whispered, "Thank you for making Syl smile again. I haven't seen her smile like this in years."

We quickly ran and boarded the ferry. We sat on deck for quite a while, with my arm around Syl. I asked, "Are you cold? Should we go inside?"

Sylvia answered, "Not at all. Just keep that arm around me."

Back in Nelson, we both ordered dinner in the hotel dining room.

"I can't remember the last time I ate here like a guest," Sylvia said. "This is kinda' neat."

"Can I ask you what you're thinking about us, and what happened last night?"

"Bob, it will take me a long time to come down from that experience. In fact, I wish it could stay fresh forever."

"I guess I mean I'm worried about you. What happens if I never come back?"

"I can see you don't understand, Bob. I never thought this was more than what we had, just for last night. The last thing I'd want to do is make you feel like you had to stay, or even have to come back. I knew that up front. I've dreamt about this ever since the first time I met you, and it was important for me to see if you were real. I've now learned I had judged you correctly, and I can be happy, even if I never see you again."

"You have to realize, Syl, I'm not the perfect guy

you've described. I can be very stubborn, and I've been known to argue. I don't want you to think I'm so perfect. I do have faults."

"Those are the normal things, Bob. We all have those faults. But you care about people. Do you realize that during all our conversations this week, your major concern, other than your kids' welfare, was not seeing Chris hurt? You said that over and over. I tend bar here six days a week, and over half the men I see are either divorced or in a bad relationship. None of them have a kind word to say about their ex-wife or girlfriend."

"It's really that bad?" I asked.

"As a bartender, I need to keep my criticism to a minimum, but yes, they say terrible things about their wives or partners. But you mentioned Chris 20 times, wanting to do the right thing. Even last night, you said you felt a tinge of guilt after Chris had just called you on the other side of the world to announce she was divorcing you."

"Well, she was good to me for many years," I said.

"See? There you go again. How can I not respect that?"

"But back to my question, Syl. Will you be okay when I leave?

"Bob, I'm already okay. Trust me. I'll be fine. However, my last question is this: Can we spend one more night together? Your room, with a much bigger bed? And I promise to let you get a little more sleep, so you're not a zombie at the shipyard tomorrow."

"Well, I think you cured me of feeling guilty. And I can always sleep on the two flights tomorrow. I think my flight is at 1300 from Nelson, and I have the 1800 Redeye to Los Angeles. I forget if I am staying in LA, or maybe I have another flight booked to Chicago. See, you have me frazzled."

"Can I ask you a bit of an embarrassing question, Bob?"

"At this point in our relationship, I'm not sure what could be too embarrassing," I said, smiling.

"Well then, I'll get right to the point. What do you think about oral sex?"

I immediately blushed, but responded, "Well, I'm not sure what to think. I suggested it to Chris one time, but she was uncomfortable with the idea, so we never got into it. I have no experience at all."

"I also have no experience with it," Sylvia responded, blushing. "But seeing we are so comfortable with one another; can we try it tonight? If either of us becomes uncomfortable, we can stop. But I cannot think of a better person to learn with than you."

"I must admit, it sounds great with you suggesting it. I'm already feeling excited, so I think the answer is yes!"

"So, let's wolf down this dinner for strength, and get to your room then. Time is a-wasting!" Sylvia said.

It was great to see Sylvia so happy. But I was still worried about her.

The next morning, she was just bubbling over. "Now my problem is going to be finding a guy who knows my body as good as you do. I think we did pretty well for two novices. What about you?"

"I didn't know I would climax just while being down on you," I said. "Sorry, but that was an incredible feeling when I felt you climax."

"Well, we have time for one normal roll in the hay, before you head to the shipyard if you are still in the mood?"

"Oh my God, woman. You are driving me crazy! Of course, the answer is yes!"

Sylvia ate breakfast with me, helped me pack my suitcase, and followed me out to my car.

Then she walked up to me, hugged me gently, and said, "Now go home, be nice to Chris, take care of your kids, and promise me you'll find a woman who likes oral sex." She blew me a kiss as she walked away.

BACK HOME

———

I ARRIVED HOME LATE on Wednesday night, and the family was asleep. I wasn't sure if I should be sleeping on the sofa under the circumstances, but I dropped my bags by the front door and went upstairs to the bedroom where I undressed and crawled into bed. I could tell that Chris was awake, but she didn't say anything.

Waking the next morning, the smell of coffee filled the air. I went downstairs to find Chris and the three kids in the kitchen. At first glance, things appeared normal. The kids were discussing the next week's events, but Chris remained quiet.

"Isn't this a school day? Everybody's home?" I asked.

Melanie was the first one to talk, and said, "Teacher conferences. So, Dad. How was New Zealand? Did you see any kiwi birds?"

I wondered if Chris had told the girls about the divorce, seeing Melanie seemed so upbeat.

Then Lilah jumped in. "This was the tuna fishing stuff, right Dad? Are the fishing ships all repaired now?"

I gave them a real brief run-down of the trip, included a quick description of the ballet in Wellington, and gave them the souvenir books.

Chris then chimed in, "It's their fall season down there now. How was the weather?"

"Beautiful weather," I responded.

I was starting to wonder if Chris had changed her mind. Things were just too normal.

Then Todd spoke up, saying, "Come on girls. Let's go upstairs. I think Mom and Dad need to talk."

The two girls each gave me a peck on the cheek as they passed, and Todd patted me on the small of my back, as the three left the kitchen.

"So, you did speak to the girls. I was starting to think you hadn't," I said to Chris.

"Yes, the four of us all talked together yesterday. I needed Todd to help me. I just couldn't do it alone. Melanie and Lilah adore you, and I was afraid of what they might say, or do. Todd sure has his head screwed on straight. He actually did most of the talking."

"Where do things stand now?" I asked.

"I explained to them that I don't hate you, and neither of us had done anything wrong. It was Todd who explained the part about my frustration with being alone most of the time. He heard my voice failing, and after my conversation with him last week, he seemed to understand, and was able to tell the girls the situation as well as I could've."

"We sure raised some great kids, Chris. That's what worries me now. If you go through with this divorce, what will it do to the kids?"

"I know Todd will be fine. He's not taking sides. The girls are both upset with my decision, which I was worried about. After they convinced me to go to Miami, I realized just how devoted they were to you. Whatever we decide to do, please tell me you'll keep those girls in your life. I know I'm making that difficult for you, but they'll be okay if you keep calling, emailing, and seeing them as often as possible."

"Oh, of course. You know I adore all three kids, and their reaction to this divorce just makes me love and respect them more than ever. But what have you decided? How are you proceeding?"

"Bob, if one of us had cheated on the other, or if you were otherwise a terrible husband, I would sue for a ton of alimony. You have always been good to me, and I feel terrible for what I'm doing to you. I just can't see myself growing older, and spending most of my life alone."

"Does that mean you're going to look for a new love in your life? Divorcing me doesn't change your alone time."

"Bob, really! That has not even crossed my mind. Right now, I'm trying to see how to keep the family together, without you as my husband. I plan to go back into the real estate business. My old boss, Libby, said she'd love to have me back. I don't think we need this big house once Todd is in college, and the girls and I can either get an apartment or at least a smaller house until they head off to college. I don't want to punish you by keeping this big house and taking all your money."

"That means I need a place to live as well, so it will still be two residences. But, with all my travels, I don't need much."

"Bob, this would have been easier had you been a terrible husband and father." Chris smiled sadly when she said that.

"I'd ask you to change your mind, but I guess it's too late for that?"

"Yes. It's better now than later, slowly beginning to hate you. I know you don't fully understand, but I want us to part as friends, not enemies. Okay?"

"I actually do understand. I've seen this coming but was hoping it would never happen. I see couples on these cruise ships, spending a week together, and not even talking to one another. I wouldn't want to see us like that. The divorce is not what I wanted, but better than starting to hate one another."

"You asked me about looking for a new love in my

life. It's my turn to ask you that question."

"Not now, Chris. But I think I need a woman in my life. I just can't even think that way right now."

"I brought it up because I understand that side of you, Bob. If you do find someone, just know that I'll understand. You have a lot of love to give, and I'll tell the kids I want you to find someone. Just be sure she'll accept our children and treat them well."

"I'm going to miss our times together, Chris. You've always been responsive to my needs."

"In a strange way, I'll miss it too," Chris said.

"So, what shall I say to the kids now?" I asked.

"I told them they could ask you questions, but they promised not to say too much. They know this will be tough on you, and they want to keep it low-key."

"Okay, I'd better go see them," I said. Then I turned and added, "I don't know how you want me to treat you. Can I kiss you, hug you? This change is just too final."

Chris grabbed my hand and pulled me to her and gave me a big hug, and a peck on the cheek. "I am sorry!" she said.

I went upstairs and found the two girls sitting in Todd's room.

"Well, this is unusual. I thought Todd's room was off-limits to you girls?"

"We're talking about you and Mom," Todd said in reply. "How did it go? Did it go okay?"

"I think we understand each other," I told them. "I'm not happy of course, but Mom and I don't hate each other. Our lifestyles just became very different over the years, and I can see why Mom couldn't deal with it forever. At least this way, I think we can remain friends. Do you have any questions? Mom said you had a great discussion yesterday, and I'm so proud of you for trying to understand. Please don't hate either of us for this happening."

All three children tried to talk at once, but Lilah broke in first. "Dad, we could never hate you," she said, sincerely. "We're upset with Mom, but we don't hate her either. Todd explained how hard it was for Mom to be alone so much. And we would not expect you to give up your career. We just want to be part of your life after this."

Then Melanie continued, "That's the important thing, Dad. If you're not living with us, will we still see you? Where will you live?"

"I'll find a small apartment near where you guys end up living. Mom thinks it's time to sell this big house, so once you move, I'll stay close by."

Todd then got his turn, saying, "Dad, we understand, and we love you guys. Even in this bad time, both you and Mom have tried to protect us. We know it's tough on you both, and we want to help you, not make it more difficult."

"Wow, how could anyone ask for better kids!" I said with tears welling up in my eyes.

The children must have seen my tears because all three of them stood up and embraced me in a great group hug.

BACK TO THE CRUISE SHIPS

I WENT BACK TO the next cruise ship audit with a new outlook on what life had in store for me. I wasn't happy about my impending divorce, but it was happening, and I was ready to move on.

After two days of busy audits, opening meetings, ship tours, and getting started on record reviews, I was looking for an opportunity to get alone with Jody. I felt she had been avoiding me, or so I thought.

As the team broke up from our evening dinner discussion about the events of the day, I finally caught her alone. "It's my turn to ask. Can we talk?" I said to her.

"Well, I was going to get a good night's sleep, but maybe a short one," Jody replied.

"I spend all my time in the engine room, so I haven't found the good, quiet spots yet. Do you know one?" I asked.

"On a Sea-Day, and this ship is small. If you don't mind, can we sit in my cabin? I got a balcony cabin on this trip, due to a passenger cancellation."

"That's fine," I said. "Lead the way."

We entered her cabin. Jody offered me a seat by the balcony door. "It's pretty windy out on the balcony, but let's open the door for some fresh air," she said, sliding the door open to let in some air. "Why don't you pull the easy chairs up near the balcony patio door, I have nothing but a glass of water to offer you. Is that okay?"

"Water sounds great. My dinner was good, but the veggies on the plate were quite salty. I could use the water."

"So, what's up?" Jody asked me as she handed me the glass of water.

"Jody, I don't want to force myself into your personal life, but after our frank conversations on the first few cruises, you have me concerned. I can tell you're not your normal, outgoing self this week. I always respect your no-nonsense business approach, but something has changed. Can I ask what's going on, or don't you want me to butt in?"

"I don't want to burden you. You have enough on your plate with Chris, so I decided it wouldn't be right to add my problems to yours. Let's just talk about your trip to New Zealand. How did Chris enjoy the trip?"

"So that's it. Then let's get that question out of the way right now. Chris didn't go to New Zealand after all. She said that Lilah had an important school trip planned, and she had promised to be a chaperone. She refused to go with me."

Jody leaned forward in her chair, her eyes asking questions.

"My son called me on my flight over there and said he felt he had to warn me about something serious. Apparently, he had overheard Chris talking to her old boss and overheard her saying she was going to divorce me."

"Oh my!" Jody said. "Things had looked so positive when we talked last."

"Chris called me when I was in New Zealand and informed me of her intentions to file for a divorce. She said that she was sorry. That seems like a weird thing to say, when you divorce someone, right."

"Well, it depends on the kind of person you're divorcing, I suppose."

"Well, that's exactly what she kept saying. She kept apologizing and saying she felt bad because I was a good father and husband."

"Wow, that's sad," Jody said. "So did it just progress from frustration to divorce in just a couple weeks?"

"No, this had been ongoing for a while. I sensed that things weren't right, but I just couldn't put my finger on it. When I returned home on Wednesday, I was served with divorce papers. She had called it quits after all."

"Oh God, I'm so sorry. In Miami, I thought things were so positive," said Jody.

"I asked Chris about that too, and as it turned out my two girls were the ones who told her she was not treating me right, and Lilah & Melanie made her go to Miami. Can you believe my kids? Chris did say that she gave things an honest effort while we were together in Miami, but she still felt she was second fiddle to my work, and she didn't want to try anymore. This has been festering for a long time, and although I'm upset it has come to this, I don't feel as depressed as I think I should right now. I almost feel relieved. But there are a lot of unanswered questions. I had only two days before heading over here for this audit, so nothing has been settled. In fact, Chris told me this was a good example of why she made her decision. She said most people could just call into work in this situation and take a vacation or an emergency leave of absence, but here I was headed off on another trip two days after my wife says she's divorcing me."

Jody shook her head.

She understands why I couldn't do that, but this devotion to duty was actually what she didn't want from a husband."

"So, what happens now? Jody asked.

"Oh, no … not so quick. I was the one who asked you what was wrong. We have all week, and I have no detailed Chris-versus-Bob answers right now. What's with you?"

"Oh, I'm sorry if I've been wearing my feelings on my sleeve. It's hard for me to hide, I guess. After my conversations with you last month, I had it all planned to go home, discuss Les's work worries, and get things back on track. But while Les didn't ask for a divorce, he admitted that he's found someone else. As he said, 'he just needed a pretty face who would be home every night.' He said he could deal with my travels when he was also traveling, but having a strong, businesswoman as his partner was not satisfying for him."

"That's terrible," I interjected. "It sounds like your situation is worse than mine. Can you believe Chris said she still loves me yet wants the divorce? And I think I understand how she feels, which is weird. But in your case, Les admitted he has someone else. Do you even think he still cares for you? That must be tearing your heart out…"

"No, not really. I suspected for a long time that it was over and that he might be seeing someone else. At first, the mini honeymoons seemed nice when we both got together, but I suspected something was not right. Guys don't have headaches when their wives suggest having sex! Like you, I'm proud of my work, and when I talked to Les about an important project that I was handling, he would always make wise cracks about being the big, important woman on the job. At first, I thought he meant it as a compliment, but then I started to see he felt threatened by my success and my position of authority."

"That had to be tough. How did you deal with it?"

"I stopped talking about what I was doing at work and talked about his work. He was a mechanic in the Air Force, and when he retired at forty-one, he had trouble finding work. Air Force mechanics need a lot of additional training to qualify for an airline mechanic's job, and Les hated the idea of doing more training. I think he was great in the military, but not suited for civilian life."

"Boy, do I understand that problem. At first, I talked to Chris about my work but avoided it when I saw her looking bored. When you love your job, like we both do, you want to talk about it. My problem was when the kids got older and started to ask questions when I came home. They, particularly the two girls, always seemed proud of what I was doing, and they always wanted a blow-by-blow description of my jobs and travels when I came home. Chris never stopped them, but she usually left the room when we started these kinds of conversations. That is apparently why the girls told Chris she needed to go to Miami with me. Damn, I love those kids for trying."

"Yes, you seem to have a great relationship with your kids. How will you handle that if she gets her divorce?" asked Jody.

"That's my biggest worry. I know my son will be okay. He told me he understands that nothing bad happened and that he loves me. I actually cried when he talked to me. It was like he was consoling me, not the other way around. The girls talked with Chris and Todd the day before I returned from New Zealand. I'd told Chris, I was not going to be the one to explain it to them and she promised to have them ready for a talk when I got home. But Jody, you have two daughters, don't you? I haven't heard you talk about them much. How will this dilemma with Les affect them?"

"My daughters' lives have always been affected by my career. I had them early, and my sister and my mom raised them as much as I did, while Les was in the Air Force. We have a good relationship, but when I was working or traveling, they were part of my sister's family. When my sister was not available, my mom stepped in. They may not even be shocked by Les leaving me.

He was seldom home. They love him as their father, but he has never been a big influence in their lives. I think they'd be more upset if my sister's husband left her," Jody said, chuckling.

I chuckled too. "My God, Jody," I said. "Are we screwed up or what? I wish I knew what my future holds. Things are pretty screwed up in my world right now. Even though I saw it looming for some time, I was trying to divert a confrontation. I'm very worried about my kids, particularly the girls. I can't wait until we go home on Friday so I can talk with them again."

"Bob, now that we have both of our situations out in the open, let's keep talking. We have different problems, but both are related to our nomadic lifestyles. My situation is over. Les found his truck-stop waitress, and she'll be home every night when he wants her to be. I need to move on. But your situation is still very volatile, and if you need advice or just a sounding board for your thoughts, just let me know. I really like you, and I want you to come out of this with as little damage as possible."

"Thanks, Jody. I'm glad we now have all of this out in the open."

I walked back to my cabin feeling much better than before. Having someone who understood my problems was very therapeutic. My thoughts went back to Sylvia, back in New Zealand, and for the first time, I realized I was very attracted to Jody. Our relationship had progressed from respect to friendship over the first few cruises, but now, I was feeling an emotional attraction. It was too early to decide how I should react to that attraction, and both of us were much too vulnerable at this point in our relationship to make a good decision. I thought it was best to just put it out of my head!

"WOW, Bob!" I said. "That's one hell of a story. I assume you and Jody worked out your problems, seeing you're now husband and wife."

"Obviously. It took a while," Bob said. "That was also an interesting story, and maybe I can continue this tomorrow. By the way, I'm feeling a little queasy. Is the weather changing? You know my problem with motion sickness. Shall I pop a pill?"

"This tug doesn't have weather-tracker electronics yet, so I'll call Captain Wright on the *Samantha*, and ask what the weather looks like along our way to the Soo. We're in no hurry on this trip, and I don't want to lose these barges. So, if the weather is looking dicey, we can pull into Muskegon or Ludington to let the weather pass."

"Thanks, Curt. I'd hate to have you see me at my worst. I don't deal well with motion."

"Not a problem, Bob. I have never been sea-sick but had guys in the Coast Guard who never got over it. Just for safety reasons, I'll delay the trip if Captain Wright recommends it. So, why not pop that pill and go down to the lower berthing area. There's a lot less motion down low in the vessel, you realize."

"I'll do that. Thanks. I didn't have the luxury of sleeping below deck on those cruise ships. Remind me to tell you my story about riding a 1200-foot supertanker across the Atlantic. Those things also roll when the weather changes. I didn't get sick but felt queasy the entire five days out in the open sea."

When Bob went down to his bunk, I called Captain Wright. "Hey Cap, I'm on my way to the Soo with these two scows. I don't have a weather tracker on this tug, and we can feel the motion picking up a little. I don't want to lose these barges if the weather kicks up quickly, so I figured I'd better call and have you check on the weather. I'm off Saugatuck right now and could duck into Muskegon or Ludington if you think it'd be a good idea. There's no hurry for us to reach the Soo. Bill wants me to spend a week at MCM, drydocking the tug and inspecting the barges."

"I'm in the pilothouse right now, let me check," Noel said. "Yes, I see a front moving in from the northwest. It's not a bad one, but with your two barges being light, I wouldn't risk it. If you were running the west, Wisconsin side, you'd be okay, but along the Michigan shoreline, it'll get rough. It's not a big storm, so why not duck into Muskegon, spend a comfortable night, and check with me tomorrow morning. It should have passed by then, and I'll check the NOAA weather buoys at that time for wave heights, so you can decide when to resume the trip."

"Hey, thanks a lot, Cap. I also have Bob Evers aboard for this trip, and if you remember him from talking that night in Norfolk, he doesn't deal well with rough weather. He'll be happy we're spending a motionless night at the dock."

"Glad to help, Curt. By the way, I hear you have Lonnie Willis with you on this trip. I understand he'll be coming over to the *Samantha* for a few rotations next month. I also understand his wife just had her baby girl. Tell him I send my congratulations, and I'm looking forward to working with him."

"Well, Noel. I'll contact you in the morning. What's your watch schedule so I don't wake you up?"

"I'll be having coffee by 0600, so call anytime. If you have any problems, even middle of the night, it's okay as well."

"Thanks, Cap. Talk to you then."

After calling Bill Strauss to tell him about the weather, and our plans to stay overnight in Muskegon, I called the local tug company in Muskegon, who were friends of Bill, and we pulled into their slip. It was nice to have Lonnie aboard because after working together in Toledo, we understood one another, and Lonnie said he'd work with the deckhands to get the barges secured to the dock. We then tied the tug to the dock, protected by the barges, so Bob would have a peaceful, non-motion evening.

I went below and found Bob fast asleep, so I told Lonnie and the two deckhands about a great little bar, just two blocks away, that served great burgers. I told them they could go over there for dinner, and I'd take the first watch. They offered to bring back a burger for me, and figuring Bob may be awake by then, I told them to bring one back for him as well.

As I figured, Bob came up to the galley about a half-hour later asking why the motion had stopped. I told him the weather was building, and we were safely nestled into Muskegon Harbor until morning.

"I was about to make a fresh pot of coffee, and Lonnie and the guys are bringing back a hamburger for each of us. Wait 'til you see these burgers! They can each feed two people. I can't wait to hear the boys' reactions, because I didn't warn them about the size of these things. That little bar has catered to sailors' appetites for over fifty years, and they still have a great following," I said to him.

"I must say, I am hungry. That's what woke me up," Bob said. "So, the weather was turning bad? Is it a big storm?"

"Nothing terrible," I assured him, "but with this smaller tug and those two light barges trailing behind us, Captain Wright recommended that we play it safe, and Bill Strauss agreed."

"Well, my stomach has calmed down now, and I'm glad we're here."

"You know, Bob, you stopped your story at the point where it looked like you and Jody were becoming attracted to one another. Would you like to continue your story? After having met Chris, Jody, and your kids, I'm interested to know how things fell together."

"I don't want to bore you, Curt. Some of my cruise ship crew-member stories are more interesting. Some are quite exotic and juicy!

"I want to hear those as well, but I need to know why your youngest son with Chris was born after you married Jody. That sounds intriguing."

Not as intriguing as you might think, actually. Okay then, here's the rest of my story. Then we move on to the more interesting stuff."

CONFRONTATION

——————

AFTER A SHORT week at home after my New Zealand trip, I was off to Miami for the fifth cruise ship
audit. This was the training audit for my mentor, John
Bryce, who happened to be working for me this time.
The goal was for him to be an occasional relief on this
cruise ship project. We both had other projects going,
so neither one of us could be exclusively tied to these
cruise ship audits. As usual, Jody asked for a meeting at
the hotel on Friday night before boarding the ship the
following morning, to discuss the previous audits and
decide if any changes were needed on the next audit.
She had flown in from LA on Thursday to discuss other
projects in their Miami office, so she was waiting for
me in the hotel lobby when I arrived. After I checked in,
Jody motioned me over to where she was sitting.

"Let's not get into too much detail now, because the
others will be walking in soon," Jody said to me. "But in
general, how did things go at home?" she asked

"You know, if we weren't talking about a divorce, I
would say it was fantastic. Isn't that weird?"

"Oh, my! I can't wait to hear more. Can we talk later?
I've been worried all week."

"Sure......" I started to respond, and just then, Sam
came into the lobby.

Sam hugged me and whispered in my ear, "Be sure

to let me know how things work out at home. I've been worried about you since you told me about the divorce on the last cruise."

I realized just how good of a friend Samantha had become to me, especially knowing that she had doubted my integrity at the start of this project.

Soon, the meeting was over, and everyone got up to leave. Jody pulled me aside and said, "Bob, we have that subject to discuss."

Following Jody, I said, "Where shall we go?"

"Due to the nature of this subject, I think the privacy of my room will be okay if you don't mind," she answered.

Together, we walked up to Jody's room and the moment we stepped inside, she turned to me and said, "Is it final? She wants the divorce?"

"Oh yes. It's final. We talked to an attorney before I left."

"A joint attorney? She isn't being terrible?"

"Not at all. She's only asking for child support, no alimony. She's going back to work in real estate, and we're selling the house to save on expenses; she's being very fair and reasonable. Truly amazing!"

I described the events of the week, my discussion with my kids, and even included Chris's wish for me to find someone to love in my life.

"You know, I liked Chris as soon as I met her," Jody said. "I thought maybe I was wrong about her during this divorce issue, but she is a good person after all."

"So, what about your situation? What happened with Les?"

"Well, Les moved out while we were on the last cruise. I called him to ask what he wanted to do, and he said it was up to me. He has no plans to marry this lady, so he said he didn't need a divorce unless I wanted one. I told him it was still a good idea, just for legal issues down the road, and he just said to go ahead, and do what I wanted."

"It hurts me just to hear how unconcerned he is," I replied.

"Remember, we've not been a couple for a long time. So, it was just a formal end to what I should have known was over a long time ago. You, on the other hand, thought you had hope until the end. That must be harder to deal with."

I nodded silently.

Then I told Jody about the hug Chris gave me when she said she was sorry. "With her actions, I almost thought she had changed her mind," I said. "But I told her about the sad couples we see on these cruises, and we agreed it was better to part now, while we are still friends. The only big issue now is, how I'm going to keep my kids in my life from now on. That'll be tough. I had once thought about moving closer to my jobs, but with East Coast, Gulf Coast, and West Coast jobs, as well as being overseas all the time, that's impossible. Flights from O'Hare cover everywhere I need to be."

"I'd like to talk about that further during this cruise, Bob. I have a similar problem, and we can get into details later. For now, we'd better get a good night's sleep. Long day tomorrow on the *Infinity*."

Jody walked me to the door, but before I opened it, she gave me a long hug. I could feel her relax. As if a load had been lifted off her. I was a bit confused by it but said nothing and left and went to my room.

INDECISION

—

THE AUDIT WENT well, and John was becoming a trusted part of the team. The ship's engineers liked and trusted him too. What's not to like about a gray-haired, old Scotsman?

On the third day, after dinner, Jody grabbed my elbow while I was leaving the dining room and said quietly, "I think we need to talk about personnel questions for the rest of this contract. John should be trained to take over some of the audits, am I right?"

"He feels ready," I replied.

"Well, do you mind coming to my cabin, so we can talk things over?" Jody asked.

"Let's go," I said.

Jody led the way to her cabin. On the way there, she joked about not having a balcony for this trip. "I think we all have inside cabins. You too?" she added.

"It sure is a comedown since the last cruise, but we're supposed to be working, right?"

We both chuckled.

"Bob, I don't know how to start this," Jody continued. "I like John, and I'm sure he can do this job, but I need you on these cruises. What am I supposed to do?"

"What do you mean, Jody? What's the problem?"

"This may be an awkward question, but what do you think of me?"

"Jody, you know I think you're great. I respect you, and like you a lot. You're doing a great job."

"Here's the embarrassing part," Jody continued. "I need to know if you are attracted to me. Not sure how to say that without looking foolish. If you're not, then I've just messed up our relationship."

"Well, I am, Jody. I just never thought we were in a situation to do anything about it, so I've tried hard to ignore that feeling. Are you saying you're attracted to me?"

"Oh, God, Bob. The first time I saw you in LA at that pre-contract meeting, I was smitten. But I knew you were married, and just hid the feeling away. You blushing in Miami, when Chris teased you about that hot and heavy night, may have impressed Sam, but it made me flutter inside wishing I was as lucky as Chris was that weekend. Then seeing you handle your failing marriage with such care for your kids and Chris, I became downright jealous of Chris."

"Let me stop you there for a minute," I interrupted. "Am I hearing you say that you're falling in love with me?"

"Bob, I think I've been in love with you since the night you counseled me on how to solve my problem with Les. I guess I already knew it was over with him, but you showed such concern for me. Then I saw your marriage fall apart, and how you handled things with such grace that I wanted so bad to have someone like you."

"So, what do we do now, Jody? You live in Southern California, and I have my three kids in Chicago. And, as you mentioned, John will be taking over many of the next cruise audits. I've been attracted to you as well, but never thought this was happening, so I need time to absorb what you've just told me."

"Bob, I talked to my daughters last week after Les left.

The oldest, Alexa, starts college in the fall, and Roberta is a senior in high school. Roberta asked if she could live with my sister's family full time. She seemed to know there was no reason to keep our home, with just her and I being part-time residents there."

"Where will you go, Jody?"

"Okay, here it comes, Bob; what would you think of me moving to Chicago? I'm not saying we live together, but I need to see more of you. I asked my company president, and they would love to have a Chicago-based consultant, and he also agreed to let me open a small office there. I wouldn't interfere with your commitments with your kids, but we could spend some quality time together. If you were to decide that you cannot love me, I'll back away, but I just can't let this opportunity pass me by."

"Okay, my turn to be embarrassed, I guess. Being this naïve person, whom you've learned I can be, I just wasn't expecting this. I now find myself somewhere between blushing and wanting to jump your bones! With more warning, I might have asked you if I could spend the night, because yes, *I am* physically attracted, but have tried hard not to be. I had no idea the feeling was mutual."

"Probably because I tried to hide it as well. But remember the hug we gave each other after our heart-to-heart at the hotel? I felt so comfortable in your arms, I almost lost my balance. That's when I decided that I needed to ask you if you could feel the same."

"Wow, I felt that relaxation during our hug. It confused me. Now I understand."

"So, you're actually tempted to stay the night? I heard you say it, didn't I?" Jody quizzed.

"Are we ready for such a big step? I don't want our first encounter to be just sexual? I'm still in shock, you know."

"So, you're going to run away from that offer? It's not a big step for me. I've been thinking this way for a long time."

"This will sound like I'm scared," I said. "And maybe I am. First of all, yes; I want you to move to Chicago. And, if you give me a day or two to get my mind around this, I would like to stay. I'm just not ready yet. You've scrambled my brain tonight. Maybe it's emotional overload."

"In one way, I'm disappointed, but knowing you, I am taking this turn-down as a compliment. It is a compliment, isn't it?"

"Trust me, it's a compliment. Our first time together needs to be special, and I want our minds to be free. I can't be that relaxed tonight. Do you understand?"

"Okay, go home to your lonely cabin then," Jody said. But she pulled me to her and gave me that same relaxed hug, and then she kissed me passionately.

"Oh no, you're not going to change my mind, though that kiss nearly did it," I said, pulling back. "Just how the hell are we going to work together tomorrow?"

"Suffer!" Jody replied. "I gave you the opportunity, but you passed it by." I'm going to enjoy the stress on your face during tomorrow's interviews."

I hugged her closely, and Jody tried for another kiss.

"Your turn to suffer," I said, as I quickly opened the door to leave. "See you at breakfast."

Watching her standing there, I knew I wasn't ready to sleep. I needed to calm down; in fact, I needed a stiff drink, so I headed to the quietest corner of the bar and ordered myself a Brandy Manhattan.

"Cognac," asked the bartender?

"God no; just bar brandy."

I was still in shock. Yes, I'd been attracted to Jody since that first LA meeting and had attributed it to her take-charge personality. I enjoyed looking at good-looking women but had always been in love with Chris, and until recently, always felt I had everything I needed at home. Even during Chris's cold period over the last year, I wanted her to stay, and deep down, I still loved her.

Now, knowing things were really over between us, and the divorce was in progress, I yearned for the long-term companionship and the physical pleasure that had been missing over the last year.

Now, other than my experience with Sylvia in New Zealand, which I knew had no future, Jody was the first person to activate those feelings in me again, and this could be the long-term relationship I needed; maybe we both needed. However, I was afraid. I didn't want to make a mistake by hurting Jody or hurting myself. I could tell that Jody was ready, but was I ready?

Then there were the kids' feelings to keep in mind. Would someone in my life, this quickly, be understandable and acceptable to them?

At that point, I wondered why this had to come so quickly, while I was still in such turmoil. But I also knew my hormones were telling me that I had just turned down a chance to let off some steam for the night. But hey… that's just not me!

CONFESSION

T HE NEXT TWO days were normal, with me getting
John prepared to take over the audits for a while.
I was not scheduled again for a cruise until several in
the Mediterranean, a couple months away. On the third
night, after dinner, Jody told me she had something
important to say, and I needed to come to her room. I
was surprised at Jody's insistence, but followed her,
wondering what was so important.

When we got to Jody's cabin, I started to say, "What's
the problem?"

Jody interrupted and said, "I need to know if we are
going to be a couple. This waiting business of yours is
no good. I don't need you to say you love me just yet,
but I'm frustrated and very horny. What's going to happen with us?"

I was blushing, and asked, "So, are you telling me we
need to sleep together?"

"In short, yes I am. So, what's your answer?"

"I guess if you put it that way, I can't say no, can I?
But first, I have two questions."

"Okay, ask your questions, but please be quick about
it. I'm ready now," Jody said.

"The first one is, have you heard of bundling?"

"You mean that ancient way of sleeping together, but
doing nothing? That's not what I want tonight, buster!"

"No, but can we start with the lights on, and keep our underclothes on, just for a while?"

"That is really strange. But sure, why not."

"The second question is a little embarrassing."

"Okay, I'm ready. But it can't be any stranger than that first one."

"I just need to know, are you into oral sex?"

"I was wrong. This one is also strange. But the answer is: I've never tried it, nor have I had it done to me, but I've always wanted to learn."

"Fantastic!" I said.

"And just why did you ask that? Was that a deal-breaker or something?"

"Maybe not. But I promised I'd ask."

"Promised who?" Jody asked.

"I promise I'll tell you some day, but not tonight."

"So, can I strip down to just my bra and panties now? Or is that too much removed?"

"That's about right. I'll just keep my shorts on for now."

"I need to ask, were you this weird with Chris?"

"No, this is different. Someday you'll understand."

CHICAGO

———

IRETURNED TO CHICAGO to deal with the divorce lawyer. I thought a no-fault divorce would be easy, and Chris was being very cooperative, but lawyers don't make anything simple.

Chris and I were looking for the financial records the lawyer had requested. Chris was also starting to pack boxes for her move, although the house had not even been listed for sale yet.

I asked her, "So, will this house be your first big sale, once you start working again?"

"We'll let the residential salespeople handle this place. Maybe I didn't tell you, but I'll be working in industrial and commercial properties. I asked Libby, my boss if I could get into that field this time, and she agreed."

"Oh, I had no idea," I said. "I remember Libby. She had you in residential before."

"I had dabbled in the commercial side a little when Todd was a baby. Then I tried to stay local, just selling residential. Of course, once Melanie came along, being a full-time Mom seemed best."

"Yes, and you are a great Mom. I always brag about the job you did with our kids, and although it was tough, I love you for putting the kids ahead of your job."

"I have no regrets. It was great being a full-time mom. But now, it's time to expand my horizons. You understand, don't you Bob?"

"Yes. During these last few months, it's been a tough learning curve for me, but I really do understand. I was married to both you and my career, so now it's your turn."

"Bob, I told you I wasn't looking for another man in my life, but have you been thinking about yourself? I know you said you didn't want to be alone."

"Well, I don't want to rush into something like that," I answered.

"Let me tell you something. After meeting those two ladies you work with on the cruise ships, I wondered if maybe one of them might be a good match for you. Does Sam still have that dark-side thing going?"

"I thought I'd told you, but maybe not, due to the shock of everything in our life. Sam resigned and she is living in Croatia with one of the environmental officers she met on the ship. It's a long story."

"That sure seems sudden. Very impulsive, I'd say."

"If you'd met the guy and seen how similar their problems in life paralleled each another, you'd understand. Both of them had terrible previous relationships because of their nomadic lifestyles, so Sam and Niko are going to hope for the best, as she said; no promises, just hope."

"Okay, so how about you and Jody? She seems to be your type."

"Well, we'll see. Jody's company is thinking about starting an office in the Chicago area, and Jody may be looking into that possibility sometime soon. I think we'd better get back to our financials."

That afternoon, Jody called to ask me what I was doing for the weekend. I told her that I was helping Chris clean out the house even though it wasn't a rush because the house hadn't even been listed yet.

"I know exactly what you were doing," Jody replied, "Chris told me."

I was stunned. "How? When? What's going on?" I stuttered.

"Don't get paranoid on me," Jody replied. "Did you know that Chris will be handling industrial real estate?"

"I just learned that today. I thought she said commercial. But I still don't know why you were talking to Chris."

"Well, Chris called me to ask for advice. She's handling a large, vacant piece of industrial land on the west side of Chicago. She has a developer interested in a shopping center, which is why she said commercial, but they want the land tested for contamination. Chris figured I would know what to do, so she called me."

Oh my God. My almost-ex and my new main-squeeze were becoming friends! That was weird and I told Jody as such. But she chuckled and said, "If you think that's weird, wait until you hear this."

"Do I even want to know?"

"It was kind of sweet, Bob. She asked me if I was attracted to you because she thought we'd be a good match."

"I can hardly believe it. She's playing matchmaker for me?"

"It sure looks that way," Jody answered.

That's when I told Jody that Chris and I had been talking while looking for records for the lawyer, and Chris had asked me if I had thought about finding someone.

"She suggested both Sam and you," I told her.

"Okay. So, that brings me back to my first question, what are you doing for the weekend?"

"I guess my answer depends on what you're doing," I replied.

"Then, first of all, are you moved into your apartment?"

"Yes, I moved yesterday, but it's a mess."

"No problem, as long as it has a bed. I miss you really bad."

"It does have a bed. So, how soon can you be here?"

"I was hoping you'd say that. I'm at LAX right now. My plane for Chicago leaves in thirty minutes."

"Fantastic! That gives me enough time to clear a path from the door to the bed and get to O'Hare before you arrive."

"So, you don't have any plans with the kids, do you?"

"Not this weekend, and I'm on a short trip, a small passenger boat inspection in Cleveland, for two days next week. Just a quick insurance survey."

"That works out well," said Jody. I'm working with Chris for a couple days, but I hadn't told her which days yet, so I'll work it around your trip."

"So, how long will you be here?" I asked.

"That's the next surprise," said Jody. "I told you my boss wanted me to start a branch office in Chicago, and when I told him about this job, he told me to stay a couple weeks, find a good location for an office, and get things moving."

"Unbelievable. I thought our liaisons would only be during our cruises for quite a while. We thought the Chicago move was months away."

"I think we have Chris to thank for this," Jody said. "Can you believe it?"

"I don't think I'm ready to tell Chris about us just yet," I said. "But it is weird that she asked both of us if we were attracted to each other. It's almost like she had a premonition."

"That's what I thought as well. At first, I wondered if you had told her about us during that last cruise. But hey, my flight is boarding. See you at O'Hare at six-fifteen. A quick dinner, and then to your messy apartment, which has a clean bed. See you soon."

I was excited. I'd planned on a boring weekend organizing my apartment. Having Jody in Chicago so quickly, with plans to move permanently, was better than I'd hoped. Jody had been in my thoughts constantly since our time on the last cruise, and I'd worried about her changing her mind, just letting the relationship slowly disappear. Hearing her excitement over the phone, I now knew she wanted our lives to remain together.

I went back to my apartment, straightened up a little, made the bed, and then headed to O'Hare.

It only took one extra circuit driving through the baggage claim area on the lower drive. On the second round, I saw Jody at the curb. I hopped out of the car to grab her bags, but Jody pushed them aside and gave me a big hug and a passionate kiss.

"I really have missed you, fella. You made one heck of an impression on me those last couple days. I'm so happy to be here."

"And I'm so glad you feel that way, Jody. I was so worried that maybe you would have thought we weren't compatible."

"Oh my God. How could you have worried about that?"

"Maybe I'm still a bit paranoid. Finding you so quickly, I was just afraid it was too good to be true."

"Hey, Buddy! Move it!" the traffic cop yelled.

"Damn! I always laugh when this happens to other people when I'm waiting for a Limo. This is the first time I've had to personally deal with the O'Hare traffic cops. We'd better get moving."

We laughed as we got into the car.

"Where shall we go to get something to eat?" Jody asked once she was comfortably seated.

"Are you in the mood for a nice meal or something quick?" I asked.

"Let's make it quick, so we can get to your apartment," Jody answered.

"I know a great place for Italian Beef, or they have Gyros if you prefer."

"I've heard you talk about Chicago's Italian Beef before. That sounds great."

"Right. We'll get one plain Italian Beef and one combo, and we can share."

"And what is a combo?"

"Oh yah, sorry. That's Italian Beef with Italian sausage. Do you prefer hot peppers or sweet peppers?"

"Spicy; I think I'm going to enjoy learning about Chicago with you."

THE BURBS

———

THE WEEKEND WENT by so quickly. Jody and I enjoyed each other's company, and my apartment never got organized. I guess Jody's priorities changed! I had to be in Cleveland on Tuesday afternoon for a quick condition survey for insurance. I was supposed to be back in Chicago by early evening on Wednesday. Jody made plans to meet with Chris on Tuesday to consult with her buyer on the property they were now working on together. Meanwhile, we had talked about Jody staying in my apartment while I was gone. When I returned, we would search for a suitable location for her office and find her a nice apartment to move into. Things were moving quite fast and becoming quite hot. One minute, I was moving out of the house I had shared with my soon-to-be ex-wife and moving in briefly with a woman I had not even yet made my girlfriend. I wanted Jody to live with me right away, but she said she needed her own space and I understood that.

"You'll be entertaining your kids, and I don't want them thinking we are a couple," she said.

That made sense to me. She had obviously thought a lot of things through before her move to Chicago. I was just happy to have her keeping me company.

"But just so you know," Jody added. "I arranged the cruise ship audit schedule so that you and I are always working together."

I looked at her and smiled.

"John will have to work with Bill, Amber, and Russ. I don't want you tempted by any of those cruise-ship floozies at the captain's table."

"Miss Lister and her room key. How can I ever forget?" I said. We both broke into fits of laughter.

We agreed to keep Chris uninformed of our arrangement until we were both ready to tell her. I assured Jody that Chris would not know if she didn't want her to know. My new apartment was only fifteen minutes away from the house Chris and I once shared, but I knew the chances of Jody bumping into Chris at my apartment were next to impossible because Chris never came to that neighborhood.

"I'll stay close to your apartment then," Jody said. "You said that greasy spoon place nearby actually has good food? I'll eat there when I'm not with Chris or her client."

———————

On Monday morning, I was working with Chris, packing boxes when her phone rang, and she answered it.

"Oh, hello Jody. When can you get to Chicago?"

I tried to look surprised, and when Chris said goodbye, I asked, "That was Jody? I gathered from your conversation that she's consulting with you. How did that come about?"

"You spoke so highly of her as an environmental expert when this contaminated property sale came into the office, I called Jody to ask her opinion. I also asked her if she could get to Chicago this week to meet with the buyer and she agreed."

"I'm sure Jody will do a great job for you and your buyer. I'm glad you thought to call her."

"She'll be here Tuesday afternoon and Wednesday.

Maybe we can meet her for dinner on Tuesday evening," Chris said.

"Oh darn. I'm leaving for Cleveland on Tuesday and don't get back until Wednesday evening. Tell Jody I said hello, but I'll see her on the next cruise."

"Too bad," said Chris. "I wanted to see you two together. I still think you'd be good together."

"Why are you playing matchmaker, Chris? It seems a little weird."

"Bob, I do feel guilty about divorcing you, and I want you to be happy. That's all."

"I guess, but it makes me feel funny, having you try to put us together."

———

Chris and her potential buyer met with Jody at a small diner in Oak Park, not far from the west-side Chicago property in question. Jody had already contacted a local environmental testing and remediation company for estimates, so she was well prepared for the meeting. They ate a quick Italian beef sandwich for lunch and Jody had to pretend she'd never eaten one before.

The three of them then drove to the property and made their brief inspection, which was all Jody needed to get a more detailed estimate from her contractor. Jody assured the buyer that she would be acting as a consultant only, and would direct the contractor in any remediation, as well as handle the paperwork with the State and Federal EPA. All seemed happy with her proposal, and they were done by mid-afternoon.

After seeing the buyer off, Chris turned to Jody and asked her what she was doing that evening. "You didn't get a hotel yet, did you?" she asked Jody. "You could stay at our place. Bob is gone for tonight, and the kids would love to meet you."

"I have a reservation at a classic, old hotel in Oak Park,

The Wright Inn. I dropped my bags there before I met you today. One of my friends told me there were a lot of unique shops in Oak Park, and I wanted to be nearby, seeing as I'm looking at the possibility of setting up an office in the Chicago area," Jody said.

"That's great," Chris responded. "Bob mentioned that you might open an office near Chicago." Why don't we have dinner, and then you can meet the kids. I can drop you off at your hotel and pick you up in the morning. Libby, my boss, wants to meet you. She said if I was serious about getting into industrial and commercial property sales, I'm going to need a good environmental consultant."

"Okay, that'll work, I guess."

Jody was starting to see how one innocent lie, can get you into trouble.

As they walked towards Chris's car, Chris asked Jody if she needed to stop at her hotel for anything.

"No, I have no need to go to the hotel."

Chris unlocked the car door and the ladies got in. "I'm picking up the girls from swimming class first. Todd is away, doing a weekend in Michigan, so he won't be at home. He's decided on their Naval Architecture program."

I'd love to meet the girls" Jody said. "Bob is always talking about them."

"Wonderful," Chris replied.

Chris pulled up in front of the high school to pick up the girls. They saw their mom's car and came running out, both hopping in the back seat when they saw that the passenger seat was occupied.

Chris turned in her seat and said, "Jody, this is Melanie, and that one is Lilah. Girls, you've heard your dad speaking about Jody, the lead auditor on those cruise ships. I needed some environmental advice on that property I'm selling, and Jody flew in to help us with that deal."

Both girls were excited and started asking questions.

Chris broke in, saying, "Let's wait until we get home you guys. Poor Jody will break her neck trying to look back to answer you."

They got to the Evers' home more quickly than Jody had expected, so she asked, "You live quite close to Oak Park, I see. What city is this."

"This is River Forest. It is a separate suburb, but we share some services, like the high school. River Forest is a little quieter, and most of the shopping is on the border streets, or in Oak Park unless you want to go further west."

"I see. I guess I never asked Bob what city he lived in."

Once inside, Melanie and Lilah showered Jody with questions, which Jody enjoyed. They had a lot of questions about Bob's involvement as well.

Chris had pretty much ignored the conversation but then broke in. "Girls, Jody and I are going to dinner. Would you like to join us?"

Melanie answered, "Remember, Mom? Lilah and I were invited to that pizza party to celebrate the end of the school year. Otherwise, I'd love to go. I have a ton more questions for Jody."

Jody then said, "Not to worry. I'm actually going to set up an office for my company, probably right next door in Oak Park. I'll get to see you again, I'm sure."

"Oh, neat!" Lilah said.

"Okay then, girls. Jody and I will have dinner, and I'll be home by nine o'clock. I expect to see you home when I get here."

"No problem, Mom. We know the rules."

Chris kissed the girls and told Jody that she was ready and together, they headed to the car.

"If we had more time, I'd suggest going into the city

for dinner, but Oak Park has a lot of good restaurants. Do you happen to like Thai food? I know the owner of a good, local Thai place."

"We really learned to appreciate ethnic food on these cruise ships, particularly Asian food. So yes, I'd love a Thai dinner."

Chris and Jody settled into their booth, near the back of the restaurant, which Chris had specified to the host. She hugged the waitress and ordered two Thai Iced Teas.

"I didn't think about this before, but this place is BYOB. I should've stopped for a bottle of wine," Chris remarked.

"Not a problem. I'm not a big drinker. We drank very little on those cruise ships, and I noticed Bob was also not much of a drinker."

"That's for sure. Bob has never been a drinker. They joked about his poor ability to hold his beer back when he was in college. But seeing we're talking about Bob; can I ask you a question?"

"What question?" asked Jody.

"First, as you're aware, Bob and I are getting divorced."

"Oh yes, Bob's told me," Jody replied.

"This may seem weird to you, but I still love Bob, and want him to be happy. We just couldn't live together anymore. He loves his career, and I needed to move on, which is why I got back into real estate."

"It does seem a bit unusual for a woman to say she loves the man she is divorcing," said Jody.

"I know. And this divorce would be much easier if Bob were a bad husband or a terrible father. I want him to move on and be happy."

"That's great for you to say," said Jody. Jody was really feeling confused by this conversation, wondering what was going on.

"So, Jody, here is my question. Are you at all attracted to Bob?"

Jody, showing total shock on her face said, "Well of course I like Bob."

"I'm not talking about liking him, Jody. Could you fall in love with Bob?"

"Wow, Chris. That is a strange question for an almost ex-wife to ask?

"Well maybe. But I want Bob to be happy, and he always talked highly about you women. So, I want you to know, I'd be happy if you fell in love with Bob."

"I'll remember that you said that, Chris. But does Bob know about this?"

"I asked him the same question, Jody. He seemed very flustered when I asked, so I think the thought had crossed his mind."

"Very interesting. So, you think Bob has thought about me?"

"For sure," Chris said. "I saw him blush, which he always does when he thinks about sex."

"Really? He blushes? And he blushed when you mentioned my name?"

"He sure did. And just so you know, Bob is great in bed."

Now Jody was blushing!

"You're telling me your soon-to-be ex is great in bed? Are you aware how strange I am feeling right now?"

"I just wanted you to know, sex was not the reason for our divorce. In fact, I'll miss that part. You remember that weekend in Miami? I wasn't just joking that morning."

"I guess that's good to know, Chris. But I'm a little perplexed by this conversation. However, seeing you started it, can I ask you a question?"

"Sure, you can. Is it something about Bob?"

"Yes. Sam and I both learned to respect Bob, and how he worried about you during this impending divorce. One time on our first cruise, we were at the captain's table for dinner, and this lady sitting next to Bob was hitting on him all evening. Sam and I noticed the lady kept pushing her room key closer to Bob, four or five times. After dinner, Bob just got up and left. We both questioned Bob, and Sam even told him he should have taken the key."

"And I thought I liked her!" Chris said.

They both laughed.

"Remember, this was only a couple days after getting to know Bob, so we hadn't learned about him yet. But that night, Bob told us that even if he had noticed the key, which he didn't, he would not have taken it. He said he loved his wife and had all he needed at home."

"That's the Bob I know'" said Chris. "I never worried about him fooling around. I wondered if he might think about an affair during the last year or so because I was under such stress, I was ignoring Bob's sexual needs. But from what you just told me, he stuck by me as long as he could."

"You were so lucky to have him, Chris. Do you realize how rare guys like Bob have become?"

"I know, I know," Chris said. "That's why I want to find him a good woman."

Luckily, their dinner came, and Jody was happy not to be talking about her new love with his old love. This was one of the strangest, heart-to-heart talks she'd had in her entire life.

After dinner, Chris wanted to drop Jody off at her hotel, but Jody asked to be dropped off in the shopping area in downtown Oak Park, so she could scout out the stores. Then Chris offered to pick Jody up the next morning to take her to her office to meet Libby. Jody said she needed to learn her way around the suburbs, so she would take a taxi. Again, Jody was starting to feel very self-conscious about her little white lies.

The next morning, Jody tried to rearrange Bob's

apartment but had to give up. She could make no sense of what he had started and realized she didn't have time to fix what Bob had already done. Jody was not a neat freak, but she could see that having her own apartment nearby would be a good idea.

The next morning, Jody tried the greasy spoon diner, a great place called George's, which Bob had recommended, and then found her way to Chris's real estate office. Again, she had to side-step Chris's offer to take her back to her hotel.

"When are you flying back to California?" Chris asked.

"I think I'd mentioned that my boss in Los Angeles has asked me to check out the possibility of setting up a small consulting office in Chicago. Now that I've seen the area around Oak Park, I'm thinking this would be a great, centrally located spot for the office. I'd talked with Bob about the idea before, and he offered to help me find a good office location, and then I'll look at the apartment situation."

"Oak Park has a lot of buildings with small offices like you're looking for. And maybe you can look at Bob's apartment building. Remember what I told you last night," Chris responded.

"Oh, right! We'll just have to see what happens. I guess."

"If you're going to be around a few days, let me know your plans. Maybe you, Bob, and I can have dinner together sometime before you leave."

"I'll let Bob know when I talk to him. When did you say he was coming home?" Jody asked.

"Early this evening, I think. I learned to ignore his travel plans over the years because they always changed anyway. When he walked in the door, I knew he was home."

Around three-thirty that afternoon, I called Jody to let

her know that I was already at my gate in Cleveland and that the flight would board in thirty minutes.

"This is one of those flights that lands about the time it takes off," I told her. "We call the Detroit flights, Einstein flights because you actually land before you take off."

"And why is this important?" Jody asked.

"Not important at all, but I always found it funny."

"What are we doing tonight?" Jody asked. "I have to tell you about some very strange conversations I had with your soon-to-be ex. And by the way, I met your delightful daughters."

"Oh, Oh. Chris was on a rampage? Not in front of the girls, I hope."

"No. Just the opposite. She has submitted you for sainthood."

"You're right, we need to talk. Glad you got to meet my two dolls. Aren't they great? I know a nice little Thai place in Oak Park where we can go. Real quiet."

"Think of somewhere else, Bob. I think you just described the place we went to last night. The place on Madison? They won't want us in there rehashing what they might have overheard last night."

"That's right. Chris's friend owns that place. I'll think of something else. Gotta run. They just announced my boarding group. See you soon. And by the way, can I start to say, I love you when I hang up?"

"I think it's time. I love you too."

I walked into my apartment just after six o'clock that evening to find Jody sitting on the couch. "Sorry, but the parking lot at O'Hare was a mess, and then River Road has flooded again. I had to take the long way around."

"What's our plan for dinner?" Jody asked, as she hugged and kissed me.

"I'm not a big fan of pizza, but we have some good, family-owned places around here. I know one where we can get a secluded booth. You need to try a good Chicago pizza. This one is thin crust, which I prefer, more than the typical Chicago style, deep-dish and thick crust."

"Don't try fattening me up while I'm here. I'm having enough problems avoiding food on those cruises."

"Well, I guess we'll have to work hard tonight to wear off some of those calories."

"And just what does that imply?" Jody asked, smacking me playfully on my shoulder.

Dinner was interesting. Jody described Chris's attempts to match us romantically, but Jody kept the information about how loyal I had been to herself, at least for that time. She only told me that after we were married. Jody also told me how hard it had been to hide the fact she was staying in my apartment.

"Oh, man. It never occurred to me she would want to drop you at your hotel."

"It was okay, though. It gave me a chance to walk around Oak Park. I think this location, between two Chicago L-lines, and close to the Eisenhower expressway, will be the perfect location for my office. And by the way, I didn't realize your home was so close. Where is Chris planning to move?"

"We'll probably all be neighbors. She's looking at apartments right here in Oak Park."

SHOCK

—

M Y LIFE WAS finally going well. Jody and I were now a couple, and the divorce was almost final. To make things better, I was still friends with my soon-to-be ex, and both Chris and Jody had become friends and business associates. My three children seemed content with the situation, and they also seemed to like Jody. The kids were just happy to see both of their parents happy, and the stress gone.

Jody was moving into her new apartment less than two blocks from my place, which was now somewhat organized. We were unpacking boxes when my cell phone rang. It was Chris.

"Hi, Chris. How are things? I haven't heard from you in a while."

"Busy finalizing that new shopping mall Jody helped me with. Looks like I could get a property management contract out of this one as well. But the reason I called, I need to talk to you, and I think Jody needs to be there as well. When will she be back in Chicago?"

"Well, funny you should ask; I'm helping her unpack boxes right now. She found a nice apartment in Oak Park within walking distance of her office. Sounds important. What's up?"

"I think we'd better wait until we can be together. Are you both available tonight?"

"Sure. We have no plans. We can drop by the house later. What time?"

"I think it would be better not to be at home. How about our Thai place? It's quiet."

"Okay. What time?"

"I pick up the girls from dance class at four-thirty. Is five okay?"

"We'll be there," I said.

"Just hearing part of that conversation, it sounded serious. What do you think is going on?" Jody asked.

"To be honest, I have no idea. If it was a health issue or a problem with one of the kids, she'd be crying, or frantic. She seemed calm, so I'm totally stumped. Funny though, she recommended the same place where she was talking you into grabbing me."

"I missed that from what I overheard. That poor friend of hers at the restaurant will be shocked to see the three of us walk in."

"That's what I was thinking. So, let's finish up here and grab a quick shower. It's after three already."

"I'd been hoping for a long shower. Maybe not alone. But I guess that will have to wait."

"Well, we could just skip the rest of the boxes," I said.

"Just go take a cold shower and cool your jets, fella. Maybe tomorrow."

Jody and I arrived at the restaurant just before five, but Chris's car was already there.

"Chris is never this prompt. I'm surprised," I said

"I think her business life is changing that," Jody replied.

We entered and saw Chris in that same back booth, and the three of us exchanged hugs and kisses. And Jody was right; the restaurant friend looked very confused when Jody and I sat together across from Chris.

"I'm sorry. Again, I forgot to ask you to pick up a bottle of wine. I keep forgetting that this is BYOB. But I wouldn't be drinking anyway. You remember, I never drank while I was pregnant."

We both sat in total silence, staring at Chris.

"You're serious? You're pregnant?" I asked.

"Yes. Just found out this morning. I thought I had stomach flu lately, but it wouldn't go away, so I went to see my doctor this morning. He said the symptoms I was describing sounded like I was pregnant, so he did the quick test. It was positive. I had also wondered why I seemed to be gaining some weight."

"How? When? I don't understand," I said. I was obviously in total shock.

"Remember our great weekend in Miami? I'd stopped using anything, because we hadn't been making whoopee much those days, and it slipped my mind that this could happen."

"What shall we do?" said Bob. "I know neither of us believes in abortion."

"Oh, no! I would never consider abortion. I'm going to have the baby, of course."

"Then what do you want me to do?" I asked.

"Just be supportive and be as good a dad to this one, as you've been with the others. This doesn't change anything. I still want the divorce, and I don't want to hurt your chances of being happy with Jody."

Jody had been silent, but she spoke now, "Chris, you are one amazing lady. Most women in these circumstances would be screaming at Bob."

"Hey, it was my fault. Bob was just a willing participant. You were there that weekend. I wasn't exactly ignoring Bob's advances. Damn, I even bragged about it. I'm just sorry if this hurts your chances to be happy."

"Chris, with you as our cheerleader, how could we not be happy? And we both know this guy well enough, so he would never think of not supporting you through this. My kids are nearly grown, so I might enjoy having a baby around some of the time. We can even babysit when we're in town."

"I hoped you'd think that way, Jody. Thank you. Remember, I have two trained and certified babysitters in the family already, but I'm glad I hadn't settled on an apartment just yet. This is going to require a much bigger place than the apartment I had my eye on, and I'm now going to avoid anything above the first floor unless it has an elevator."

"So, I'm assuming the kids don't know at this point?" I asked.

"Not yet. All three are home tonight, and I was hoping the three of us could tell them together after dinner."

"Are you sure you want me to be there?" Jody asked.

"Sure do," Chris answered, "They know you're now part of their lives, even my life too, and I want them to see this can be a happy event in our lives. None of us did anything wrong, and the baby will be something to look forward to."

"Maybe this one can even take over my business someday," I said.

"By the way. When are you two planning to get married?" Chris asked.

The three of us broke into laughter.

———

Chris has built a good real estate sales business and supports herself. She's remained single so far and says she doesn't need a man in her life to be happy. Of course, I'm still there if she needs me. We both participate in our children's lives, and we plan to dance together at their weddings.

"And Jody's good with all that?" I asked.

"Of course. She and Chris have developed a very weird bond. I'm sure I have no secrets with either of them."

"Todd did go to the University of Michigan, studying Naval Architecture. He said he doesn't want to travel like me but wants to work in a large shipbuilding company. You met the girls, and Melanie is now a senior in High School and is planning to attend Loyola University in Chicago, to become a registered nurse. She gave up dance but is active in student government. Lilah is now in High School but has not yet decided what she wants to do afterwards. She still takes ballet lessons and has performed several children's roles in the Chicago Nutcracker during the Holidays."

"I'm curious, Bob. Did you ever hear any more from Sylvia, over in New Zealand?"

"As I promised her friend, Anita, I kept in touch with Sylvia. She decided to leave Nelson and move to Wellington, where she found a better class of friends, which were her words. She now has a new man in her life, and she thanked me for showing her there were good men in the world. She said she used the 'blush test' to find the right guy."

"It's really wonderful, Bob. You should write that book you talked about."

"Well, this personal stuff might not go into the book. It could be embarrassing for the kids. I didn't mind telling you the story, because you've told me a lot about you and your wife getting together, and some of the odd things that happened to both of you. I loved Lois's reaction to you wanting to see your lady friend from Miami, the one you helped move to Atlanta. If you hadn't been involved in her life, she probably would never have found her new husband. What's that term, serendipity? I think those things happen in our lives as long as we act sincerely with those around us. Maybe we don't partner with that person, but we can somehow be responsible for their happiness with someone else. As you told me, the terrible events you experienced together, resulted in her eventual happiness."

"You're right, Bob. I remember Estrella telling me I could just leave her, but I could never do that to anyone when I was responsible for our predicament. Without that event occurring, she and her kids might have stayed in that dangerous Miami neighborhood. I was so relieved when I saw her new family, and how happy they were."

"And that's why I wanted to tell you my story, Curt. I knew you'd understand."

We heard the noise out on deck as Lonnie came into the galley with the two deckhands. They were laughing and having a good time.

"I hope you guys didn't drink too much. We hope to leave in the morning," I said, half-jokingly.

"No way, Curt. One beer each. I told the guys about Strauss's strict rules on drinking."

"So, what was all the laughing about? Did we miss something good?"

"We were still amazed at the size of those burgers. And we had to leave half the fries and salad."

"But you actually finished the burger? Aren't they huge?"

Tony, one of the new deckhands said, "Coming from Chicago, I thought I'd seen big sandwiches, but this one takes the cake. I thought the meat was a full pound, but the waitress said it was only three-quarters. But all the onions, lettuce, pickles, and other stuff they pile on that bun; it literally was falling off the plate."

"I knew you'd like it. That's been a sailor's haunt for many years. Now you know why. You didn't forget ours, did you?"

"Right here, Cap," the other deckhand said.

"How much do I owe someone?" I asked.

"How about you catch the bill at The Antlers in the Soo, before we leave. Have you been there?"

"No, but it sounds interesting."

"I've been there," Bob piped in. "Their poutine is to die for. Not that it's the only good thing on the menu."

"Well, I'm glad we have a crew that likes to eat," I said. "We'll get along just fine. I'll check on the weather early tomorrow morning and decide when we should head back out into the lake. I'll stay on watch until midnight, and Lonnie can take the 12-6 watch with one of you. If we leave early, all four of us can help get the tow underway, and then those two from the midnight watch can get some shut-eye after we leave. Sound okay?"

"Good plan," they all chimed in.

"So, Bob and I will attack our hamburgers, and the three of you head to bed. That is if you can sleep with all that food in your bellies."

The next morning, I called Captain Wright on the *Samantha B*, and he said the storm had fizzled. He recommended we wait until about 0900 for the waves to settle down, but then we should have an easy trip up to Sault Ste. Marie. I called Bill Strauss to fill him in on our plans and decided to let the others sleep in, so they'd be fresh for the rest of the trip. I wanted both Lonnie and a deckhand to be in the pilothouse, to keep an eye out for fishermen in the area. The smaller fiberglass boats don't always show up on the radar, so keeping a lookout is important. Fishermen usually don't understand the towing symbols on the tug's mast, and they have been known to run over the towline. If they hit it just right, they knock the lower unit off their outboard motor. Even though this is their fault, we would be delayed until the Coast Guard arrived to tow them in.

We arrived at the shipyard in Sault Ste. Marie and got a call from Bill Strauss. He asked to talk to Bob Evers. When Bob ended the call, he said, "Looks like Bill would like me to hang around to see the tug on drydock and supervise the hull thickness gauging. I told him I needed to be back in Chicago by Saturday night, so he said I could add my air fare getting home onto the invoice. He joked that he wouldn't expect a credit for my cruise up the lake."

"So, we'll have time to hear more stories. Maybe at dinner tonight at The Antlers?"

"Good idea. I have just the story for those young sailors. You'll get a kick out of this one as well."

———

We saw the tug go up on the dock that afternoon. I rented a small van to use during our stay because we wouldn't be able to sleep on the tug while it was on the dock. We secured the barges before we headed to the restaurant. The shipyard said they'd have the hull cleaned and be ready for the thickness readings the next morning. Now that she was docked, we didn't need to stand any watches, so the five of us used the van to go to The Antlers.

The Antlers has been in business since the early 1900s, family-owned for four generations. They have over 200 stuffed wild animals hanging on the walls, plus a lot of other interesting artifacts. The original name of the restaurant was supposedly The Bucket of Blood Saloon. Its front was an ice cream parlor during the prohibition days, but the government caught up with them when it was showing a huge profit of $900, way more than ice cream sales could generate in those days.

We weren't sailing the next day, so I told the crew they could have a few drinks, but I wasn't carrying anyone into the hotel. Bob had recommended the poutine and I also saw whitefish on the menu, which is one of my favorites. I saw they had bar-b-que, but I told the crew they should wait for a trip to the Detroit area, and we'd go to Mel McLaurin's church in Monroe, for some spectacular ribs.

I reminded Bob about telling another one of his stories, and Lonnie had heard about the Ship Mice story from our delivery trip of the *Samantha B*, so he also asked to hear one of Bob's tall tales.

Bob said, "Hey, these are not tall tales or sea stories. I can assure you, this really happened. Now, you two young, single guys listen closely. You might learn something about relationships from this story.

DANCE LESSONS

———

ONE DAY, WHILE nearing the end of a week-long cruise, our audit team met at the crew's mess for lunch. We'd decided to meet there, seeing as it was a sea-day. Avoiding the passengers was one thing, but the unusual food in the crew's mess was also an attraction.

"What's on the menu today," Jody asked? "I've been wondering all morning."

"I think I saw that it was Middle Eastern Day. Baba ghanoush, falafel, tabbouleh, and I think there is hummus on each table to share. I may have forgotten some items as well," said Sam.

When they had filled their plates, Jody asked me what I had accomplished, and I described the events of the morning, particularly the plastic problem in the sewage lines. Jody then asked me about my plans for the rest of the day.

After mentioning my afternoon projects, I then told Jody about my plans for the evening, which included witnessing the ship's refueling operations in St. Croix.

"How long will it take, Bob? If it isn't taking all night, I'd be interested in seeing the procedure."

"Well, my intention is to watch the first hour or so, to verify their set-up and record-keeping procedures, but I won't stay to watch the entire refueling."

"Okay, then. When and where can I meet you?"

Jody met me near the garbage room just before midnight. The starboard side bunker station was nearby, so I thought that was a good place to meet.

I introduced Jody to the engineers who would be handling the refueling, and then asked the second engineer, Mladen if he had brought the extra copy of the ship's refueling procedure.

"Got it right here," Mladen said.

"Thanks, Mladen. When you start the process, tell me verbally what you are doing, and why you do it. I will follow along in the procedure."

"So Bob, you want me to give details, like clearing the lines, placing gaskets on hoses, and other small details as well?"

"Yes, but if you need to do something quickly, or if something goes wrong, you just do it and tell me what happened afterwards. I don't want my being here to cause a problem. Understand?"

"Okay, Bob. That's good, because sometimes the refinery does things that we need to handle immediately, and it might delay me if I am searching for English words."

"Now you've got it, Mladen. I just want to be the fly on the wall, and you can explain when you have time. I'll understand as I watch you do things. You can catch up on explanations when it's less busy."

The hose hook-up, alarms, and controls were installed, and the fueling started. Mladen and I spoke when necessary, and when the action slowed.

"I thought the passengers couldn't leave the ship here? I saw several men walking ashore, dressed in fancy clothes like they were going dancing," Jody said.

Mladen said, "Those are crew members. They actually do take dance lessons here."

"Dance lessons? You're kidding," said Jody.

"Well, that is the official answer," said Mladen. "They do go to a bar up the street, and they dance with a couple the girls. We're pretty sure they leave the bar with them."

"What about clearing immigration?" I asked.

"Technically, all of the engine room staff are cleared by immigration when we come to St. Croix because we have to be off the ship to assist in bunkering. Those guys trade watches with other engine room crew, so they can take dance lessons each time we hit St. Croix."

"So, what I think I'm hearing is, these guys have girl-friends on the island?"

"I guess they're girlfriends. I know these guys see the same girl each time. These are guys who don't like these shipboard romances you've probably heard about. They have developed a relationship with an island girl in St. Croix, and because we refuel here regularly during the season, they are seeing their girlfriend almost every week. The girls must like their attention; because they leave work when our guys go into the bar."

Jody then asked, "And what happens at the end of the season, when your ship repositions to a different itin-erary? These guys must go home, or at least they no longer come to St. Croix for a long time. The girl does not see them during the off-season."

"A couple of the guys have actually spent their vaca-tions here, living with their dance teachers. But I must admit, some just go home to the Philippines, or wher-ever they live, and maybe start again next season, where they left off on their last contract," Mladen answered. "I think they love and respect these ladies, but they understand they can't marry them. And the women have someone who treats them, and their children well, and also helps to support them. Life is hard for the poor on these islands."

"I guess, speaking as a woman, I don't understand why these women would want a relationship like that," said Jody.

"I don't want to sound like I'm defending our crew guys, but I've met some of their girlfriends, and they do not have the best life on this island. The crewmember treats them well, and they help them pay for rent and food. Some of the women have children, and I've seen the crewmen carrying them down to the ship when he comes back. He treats them like family, and maybe he is the only good father figure in their life. I've never heard of any abuse by our crew, and if there was, local authorities would report it to the cruise line."

"Now that I hear your explanation, I think I understand. Maybe we Americans try to impose our moralities on the rest of the world when our own are failing us. It sounds like these men are actually helping some of these women, strangely. Do you think these crewmen love and respect these women, Mladen?"

"I know some of them do, I'm not sure about all of them. But they're no worse than the rest of society, from what I see. Maybe even better, because they're honest with their girlfriends," Mladen said.

"I sure can't argue with that!" said Jody.

I told Mladen, "I think I've seen enough of the bunkering operation. Do you have any further explanation of the procedures? It all seemed to go quite smoothly."

"No, this was a typical bunkering operation, Bob. I'll show you the written reports tomorrow."

"That's great. See you tomorrow."

As Jody and I walked to our cabins, we discussed this new revelation of shipboard life.

"It's truly amazing, the things we've learned about shipboard relationships during these audits," Jody said. "My first impression had been to only see what I thought was bad, but that is based upon my American value system. Then, after closer examination, I do think these people are handling their love life better than we are. Certainly, they seem more honest. What do you think?"

"I'm also becoming convinced of it. Other than your experience with that one bad captain and his social hostess, I think everyone we met is better off than we are in many ways. Rather than promising more than they can honestly do, and then fail in their relationships, they only offer what they know they can do. In many cases, they seem to go above and beyond. They make one another happy, with no betrayals."

"I envy many of the people we've met," said Jody. "I know so few truly honest people in our society, and we think people from other cultures and lifestyles, whom we don't understand, are somehow beneath us. In just a few months, I'm questioning my whole value system. I don't know what to think anymore. I'm totally confused, but I'm learning what it means to be honest, and respect others."

"It sure is making it tough to understand our own personal problems, isn't it? Our western marriage vows seldom last in our American society anymore."

"It turned out to be more than a bunkering experience. Thanks for inviting me, Bob."

CURT

———

THE NEXT MORNING, we were all at the shipyard. Bob Evers had a late morning flight from the Sault Ste. Marie airport back to Chicago. Bob supervised the ultrasonic thickness gauging on the hull of the tug, and I also asked him to do a quick walkaround on the two barges, to point out any areas of concern. Bill Strauss had instructed me to look them over for any problems, even though their drydocking wasn't due for two more years.

I told the other crew to keep an eye on what the shipyard found, and that I'd run Bob out to catch his flight. On the way to the airport, Bob asked me if I knew the history of the county airport serving Sault Ste. Marie, and I had to admit that I had no idea. Bob said he had flown into the airport several times on a small, charter plane, sitting in the right seat next to the pilot. During the landing, Bob said he could see the runway was extremely long, and half of it had grass growing out of the cracks in the concrete, so he asked the pilot what that was about.

The pilot told Bob, this had originally been the runway for Kincheloe Air Force Base, back during the Cold War, when it was used as a B-52 base. That was the reason for the extra-long runway. That much runway was unnecessary for small commercial airplanes, so nearly

half of the runway wasn't maintained. Another interesting fact was that NASA considered that runway as a last
resort landing strip for the Space Shuttle, in case all of
the other landing sites were either damaged or weath-
ered in. That never happened, but it would have been
interesting to see the shuttle loaded onto its 747-trans-
porter in Northern Michigan, to fly her back to Florida.

I told Bob he was just a veritable wealth of knowledge. Here I was, a Michigan native, but never knew
about that interesting piece of history. Bob then told me
to check out the airport at Marquette, Michigan, if I ever
got up there, because it was also an Air Force Base, K.I.
Sawyer, in its previous life. In the case of Marquette,
the Air Force still uses that runway, because commercial flights are very limited there. They even have an air
museum next to that airport, Bob told me.

I dropped Bob in front of the small terminal building
and thanked him profusely for his help, and told him
how much I enjoyed the stories, as well as meeting his
family. Bob promised to send me some of the stories
he'd written down. He thought both Lois and I would
enjoy reading them. He said Samantha's story was one
of the stories he's written down and that it covered how
she had ended up living a happy life in Croatia, after her
tough life journey.

After a busy spring, delivering the new tug from Norfolk, then starting up the dredging project in Toledo,
moving over to work on the *Samantha B*, and now this
trip from Chicago to the Soo, I was looking forward to
getting some time at home. I enjoyed my job, but I was
really missing my family. I had barely had time to get
to know our twins before I was off to work again. Bill
Strauss had promised me a few extra days home this
rotation, and I reminded him of that.

Bill said, "I haven't met the twins myself. Would you mind if Syl and I run over to meet them? I'll call you next week to see what your schedule is, so we won't interfere with any of your plans."

"I'd love to have you come, Bill. I doubt we have any plans, except for Lois working at school occasionally. Now that summer has arrived, she is home most of the time. We could even drop in at school to see them if necessary."

"Sounds good, Curt. You get home to your family, and I'll call you next week. Great job getting the tug and barges safely to the Soo. Bob Evers called to say they found a few minor damages to be repaired, but the hull thickness gaugings looked great. That should be a serviceable tug for us for a long time."

"We just need to improve the electronics for the Navigation systems, like Weather-Fax, and electronic charts. We don't need those things on the small tugs, but after seeing them on the *Samantha*, I think we could use them on this tug if we make more trips like this one."

"That's a good idea. Now that we're getting into these larger tugs, feel free to tell me when we need improvements. I may be the boss, but my experience is on the small, harbor tugs. I need your input on things like this."

"I'll have Captain Wright recommend the right equipment for this tug as well. I think he also has a wish-list started for the *Samantha*, and I'll ask Lonnie what he thinks we need on those smaller tugs."

"You let me know what they say. We're making money, so let's spend some on improvements. I'm having Lonnie stay at the shipyard up in the Soo until you can get back up there. Tell Lonnie to call me with updates on the repairs, and if he spots any other problems. And by the way, how do you like those two new deckhands."

"They're keepers, Bill. They work hard, and they know their way around these barges."

"Good. I'm looking for two more from that Chicago operation. We will have less training to do if we can find guys familiar with the operation of that equipment."

"See you next week, Bill. I'm having Lonnie run me down to St. Ignace. I can catch a bus from there to Cadillac."

"Curt. Just rent a car. I'll have you go back to the Soo when you go back to work. This way, you have transportation both ways."

"If that's okay with you, I will. Thanks, Bill."

"Hey, with all the extra I've been asking of you, I don't want to make you ride a bus. Just drive home safe. You can still be home tonight."

———◆———

It was good to get home. My normal two weeks had turned into nearly three on this rotation, due to the trip to Chicago and then towing the barges up the lake. I pulled into the driveway about nine-thirty and went into the house. The light was on in our bedroom, and Lois was propped up on the headboard of the bed, nursing the twins. She looked pleased to see me but mouthed for me to be "quiet!"

Lois motioned for me to come over, and she handed me one little one. I wasn't sure if it was Robert or Ellen because they had changed so much since I was last home. Lois and I silently went to the nursery, deposited the two little ones in their beds, and returned to our bedroom.

Closing the door, Lois jumped up and put her arms around my neck, and planted a big kiss on my lips. "I'm so glad you're home," she said. "Wait until Steve sees you in the morning. He has missed you a lot during this rotation. Even Steve is now saying the word rotation."

"Your Uncle Bill apologized. He is giving me some extra days off this time, so I should be here for a full week. Has everything been okay with the babies? How is Stevie taking all the changes?"

"Steve is so proud of his brother and sister. Nearly every afternoon, when we come home from school, he'll ask me if some of his friends can come in to see Robert and Ellen. And I have to tell you about the time he had Becky over to see them. She was so cute and very serious."

"So, Becky is still in the group of nerdy friends?"

"Yup. After his Birthday Party, his guy friends have accepted her quite well, and she obviously appreciates the fact that Steve made that happen. But here is the sweet part: she wanted to talk to me alone, so she told Stevie that she and I needed a glass of ice water. While Steve was out of the room, Becky said, 'You're nursing the babies, right.'"

"Why would she ask you that?"

"So, here goes, she explained that her mom nursed all seven kids in her family, and she had asked Steve if I was nursing or using a bottle. She said Steve didn't know what nursing meant, so she had to Google it to show him. She said he was very embarrassed, so if I was nursing, I needed to explain it to him."

"That's funny. So, what happened when Stevie came back?"

"I told her I was nursing, but Becky said no more. It seemed she didn't want to embarrass Steve anymore. When she left, I thanked her and gave her a wink. She smiled, so I think she knew I understood. With three older and three younger kids in her family, I assume Becky is familiar with a lot of things that Steve has never seen. I thought it was nice that Becky was concerned about his lack of experience."

"And how did you handle Stevie?"

"The next day, I mentioned to Steve that he shouldn't bring his friends to the house around four-thirty, because that's when I'm nursing the babies. I saw the blush on his face, and I asked if he knew about nursing. He told me he did, so I asked him if he wanted to watch sometime. Of course, he said no, and that Becky had shown him a picture and that was enough.'"

"I'm sure he'll pop in sometime and see you nursing. I hate to see him get embarrassed. Any idea what we should do?"

"I was thinking, maybe we could take a drive somewhere while you're home. Outside the house, he can't ignore what's happening. I guess I never realized that being alone with me for ten years, he's led a pretty sheltered life. However, that's enough about Steve, babies, and nursing for now. We have a long-overdue appointment in the shower, and then I have plans for you this evening before the two little ones wake up hungry. Are you okay with that? Or would you rather spend the night talking about tugs and barges?"

"Oh, have I missed our showers together. The tugs can wait until tomorrow. And I need to tell you about my time with Bob Evers."

"That reminds me, you have a big manila envelope out on the table. It came from Bob Evers. I assume some business stuff."

"I bet he remembered to send the stories. He said he had a few you would like to read. But that can wait. Get your fine body into the shower, and I will follow."

———➤———

The following afternoon, while Stevie was at the library, I was telling Lois about my trip, while I opened the envelope from Bob. "So, Lois. I told you that Bob Evers has all these stories about the people he met on the cruise ships he was auditing. I got to meet his wife, Jody, his ex-wife, Chris, and his four children. The wife and ex-wife are friends, and in fact, his ex-wife actually matched him up with Jody. That will be hard to explain, but maybe we can meet them all in Chicago on this next trip, and it will be easier to understand. But for now, let's take turns reading this story Bob sent, about one of his fellow auditors, Samantha. The other auditors called her Sam. She had a bad marriage early in life, and she had a 'dark side' as Bob called it.

"So, why don't you start reading, and if the babies need to be fed a little later, midway in the story, I can finish reading." Lois began to read Bob's story out loud while she snuggled up with me on the couch.

NIKO

NIKO KOVAČ WAS the ship's Environmental Officer on our first cruise. During a coffee break in the middle of our ship's tour, Jody welcomed the chance to learn more about Niko, Olaf, and Hans, away from the working environment. She asked Niko to explain how he became the ship's environmental officer, and Niko was happy to tell his story. I loved his accent, and his Eastern European way of speaking without pronouns and articles, which they don't use in their languages. I think it makes his speech very becoming, so I will try to do that in this story.

Niko said, "I am from Pula, in Istrian Peninsula of Croatia. Istria was once part of Italy, but most of us are more Croatian than Italian. Then Croatia was once part of Yugoslavia, and you are probably aware of terrible war for independence, fighting against Serbia, for twelve years."

Everyone nodded knowingly but did not want to interrupt Niko.

"My brother fought in war and was wounded. Many Croatians from eastern provinces, escaped to western provinces, and we had large refugee camp in Pula. Those were very rough years. Because I was already sailing during those years, I was not directly involved in war, but my brother worked in refugee camp after he

recovered from wounds."

Sam asked, *"Niko, have you always sailed on cruise ships as an environmental officer?"*

"No," Niko answered. *"I started sailing as cadet engineer on tank ships. I had graduated from Maritime Academy in Rijeka and was hired by Norwegian tanker company. I became second engineer with them, and then saw job advertised for second engineers at Stellaris. I was just married and thought Stellaris job would give more time at home. Some contracts on tanker fleet ran six months or more."*

"Oh my God," Jody said. *"You were gone for six months? Didn't you get home at all?"*

"No vacations until contract was over," Niko said. *"One time we delivered load of jet fuel to NATO base in Italy, and my wife came there to visit. We were only there thirty-six hours."*

"So, is your wife happier with this Stellaris lifestyle? Do you have children at home?" Sam asked?"

"Two kids, now eighteen and fifteen. But no wife! She could not take life as a sailor's wife. She left me after eight years of marriage. At first, I was very mad at her, but I have come to understand. At least two-thirds of crew on this ship are divorced. Others are single or on second or third partner."

"I can certainly understand that problem," said Sam. *We also lead a nomadic lifestyle, and it's also tough on our relationships. I'm divorced as well."*

"Many unlicensed crew members meet second wife on board ship. It is not good to start family, but if crew members marry, Stellaris does good job of keeping them together, both on same ship, and with matching contract periods, when possible. Many other cruise lines will not try to help with that," Niko explained.

"So, Niko, have you found a second wife on board?" asked Jody.

"No, I'm done with marriage," Niko said. "I just keep a ship mouse."

"A ship mouse?" Sam asked.

"Well, I hope you will understand. Many of us are divorced, or permanently single, and we still want companionship. If we are attracted to someone, we spend time in one another's cabins. For officers, it is easier, because most of us have private cabins. We do not make any commitments, but just enjoy each other's company during our contract. On next contract, we find another ship mouse, unless we see one who we already know, from previous contracts."

"Don't you decide to marry them and ask Stellaris to keep you together?" asked Jody.

"That works for two unlicensed crew members, but officer contracts are four months, and unlicensed crew has eight-month contracts. The crew know, if they become a ship mouse, it is over when officer's contract ends."

"It doesn't sound very fair for the ship mice," Sam interjected.

"I know it sounds bad," Niko said, "but both of us know rules, and agree to rules before. The ship mouse is treated with respect by most officers I've known. We find them extra jobs to increase their pay, and most guys I know, give gifts to their mouse partners. Once in a while, the officer will marry his mouse, and she starts a family back home, usually in her home country. She can then sail with her husband as much as possible, to be sure he doesn't find another ship mouse."

Once the ship tour was over, Jody asked the other three to meet in a small bar we had noticed during the tour.

"Looks like we'll learn more than just environmental

issues on this job. It's too much!" Jody said.

Everyone chuckled, seeing the exasperated look on Jody's face.

"Let's go to dinner," I said. "We have the early seating, which is good. We'll need to get an early start in the morning, and I'm tired already."

After working hours, the audit team was being treated like passengers. We could attend shows if we wanted, but with the early start on Sunday morning, we decided it might not be a good idea to attend the show on this first night aboard. Instead, the four of us were at a table for four. Jody suggested that we meet the two Stellaris guys each morning for breakfast, and again at lunch, in order to keep the various tasks coordinated, but keep dinner private for us to discuss things.

Sam said, "I was very impressed by Niko, Olaf, and Hans. They all seemed to be taking our presence positively."

"I've always found the Scandinavian and Croatian sailors to be straight shooters. Something about their culture, I guess," I said.

"What about the guys who brag about their conquests?" Sam said, with a smirk on her face.

I wasn't sure what prompted Sam's remark, but I turned red and said, "Actually, my wife and I were discussing that very thing not long ago. An acquaintance of ours, who always insinuates he has a new girl every weekend, we know for a fact can't get a woman to give him a second look. Maybe you ladies should tell me, what attracts you to someone?"

Sam answered, "Well, I may not speak for womankind, but the old saying about still waters running deep, has a lot of truth in it. Not making a pass or anything, Bob, but I am attracted to guys who blush when sex is discussed. You were really cute in Miami when your wife was telling us about your wild night. You really turned red!"

I ignored Sam's comment and observed a couple sitting nearby, early fifties maybe, and they were eating dinner without talking; not even looking at one another. I said, "What's wrong with that couple? I've been watching them, and they don't talk or even look one another in the eye. They paid for a cruise to enjoy a vacation together, but there's nothing between them. Really sad!"

Jody then said, "Good way to avoid Sam's comment about you turning red, Bob. But I also noticed that couple earlier. They each smile at their waiter, but never at one another."

Then Sam added, "It happens to a lot of couples when their kids leave home. The wife was involved with their children, and the guy was consumed by his job. When the kids are gone, or at least old enough to be independent, the couple realizes they have nothing left in common. They come on a cruise, thinking it'll spark something, but now they're stuck with one another twenty-four hours a day for a week, and instead of a spark, they feel tense, having nothing to say. It's really sad."

I contemplated the events of the day. I had worked on ships most of my career, but today was the first time I had heard about all of these romantic problems. I was happy to avoid my father's career, who was a career sailor. Life was tough enough with a shore job, trying to earn enough for a family with growing expenses. The life of a sailor would be much harder.

SAM

———

*I*HAD ORIGINALLY MET Sam during a meeting at the *Stellaris Cruise Line offices in Long Beach, long before these cruise ship audits began. I had offered Sam a ride to LAX in my rental car, so the other auditors, Jody and Bill, would not have to drive out of their way. Sam was not from LA, and I was on my way back to Chicago.*

I asked if anyone needed a ride, and Sam agreed to the offer since Bill lived near San Diego and Jody also lived south.

The drive to the airport was a good chance for me to get to know Sam Hough. Sam said she had the same environmental credentials as Jody Cooper, but with much less experience. Sam liked Jody a lot and considered her a great mentor. I noticed that Sam tried to hide her feminine side by talking with a businesslike tone, but her good looks and great smile were hard not to notice. She was tall, with dark hair pulled into a bun. Her facial features were striking, with a dark skin tone, which I thought might be Greek.

"Funny, I just assumed the three of you Stolton guys were from the Los Angeles area. With the rush into the meeting, and the problems to discuss afterwards, we never had a chance to mention any personal information. So, where do you live?" I asked.

"I live in Atlanta," Sam told me. "Jody wanted me on the team for this job. If we get the contract, there might be other Stolton people flying from various locations to meet the ships for these audits. It depends on what problems we find onboard. Are you familiar with Rickra, Bob? Officially that is RCRA, but we all just say Rickra."

"Never heard of Rickra," I said. "Looks like I'll have a lot to learn. What's Rickra?"

"You won't need to worry about Rickra. It deals with hazardous waste disposal. It stands for Resource Conservation and Recovery Act. There are a bunch of records to be kept, and Jody figures they have not been properly maintained by Stellaris. That's why she wants me on the team because Rickra is my main focus at Stolton. We need you because none of us are experts on shipboard oily wastewater treatment, and the record-keeping required in the machinery spaces on these ships."

"Well, I'll probably take the job, if offered, but I'm already in trouble at home, just for this trip. I'm not sure how I'll handle a long-term project like this one."

"Oh, Bob! I'm sorry this trip caused you trouble! What happened?"

I told Sam about missing my daughters' dance recital, and my wife's displeasure.

"Well, I see you're also experiencing the downside of the nomadic life. We joke about it all the time at Stolton because most of us travel regularly, and our spouses are not happy. It's common amongst us nomadic consultants."

"I guess I never heard it referred to as a nomadic life before, but mine sure has been a problem lately. My ship inspections have taken me outside the country a lot the last few years, and my wife seems to be more upset with my travels than before. It does heap a lot of responsibility on her."

"Well, not that it'll make you feel any better, but I'm divorced, and Jody's marriage is pretty shaky as well. My husband had a nine-to-five job and was home every weekend. My travels kept me away for several days at a time, and sometimes over a week. My husband found someone who was home when he came home. Starting a family with my work schedule was out of the question, so our marriage lasted only a little over two years."

"Very sorry to hear that," I said. "Chris and I have been married eighteen years, and we have three kids. It seems like the kids understand my work and travels more than Chris does. I've tried to get her to travel with me, but she's very devoted to the kids, and she won't leave them with friends while we travel."

"The one lucky person on our team today is Bill," said Sam. "He's not married and having seen our relationship problems; he says he'll never get married unless it's to another nomad. There are a lot of these love problems at Stolton."

"So, how many people work for Stolton? Obviously, it's not just a California company."

"Oh, hell no!" said Sam. Stolton has over three hundred employees, and we have seventeen offices in the United States, and they're thinking about expansion overseas. Not all three hundred are nomads, but around one hundred meet that definition. I know over half of them have strained marriages. It's a tough life to be on the road, as you're finding out."

"I guess I'd better ask what airline you're flying. You said Atlanta, so do I assume it's Delta?"

"Sure. You know the joke about going to heaven? You need to change planes in Atlanta on the way there! I decided living near Hartsfield was smart. I don't even own a car. No need with all my travels."

As Sam got out of the car, I started thinking how nice it might be to work with these two great women. They looked good, smelled good, and did not swear con-stantly, unlike all of my normal shipboard clients. It could be a great experience.

SAM & NIKO

———

*A*FTER WE STARTED *that first audit and were introduced to Niko, Sam was the auditor assigned to
work with Niko, because he was the person onboard who
kept all those crazy, but important "Rickra" records, as
well as other waste disposal files.*

*We were impressed by Niko immediately, because of
the following conversation, occurring after the opening
meeting in the captain's conference room, with the captain still in attendance:*

*Olaf, the Miami operations manager, suggested the
environmental officer, Niko Kovač, should act as our
tour guide, seeing our focus was environmental. Niko
asked Jody to describe the areas of concern, and it was
obvious that Niko was giving due respect to Jody's position as the audit group leader, unlike the captain, who
seemed to snub Jody.*

*Jody presented the areas to be seen during the tour,
saying, "We will want to visit the navigation bridge,
and please show us where logbooks and environmental
records are kept. A quick run past the swimming pool, to
look at spa chemicals, and records of when the water is
discharged. Next, we can briefly look at the food prepa-
ration areas, particularly the dish cleaning and trash
separation areas. Then, a short visit to the main garbage room and storage area, including the overboard*

discharge chutes. If we can, give us a brief look at the refueling area, piping systems, and how records are kept for the fuel taken aboard."

The captain interrupted, saying, "This will be a lot to accomplish in just your first afternoon."

Jody replied, "Captain, this tour is meant to be just a brief walk-by, so we will know where to concentrate our efforts during the rest of the week. We will not be checking records during this tour, but asking where they are stored, so we can plan our work for the next few days."

"Now I understand," the captain replied.

Jody then continued, "If we have time, we also need to see the sewage treatment system, including where maintenance records and discharge records are stored. Then the engine room, including the bilge oily water separators, and where the records of overboard discharges are kept, as well as shore discharge of waste oil. Only if we pass by, the chemical storage areas, paint lockers, and other hazardous chemicals used onboard, as well as your photo development laboratory, and any printing facilities. I don't think we need to visit the medical facility or the laundry today, but we will want to visit them during the week."

Niko then spoke up, after Jody had finished her list, saying, "Excuse my broken English, Miss Cooper, but you have done your homework. Those are areas I check on almost daily basis. I look forward to any comments you might have. I think I am doing good job, but one is never too experienced to learn something new."

I looked at Sam and Bill, and their glances included a smile. We all understood, it was good to see Niko giving a positive spin to the audit. Better to look for advice than think you already know everything.

It was during this tour, the conversation about ship mice occurred. It was obvious that Sam and Jody were a little upset by the "Ship Mouse" affairs that Niko had described. *I think we all thought this was a way for the men in the crew to satisfy their sexual needs, at the expense of the less fortunate women crewmembers. Sam in particular had shown her displeasure on her face.*

Although Sam was very likeable, she seemed to have a 'dark side", which she showed when she was not directly involved in a conversation. It appeared to me as being 'moody', yet as soon as you got her involved in the conversation, the dark side quickly disappeared.

However, Sam was the disposal record expert, and she would be working with Niko, despite his use of ship mice.

The next morning, while dividing up responsibilities for the audit, Jody said, "Niko mentioned the garbage record books and the Rickra hazardous waste records are kept in the office, behind the bridge. We should not be on the bridge while at sea. Because the captain offered to let us use his conference room, I suggest those records be taken there for Sam and Bill to review. Does that sound okay, Niko?"

Niko nodded his approval, and Jody continued, "I'll start with a review of your environmental policies, your crew training programs, and if there is time, look into chemical storage. Then maybe we can meet in the crew's mess again for lunch? We enjoyed the food there yesterday, and we can discuss our progress without the passengers wondering about us. I don't want us to be a distraction while onboard. Tomorrow, when we're in port, we can make our inspections in the public areas, when the passengers are ashore on excursions."

"That all sounds great, Jody," said Olaf. "Niko can work with Samantha and Bill on those records, which he keeps anyway. Hans can get Bob started in the engine room, and I'll stick with you. Some of those documents are electronic, like training manuals, for easy access by the crew. I'll be able to show those to you on a ship-

board training computer."

After breakfast, the team split up as discussed.

That evening, during dinner, Sam related their progress, "Bill started reviewing the garbage record books, and I worked with Niko on his Rickra records. I was surprised by how much hazardous waste is discharged. They're saving all the hazardous waste for discharge in the United States while operating in the Caribbean. When in Europe, they prefer to use the more regulated countries, to be sure there is a proper paper trail. Niko told me Stellaris was accused of dumping haz-waste overboard in the Mediterranean, even though they had a receipt showing it'd been accepted by a waste hauler in Greece. Apparently, the waste hauler's record-keeping was lacking. Since then, they pay more to assure a good paper-trail, from more reputable waste haulers, usually in Barcelona."

Bill then jumped in, "I was impressed by Niko's garbage discharge records. He's been very meticulous in recording the positions of any overboard discharges of food waste, and the galley staff has been trained to remove any plastic items. The ship now uses paper straws, and no plastic butter packaging is used, so the risk of plastic going overboard has been greatly reduced. Niko personally checks the discharge positions on the bridge, before the overboard chute is opened. That chute is locked, and only Niko has the key. Tomorrow, I'd like to start on glass, plastic, tin, and paper recycling records."

Sam then added, "I'm very impressed by Niko. His records are impeccable, and he actually understands the Rickra requirements. He's a pleasure to work with. I just hope the other Environmental Officers in the fleet are as organized."

The next morning at breakfast, Jody told Olaf and Hans her plan for the day.

"I'm ready to go back to the record reviews. Do I get to keep Niko?" Sam added with a chuckle.

Jody, Bill, and I began to see Sam's attitude changing. The dark side I had seen, now seldom appeared, like it had earlier in the week.

One night at dinner, Sam announced, "I've been invited to the crew's bar for a drink tonight. Would anyone else want to go?"

Everyone declined, but Bill asked, "So, who invited you? Niko, I assume?"

Sam gave Bill a weird look, said nothing, and left the table.

I was starting to notice some friction between Sam and Bill but was unable to figure out why.

NIKO & THE CREW

———

*O*N THE THIRD *morning of the audit, it was the day we had set aside for interviews with the non-licensed crew. Jody had made random selections of people on the crew list, and Hans had organized the crew to come at certain intervals.*

"For today's task, we have notified all the crew members you selected, to come to the two small meeting rooms, near the main bar," Hans said. "Those rooms are comfortable and quiet, and you will have total privacy."

"Thanks, Hans. I saw those rooms during our tour, and they're perfect. I decided we would do the interviews in teams of two, so the crew members will not feel threatened or self-conscious in any way. I will work with Bill, and I want Bob to work with Sam. Most of Bob's interviews are with Engineering officers later this week, so he doesn't need to interview engine room staff today," Jody instructed.

"That's a great idea," Bill said. I was worried that a young girl might feel nervous being interviewed by a guy, and vice-versa."

"Well, they're all nervous anyway," Hans explained. "Some of them looked quite shaky when I told them about their interviews. They're all afraid of making a mistake and getting fired."

"We talked about this exact problem before we left Miami," I said. *"We even played out some interviews to practice putting the crew members at ease. I think we'll do fine, and so will the crew."*

"Thank you," said Hans. *"Many of them are very worried."*

"How do we want to divide up the crew for the interviews?" Sam asked.

"I gave a lot of thought to that last night," Jody responded, *"and at first I thought each team should take some from each department. Then I thought, we'll learn some details about each job, which we can expand upon during the subsequent interviews. With that in mind, Bill and I will take the galley crew and cleaners, and Sam and Bob will take the room stewards and deck crew."*

"That's a good plan," I said. *"Shall we get started?"*

We left the dining room and headed for the meeting rooms. When we arrived, there were already a half-dozen crew members waiting, and Hans was right, every one of them looked tense. Hans separated the crew into the two groups Jody had mentioned, and Hans said he would stay outside to direct them into the correct rooms.

Hans asked, *"How long do you think each interview will take? Some of the room stewards and cleaners have their jobs to complete, and some are worried they will get in trouble with their supervisor. I plan to call a couple of them at a time, so they are not away from their work too long."*

Jody asked the other team members, *"Don't you think we can ask what we need in ten minutes or so?"*

Everyone nodded in agreement. *"We'll try to keep the chit-chat to a minimum,"* I added, *"although that is an important part of the interview."*

"Okay, let's get started," said Jody. *"Let's plan on a break around 11:30 and see how we're doing. We can decide what to do after that."*

I asked Hans to send in the first person, who happened to be a room stewardess. She was a young woman, small in stature, and I guessed she was from the Philippines. I stood to greet her, asked her to be seated, and then asked, "Would you give us your name, and tell us a little about yourself?"

The young woman said, "Marina, and I am a room stewardess. I clean………"

Sam then interrupted and said, "No, Marina, we'd like to know where you are from. Do you have a family back home?"

Marina's face brightened a little, and she then continued, "I am from the Philippines, in a city named Olongapo."

"I have only been to Manila," I said. "Is Olongapo near Manila?"

Marina was obviously more at ease, and answered, "It is about a three-hour drive away. Olongapo is along the sea, and I worked in the hotels there, cleaning rooms."

"Oh, so that is how you got the training to work on the ships?" Sam asked. "How long have you been on the ships?"

"Yes, a friend went to work on the ships and told me to contact the agent in Manila, because the money was good. This is my second contract on Stellaris. I was on the Stellaris Queen before."

"How long is your contract?" I asked.

"Room stewardess contracts are eight months," Marina answered.

"So, you do not see your family for eight months?" Sam said.

"My mother takes my baby. She is three years old."

"What about your husband?" I then asked.

"He sails too, but for cargo company. We try to get our vacations at same time."

"That is tough for a family. We also travel a lot, but

not as much as you," Sam consoled. *"But do you like working on the cruise ships? Does Stellaris treat the crew well?"*

Marina answered, *"I like my job, but hours are very long. It is also hard work to carry passenger suitcases on turn-around day, so, I need to pay one cleaner to help me."*

"You have to pay the cleaner?" I exclaimed. "Where do you get the money?"

"I use my tip money, or sometimes I work extra jobs to make money. If a worker friend is sick, I help her and she shares her money," answered Marina.

"What about your supervisors and the officers? Do they give you good training and help you?" asked Sam.

"My supervisors show me training computers and tell me we must know everything. But we get good training from agent in Manila before we come on the first contract. The agent knows what Stellaris wants us to do, and all Stellaris' rules."

"What do you do if you have questions, or see something wrong?" I then asked.

"I go to ask Niko, our environmental officer. Niko always helps us. He is good man!"

Sam smiled, and then asked, *"Does Niko help everyone?"*

"Yes, Niko always says, 'I don't want you to get in trouble, so please tell me about your problems.' He helps the Blue-Boys, stewardesses, galley-men; anyone who asks for help."

"That's wonderful," said Sam. *"But what if Niko is not here? What if he is on his vacation? And oh yes, what is a Blue-Boy?"*

"Most environmental officers are helpful, but Niko is best. He even tells us to send him e-mail if we need help when he is gone. They call deck crew boys, Blue-Boys, because all wear blue coveralls when doing dirty

work."

"That is great," I said. "Why don't you tell us a little about your job, what chemicals you use, where you dump waste and chemicals, and so on. Maybe start with your morning duties and tell us how your day goes."

Now that Marina was very calm, and did not feel threatened by Sam and me, she gave a good description of her duties, the chemical storage, garbage room, and even mentioned some things she worried about, such as dumping chemicals into the sinks and toilets. Sam and I had a few questions, but we finished this first interview in just over twelve minutes.

As Marina left the room, we heard her speaking in Tagalog to the next person coming in, who was one of the Blue-Boys. Sam remembered the fearful look on his face when she saw him waiting earlier, but whatever Marina said to him, his worried look disappeared.

Again, Sam and I stood to greet this next crew member and asked him to be seated. "This time, Sam took the lead and asked, "Would you give us your name, and tell us a little about yourself."

The Blue-Boy said, "Rodolfo. I work in the Bos'n crew and...."

This time, I interrupted, saying, "Rodolfo, first we'd like to know where you are from. Do you have a family back home?"

Rodolfo then opened up freely, maybe understanding what Marina had told him in Tagalog. He gave so much personal information, I finally had to interrupt him, saying, "So, you are one of the great Blue-Boys I have heard so much about. Do you mind being called a Blue-Boy?"

"No, we are Blue-Boys. We even call each other Blue-Boy. It is just our coverall color, so no problem. We do wear white coveralls if we work around passengers."

Then Sam asked, "What is the Bos'n crew? I am not

a marine person. Bob probably knows, but I have not heard that term before."

Rodolfo explained, *"Bos'n runs all of the deck repairs, outside cleaning, and painting. He gives us our jobs each morning and we report to him any damages we see."*

"How do you like working for the Bos'n?" I then asked. *"Where is he from, by the way?"*

"We really like this Bos'n. He is tough but fair. As long as we work hard, he takes care of us. Jakub is from Poland, and he has sailed for over 30 years. He's been on tankers, cargo ships, and even big fishing trawlers."

Next, it was Sam who asked, *"Do you use a lot of chemicals in your job, Rodolfo? How does Jakub store those chemicals?"*

"We use a lot of chemicals. We use a special one to remove rust on the ship. It burns our hands. We also use lots of paint. I guess that is chemical?"

"Tomorrow we are going to visit the Bos'n Locker," I said. *"Maybe you can show us the chemical that burns your hands when we go there. What do you do with the chemicals if you don't use them all? And oh yes, what do you do with empty paint cans and old brushes? I also wanted to ask you, Rodolfo, are you part of the emergency evacuation team?"*

"If we are at sea, we just dump chemical left in our pails over the side, but not paint. If we are in port, we dump chemicals in sink in work room. Jakub is very clear about paint cans; we must set them out to dry, and then can put them in the garbage. We keep paint brushes in cans with thinner, if going to use them again. Old brushes are dried, just like paint cans, and then can throw in garbage. And yes, all Blue-Boys are part of emergency team. We launch lifeboats. We all trained for that back home before we sign contract to sail."

Sam ended by asking the same questions about train-

ing and was happy to hear the same response about how wonderful Niko treated the crew. Everyone seemed to like him!

The other interviews went similarly. Sam looked at her list, and they had interviewed three-room stewardesses, Marina from the Philippines, as well as one girl from Ukraine, and another from Thailand. All three Blu-Boys were from the Philippines.

Sam asked me, "Are there any deck crew from other countries? All three of these were from the Philippines."

I told her, "I've seen deck hands from most maritime countries on cargo ships and tankers, but I've heard the cruise lines prefer those from the Philippines because they're trained so well before they take a contract. Also, the Filipinos are very moral and loyal, as I've heard it said. They work very hard, never steal, and in an emergency, they always do their duty. Throughout history, if the ship officers failed in their duty, the Filipino crew still launched the boat and got most of the passengers safely into lifeboats. It's just part of their culture to do their assigned duties, and probably beyond."

"Oh, how wonderful to hear that," Sam said.

Each of the interviews went well, but then we saw it was already 11:45, and after the agreed time for a break. The word was obviously spreading amongst the crew: the inspectors, as we learned the crew was calling us, were very nice people. It was good to see how comfortably the crew began to speak with us, once they understood there was no threat. Sam and I did not find a single crew member who seemed to be hiding anything, and their list of potential problems, as noted during the interviews, were nearly identical. We stepped out into the bar area and found Hans was the only person waiting for them.

Hans said, "I hope you don't mind me sending in that last person. He had been waiting, and I did not want to ask him to return after lunch. I did the same thing to Bill and Jody, so they are still on their last interview."

"That's fine," Sam said. "We don't want to get them in trouble. We understand Jakub can be tough."

"Yes, I've known Jakub ever since he came to Stellaris. It's hard to find a good Bos'n anymore. They start as a deck hand and learn how everything works before they become a Bos'n. It is not a skill learned in a few years, so most deck hands quit, or die before they are experienced enough to become a Bos'n."

"Where does the name, Bos'n come from?" asked Sam. "I'd never heard it before we got on this ship. And what do you mean die? Why would they die before becoming a Bos'n?"

"The term Bos'n comes from the full word Boatswain. I think the contracted version started back in the old English sailing days," Hans replied. "They've always been the person aboard ship who was familiar with the rigging and structure of the ships, even back in sailing days. They tend to be the only person aboard ships, who everyone relies upon for practical knowledge. It was also a tough, sometimes dangerous job. They crawled in the rigging in the old sailing days, and in modern times, many died from accidents in cargo holds, snapped mooring cables, and entering other dangerous areas. Safer today, but they are still exposed to danger, more than you might think."

About that time, Jody and Bill emerged from their meeting room with their last crew member. Judging from the white topcoat, we assumed that this was one of the galley crew.

Jody immediately said, "Is anyone else hungry?"

"I think we could all use some lunch, and I really need a cup of strong coffee. These interviews were stressful for me!" I added.

Hans asked, "Where shall we eat today? The passen-

gers are ashore, so, maybe the dining room is still a good option. We can save the crew mess for tomorrow, which is another sea-day."

Bill commented, "I was thinking, we had not eaten in the buffet since boarding on the first day. Would that be a good idea for today?"

Jody replied, "Great suggestion, Bill. I had totally forgotten about the buffet. What do you think Hans?"

"The buffet it is!" Hans said as he started to walk in that direction.

After gathering their food from the buffet line, which was quite empty due to the passenger excursions, everyone gathered in a remote corner of the dining area in order to discuss their morning interviews. By this time, everyone had come to trust Hans, and except for actual potential problems, the audit team discussed their impressions of the crew.

Sam began by stating, "Bob and I first found the crew to be a little fearful, but I think we did a good job of putting them at ease, so, the rest of their interview was very fruitful. Every one of them seemed to be completely honest, and they were not afraid to mention things that they felt were either a problem or in some cases potentially dangerous. Would you agree, Bob?"

"Fully agree, Sam. I was surprised that they mentioned some of the problems they saw with chemical usage on board. Some of those problems may not be an environmental issue but should be addressed because of health and safety concerns. We still need to look at chemical storage."

Then Sam continued, "What about your interviews Jody?"

"I think Bill and I found the same issues with chemicals as you indicated. And our galley staff and cleaning personnel were very relaxed after we completed the first interview. Somehow, they seem to have communicated

with the others, we were not their enemy. It took us a while with the first galley worker to get him calmed down, but after Bill started talking with him about his home in Budapest, he opened up for us."

Sam laughed, "That's funny because Bob did the same thing with our first room stewardess, who was from the Philippines. Once we started talking to her about her home and family, she knew we were friendly, and we were not trying to get her in trouble."

"So, what are we planning for this afternoon? We accomplished quite a bit this morning," said Bill.

Jody answered, "I think we need to interview a few more crew members, but we're finding consistent answers at this point, and I see no reason to interview 12 more. I suggest at this point, we change interview partners, and each interview team talks with four more crew, and then we quit. If you have that list handy, Hans, let me randomly choose the last eight people for our interviews."

"That's a good idea," said Sam. "Remember, we need to get ready for dinner at the Captain's Table, and I've not even unpacked my good dress. It probably needs to be pressed."

"Why are you worried about looking good, Sam? Niko won't even be at the captain's table," Bill said with a chuckle in his voice.

"What the heck are you talking about?" said Sam.

"Oh, nothing!" But Bill smiled at everyone sitting at the table.

———

Just then, the babies started to cry. Lois got up to get them while I prepared to read the rest of the story. Lois gathered the two little ones and returned.

"And you say that Bob Evers actually knows these people?" Lois asked me.

"He not only knows them, but he's also now married to Jody. He told me that story when I met him and Jody in Chicago on this last trip. I also met Chris, the ex-wife. It was a strange story, but quite sweet, in a strange sort of way."

"I'll have to meet Bob. He sounds interesting."

"Bob has traveled to places I've never heard of, and those I've heard of, I had to look for them on Google, just to be sure I knew where they were. He's led an interesting life, but I wouldn't want to put up with all his travels away from home. That's why his first marriage fell apart. It's good that he and Chris are still good friends, and they are both still very involved in their kids' lives."

"Yeah, you're gone enough as it is. What makes our separations manageable, is that you come home happy because you love your job. That reminds me, it looks like your crane mechanic from last year's project, Larry Boyle, and my friend Loretta Sanchez, have stayed together. She lives with Larry in his mom's old house. Their crazy work schedules don't seem to be a problem. Sanchez spends much of her time off from the firehouse, staying with Larry at his hotels near his jobs. When they are both at home, they are into gardening and remodeling the house. They seem very happy."

"So, your match-making skills worked out well. We should try to see them during one of my times home. With these two little ones, it may be a while before you want to stay in hotels near my jobs."

"Maybe once they are toddlers. Steve will enjoy trying to keep them herded together if we make some excursions. At school, he drops by my office several times a day, just to check on them. But hey, the babies are quieted down now, so I've really gotten into this story from Bob Evers. Continue reading the saga of Sam and Niko."

"Okay. Where were we? I see, Bob was just going to meet the others at the bar."

DARK SIDE BRIGHTER

I WAS IN THE bar by six-thirty and was surprised to find the other three were already there. I said, "I guess we're all anxious to hear comments from the others. I figured we hadn't said everything in front of Hans and Olaf at lunch."

"Yeah, I guess we're all on the same page. It's like we've worked together our whole careers. I've been dying to hear what you all have to say," said Jody. "I'll let Sam start."

"As we mentioned at lunch, Bob and I were both very impressed by the honesty of the crew, and how willing they were to discuss problems which they notice on board. There seems to be a lack of good training, at least in areas related to chemical usage. Some of these could be environmental violations, but as Bob mentioned earlier, they are certainly a health and safety issue."

I then added, "Every one of our interviewees indicated that they'd go to the environmental officer with questions because their supervisors were only directing them to use the training computers on board. It was obvious from those we interviewed today, the level of English on board is minimal for the non-licensed crew, and certainly, the training in those computers is in English. Is that true, Jody?"

Jody replied, "It sure is, and although the training

modules are very complete, I also wondered at the time I reviewed them, how the crew could understand them without help."

Sam then added, "We did hear good things about Niko, helping with their questions, and as one young woman said, 'keeping them out of trouble.' She did add, the other environmental officers were also very good, but Niko was excellent. And Bill, I don't want to hear a comment about me and Niko!"

"I was just pointing out the obvious," said Bill. "You're not getting sweet on the guy, are you?"

"Oh, shut up!" she said.

The next day at lunch, Jody and Sam were discussing a very unusual story about the ship's doctor, involving his ex-wife and his attraction to the opposite sex.

Olaf looked a little worried, and said, "I hope you're not thinking everyone on our ships, or all ships in general, are bad people. Because of our being away from home for such long periods, we do tend to have unusual relationship problems, but I don't think we are bad people."

Sam answered, "Not at all, Olaf. Each of us has had our own share of relationship failures, but the doctor was a bit more unusual than most. So far, I think most of the people we've met onboard, are more caring, and concerned about one another, than most of the people I know back home. You don't need to apologize. I think we're just seeing a common human problem, and most of those onboard are simply unafraid to talk about their problems. Most people with these issues, just keep them inside, and it would probably be healthier for everyone to confide in others about our relationship problems like we're finding here."

"Oh, good," said Olaf. "I was afraid you were thinking poorly about us. We are like family, and we try to take care of each other."

"You just proved my point," said Sam, with a big smile. "I'm learning that."

After hearing this remark by Sam, I was becoming convinced that her dark side was turning much brighter. I wasn't sure why, but the change seemed to involve Niko. That was hard to believe, since Sam seemed to have such a bad first impression of Niko, after his ship mouse revelation.

Then the first cruise was over. The seven days seemed to have flown by.

After the closing meeting, again held in the captain's conference room, Jody and I noticed Sam and Niko, chatting away in one corner, in hushed tones. Everyone noticed them, but we decided to leave them alone. Even Bill kept his mouth shut for once.

We were on our way to Curacao, to meet the ship for our next audit.

During the entire cruise from Curacao to San Juan, we all noticed Sam spending a lot of time on her cell phone. We were worried about her having some problem back home, but we knew she wasn't married, so our concern became obvious. She had never done that before, and Bill overheard Jody and me discussing it.

"She's probably still swooning over Niko," Bill said.

"Swooning? Really?" Jody said.

"You guys didn't seem to notice on the last cruise, but they spent nearly every night at the crew bar after dinner last week. Sam got a little mad when I told her Niko didn't need a ship mouse last week."

"You said that to her, Bill? That's pretty insensitive!" I said.

"Well, remember I was working in the same room with those two all last week. There was a lot of whispering going on, and it sure wasn't all about Rickra."

"Knowing how Sam feels about her past relationships, and her reaction to Niko's ship mouse revelation, I'd be

surprised if she would be interested in Niko," Jody said.
"You know I've mentioned that "dark-side" thing I've
noticed in Sam. Well, I have noticed a change in that
over the last week. I wondered if Niko was responsible, but I also don't suspect she has any real interest in
Niko," I said.

"Can I be straight with you two?" Bill said. "I like
you guys, but you both think like old people. I'll bet that
Sam and Niko were getting it on last week. Just sayin'!"

"Oh, come on!" said Jody. That just isn't like her."

"The whispering I heard was serious, and not part of
the audit. Trust me!" Bill replied.

"Well, I must admit, I'm curious," I said. "She's been
on the phone all this week."

SHOCKER!

———

*J*ODY DID GET *a chance to talk with Sam but just wanted to be sure everything was OK. Jody told me Sam had no problems, but said she was just trying to organize her schedule, so she could take the next two weeks off before we made our next cruise audit. We just forgot about the phone calls and Bill's theory. Bill always seemed to look for the kinky side of things anyway.*

I was on my way to New Zealand for a job and had talked my wife into going along. Jody had some oil refinery clients to attend to back in California. We never ask what Bill is going to do, for fear he might give us a weird answer.

Jody called me to say we had two new Stolton auditors joining us on the California cruise. As usual, we met in a hotel the night before the audit to discuss any problems from the last cruise, and to plan how the next audit should proceed.

I came into the hotel bar after checking in and saw Jody sitting in a booth, near the back corner. I was very curious about our new team members, so I went right over and asked, "So, who are the new people?"

"In addition to Amber, who trained with us in Curacao, we have a new lady, Leslie Bowles. She will be training with us on this audit. Amber will be our new

Rickra expert, and we will be needing her since Sam has submitted her resignation."

"Sam resigned?" I said, almost in shock. "Why?"

"I'll let her explain. I was surprised as well. I tried to talk her out of this, but her mind is made up."

"So, tell me a little about Leslie," I said.

At that point, Sam came through the door. She had a big smile on her face and seemed to have lost that "dark side" appearance entirely, which both my wife and I had noticed in Miami when we first met Sam. Jody remained seated, but the others all rose to greet Sam. I could see that Jody was not in a good mood.

Everyone seemed hesitant to ask the question, so Jody finally said, "So, will you tell them........I haven't told them anything except that you are leaving."

"Yes, spill the beans," said Bill. "Did you hate working with us last month?"

"Well, with all the crap you were giving me, Bill...," jeered Sam. "But you did seem to pick up on what was happening."

"I knew it!" Bill chided.

"Okay. I was working closely with Niko, and he started asking me why I was so aloof. I never thought of myself that way, but he kept pointing out that I seemed to be a man-hater. I told him it was not men in general, but just that every love interest in my life turned into crap. Divorced in only two years, so I gave up."

"What am I missing here?" I asked.

"You really are naive, Bob," Jody said with a laugh. "The rest of us saw it."

This was the first time I saw Jody smile that day.

Sam continued, "On the second day, Niko started relating his sad love story to me, and we saw our lives were very parallel in romantic failures. We started meeting after the workday, and we felt a real kinship. In just a week, I understood more about my life problems than

I ever had before, getting advice from someone who was just as big a failure as I was."

"OK, you connected," I said. "But why are you resigning?"

"Now for the weird thing," said Sam.

"And this wasn't weird?" Bill said.

"You asked for an explanation, so shut up, Bill. Here it is. You may remember, I took a two-week vacation after the second audit. The last night on the Stellaris cruise, I met Niko after the closing meeting. I asked him if he was concerned about me, or was this just his Croatian bravado? Niko said he was wishing he had met me earlier in his life and wanted to stay in touch. I described my terrible nomadic work life, and I knew his was the same. But I told him, we had started something I did not want to let go of. Niko agreed and asked what we could do about it."

"So, you'd been sleeping with each other all week?" Bill again interrupted.

"Bill, you are a real jerk," Amber suddenly said.

"Thanks, Amber. That saved me from saying something worse," said Sam.

"Please continue," I said. "We still haven't heard about your resignation."

"On that last night, after both Niko and I agreed we may have found something important between the two of us, I asked him if there was a way for me to return to the Prince after our Curacao audit, so we could decide if we should continue our relationship. Niko said he could request passage for me as a family member. So, the last two weeks, I sailed on the Prince, and Niko and I learned more about our similar problems. Having a kindred spirit was very therapeutic."

Amber now asked, "And how can you carry on a long-distance relationship with Niko? Why are you resigning?"

"I know this seems crazy. And Bill, it was not a sex-filled two weeks! But after those two weeks, we decided we had something, and neither of us was willing to let it go. Niko's contract ends in two more weeks, and I'm meeting him in Miami. He's taking me to Croatia, and we'll spend his off time together, getting to see what life would be like, if we stayed together. At the end of his four-month vacation, we will make a final decision."

Jody chimed in, *"What about his ship mice, Sam?"*

"We discussed that as well. He had far fewer ship mice than he first told us about, but I told him, there would be none of that if we stayed together. Niko agreed and asked if I would mind spending most of his contracts on board the ship with him. That is what we plan to do for the foreseeable future. But then, we may look at starting an environmental consulting business in Croatia, so he can quit sailing. Although sailing is in his blood, Niko said he never had a reason before to stay ashore, so he could probably change his mind."

"What if it doesn't work out?" I asked.

"I'd certainly be no more messed up than I was before," said Sam. *"But we're not basing this relationship on promises. We are being honest with one another, and basing things on hope. We both wanted something better and have experienced similar problems in each of our past relationships. Because we understand that, it is our mutual problem, we have a good basis to start working on."*

"Wow!" I said. *"I never expected this, but I sure hope things work out for you both. It seems you're taking a big chance, but you sound convinced."*

"OK," said Jody. *"Can we get down to business and muddle through the papers for this audit? Amber, have you reviewed the protocols and questionnaires? Sam can get you up to speed on her Rickra findings from the last two audits before she leaves next week."*

The rest of the afternoon was spent on purely business terms, and I could see that Jody was not interested in anyone's personal life, after Sam's revelation.

The next morning, we boarded the ship in San Pedro.

After two days of busy audit business, opening meeting, ship's tour, and getting started on records, I saw my opportunity to get Jody alone. Sam was constantly e-mailing and messaging Niko about their upcoming plans for their first Croatia trip together. That left Jody and me pretty much on our own, but Jody had been avoiding me, or so I thought. I finally asked for a good talk, and Jody agreed.

"I'm happy for Sam," Jody said. "I've been worried about her for a long time. She warmed up to you, but she had this strange, deep aura about her, which I always translated as being a man-hater. I was surprised to see she liked you, but once I saw how honest and concerned you were about your wife and your own problems, I think Sam respected you."

"In Miami, my wife said Sam had a dark side, which she didn't understand. That must be the same deep aura you mention. Amazing that you both saw the same thing. I noticed today that the deep, dark side seemed gone. How could two weeks with Niko change her so much?"

"Bob, I think it's the hope thing that Sam mentioned. Having someone in your life who understands you, both the good and the bad is just so important. Sam and Niko had each reached a point in their lives where they no longer trusted the opposite sex. Knowing they were not alone and finding someone from the opposite sex feeling the same, opened their eyes to possibilities they had never thought could come their way. I liked what Sam said about their relationship would be based on hope, and not based on promises. I think they will both be honest with one another, and I have a good feeling about their future."

I walked back to my cabin, feeling much better than before. Maybe just like Sam and Niko, having someone who understood my problems, really was therapeutic.

OFF TO CROATIA

———◆———

*I*WAS OFF TO *Miami for the fifth audit. This was the training audit for John Bryce. As usual, Jody asked for a meeting at the hotel on Friday night to discuss the previous audits and any changes needed on the next one.*

I started to respond to one of Jody's questions about John Bryce, and then Sam came into the lobby.

"I thought you'd resigned," I said. "Missed us already?"

"My resignation was official this afternoon. I wanted to come to this last meeting and say goodbye to everyone."

"And what happens next?" I asked.

"Niko's contract is over tomorrow when the Prince arrives in Miami. We both have flights booked to Zagreb. He has a friend there who keeps his car, so we drive from Zagreb to Pula. We have the next four months to decide what comes next."

"I'm really happy, and hopeful, for you, Sam. I think you two have the right attitude, and you'll figure this out together. What will happen when Niko's next contract starts?"

"We're talking about that," Sam replied. "Stellaris has agreed to let me ride ship with him as much as I want. However, Niko said he likes my idea of starting a

consulting business in Croatia. Now that they are in the EU, their environmental requirements are stiffening. If we see opportunities, I'll stay in Croatia for a while, to see if some consulting work is possible. But I'll ride ship with Niko as much as I can until it is time for him to quit sailing. No more ship mice for that man!"

"Okay, let's get this meeting over with so we can have our last dinner together, and fill in John Bryce on all the history," Jody said. "I hate to see Sam leaving us, but she said Amber is right up to speed on the project, so we'll be fine."

The meeting went quickly, and dinner was very jovial, with no business discussed. Everyone wanted details from Sam about her plans with Niko, and Sam was willing to give lengthy answers. I could see no signs left of Sam's dark side, and knew she'd be just fine. I was very happy for her.

As they were leaving dinner, everyone hugged Sam and wished her well. Jody told the others when to meet in the morning, so they could get to the ship on time.

Sam came to me and gave me a big hug, then whispered in my ear, "Be sure to let me know how things work out at home. I've worried about you since you told me about the divorce on the last cruise. A long email when you can, but we will see one another again somewhere, I'm sure."

"I sure want to keep in touch. Maybe I can learn from what I saw you experience over the last month or so. This nomadic life is terrible for relationships, but you found a solution. Maybe I can do the same.

Sam and Niko have remained in Croatia and continue to be hopeful. With Niko's contacts, Sam was able to start an environmental consulting company, and the two of them work together. Sam told Jody, "Life is good!"

STRAUSS COMPANY REUNION

———◆———

WHEN LOIS AND I finished reading the story Bob had sent to us in the mail, Lois sat up. I could tell that she had enjoyed it, and so did I.

"That is an incredible story!" she exclaimed. "I've never met Samantha, of course, but both Chris and Jody saw that dark side of hers. It sounds familiar to the way I was feeling just before you and I got back together. All it takes is a couple of bad relationships to sour a person and to start thinking that everyone is bad. I'm just thrilled that Sam has found someone with whom she can work through her problems."

"My next trip to Chicago, let's try to get all five of us down there," I said to her. "You would love to meet Bob and his two wives."

"You do realize how kinky that sounds?"

We both chuckled.

"I know, but it's something that Bob Evers would say. Did I mention that Bob's son, Todd, is at the University of Michigan studying Naval Architecture? Since Stevie has been talking about that same line of study, I'll ask Bob when Todd will be home, so the two of them can get together during our next trip."

"That's a great idea. I understand from Will, Steve's friend at the high school who is mentoring him with that CAD program, that Steve is really taking to it. Will said that there are kids in his high school class who could learn by watching Steve."

"That's amazing. I'll have to ask Stevie to show me. I use CAD drawings at work, but I'd have no idea how to produce them."

I had a feeling Bill would be sending me on another trip soon. The shoreline protection project in Sault Ste. Marie was going well, but maybe too well. Several more properties near our worksite saw the work going on, and Bill started getting calls for quotes to work at those locations. Bill realized his crew at the Soo could not handle all this work, so he asked Mel McLaurin and me to go to Chicago, where there was a crane barge and another tug for sale. Bill wanted Mel and me to stay in Chicago long enough for both pieces of equipment to be drydocked, repaired, and ready to start work when they arrived at the Soo.

Bill told me to call Bob Evers and arrange a schedule where Bob and the shipyard were available at the same time. Bob had already recommended that the equipment was worth buying, but Bob told Bill he wanted a good crane-man to look at the crane because that was not his area of expertise. Mel then suggested that we have Larry Boyle along on the trip, to look carefully at the mechanical condition of the crane.

I knew that Lois and the three kids wouldn't be able to stay with me the entire time in Chicago, but I asked Bob when the best time would be for Stevie to meet his son, Todd. Bob said that Todd was working a summer job, but it was right there in Chicago, so he would ask him to be available a couple evenings to speak with Stevie.

Lois was excited about the trip. She had not been able to stay with me at job sites since the twins were born, so she was excited to stay as long as possible. If she needed to get home, there was a train they could take to Lansing or Grand Rapids from Chicago, and either her parents or her friend, Jenny, could pick them up and take her back to Cadillac.

Stevie was very excited to get back to Chicago. He had been telling his friends about the good food he'd tried there on our trip last summer, and he wanted to try some new things, in addition to more Italian Beef, which he had come to love. When I told Stevie about Todd Evers being a Naval Architecture student at the U-of-M, he could hardly wait for us to get to Chicago.

Bill had me rent two vans for the trip. My family of five took up an entire van. Although Mel could not get his wife, Sarita, to come along for the entire trip, she decided that she could come over for a quick get-together and return home on Amtrak after a short stay in Chicago. Larry Boyle was also coming with his lady friend, Loretta Sanchez, for a few days. I was glad to have a chance to get to know Loretta a bit better, having only seen her a couple of times. She seemed to have changed Larry's outlook on life.

Bob Evers arranged for all of us to meet at a nice little Oak Park Greek restaurant, who let our group gather in a small, private dining room in the back. Chris joined the party sometime later that evening. She had the four Evers children with her, including Todd. I hadn't told Stevie about the possibility in case the plans didn't come together. We made all the introductions and had Stevie sit at one end of the large table with Todd, so they could talk without having to hear all the boring adult conversation. With our twins, Chris & Bob's toddler, Sarita's baby, and the four older children, it was quite a large roomful of people. Bill had told me to pay the entire tab, and I hoped he wouldn't be shocked by the total. At least we had a room full of non-drinkers, due to our jobs or the nursing mothers, so it could have been worse.

However, Bob's two daughters, Melanie, and Lilah seemed very interested in meeting Stormi, our woman captain, and Loretta, the EMT. The young girls listened attentively to the conversations and asked both Stormi and Loretta some great questions about what had led them into their careers. Melanie had already started nursing school, and Lilah was at the point in her high school studies that she was thinking about her career path. It was obvious from their questions that they were both very interested in how these two women had chosen atypical careers.

One of the topics of discussion revolved around the fact that Bob and Chris Evers had a child born during their divorce proceedings, and that Chris had played matchmaker to get Bob and his new wife, Jody, together before the divorce was even final. The three of them remain friends and even babysit the new baby when Chris and their older children are busy. As Chris told us, "Growing out of compatibility with Bob, did not mean I didn't like him, and I wanted him to be happy. Jody was an obvious choice, and I liked her. It all made sense, and we all remained friends."

We all had to go to work the next morning, so we left the restaurant early that evening. The next morning, Bob Evers met us at our Hammond, Indiana hotel, and led us to a slip along the Calumet River in South Chicago, which we never would have been able to find on our own.

There was an old crane barge in the slip, but Bob told us it was well maintained, with three spuds, one of which was a 'walking spud.' Bill Strauss didn't want to make the deal on buying the barge until Mel McLaurin and Larry Boyle said the crane was in good shape. The crane was half the value of the combined piece of equipment. As Bill said, this was the most expensive piece of equipment he'd ever purchased, so he wanted to be sure everything was in good shape. Once we knew the crane was worth it, then we'd drydock the barge. The barge also had a generator and a large air compressor in a compartment below deck, so Larry had his work cut out for him on this trip, checking out all the mechanical equipment.

Bill Strauss had already closed part of the deal, buying another 85-foot tug, which was in the same slip. Bill asked me to inspect the tug with Bob Evers and make a list of new equipment and any upgrades we felt were necessary.

Lois, Stevie, and the twins were at a hotel in Hammond, not far away, so they were close to my work for the week. Lois and the kids would take the train to Lansing when we started up the lake. My parents offered to drive down to Lansing and drive them back to Cadillac. I told Lois that once we had things under control, I wanted Stevie to spend a day with me. While I was working on the barge, Stevie could hang out on the tug, which would have power and air conditioning, to keep it comfortable. Lois said she didn't want to spend too much time there but thought the tug would be just as comfortable as the hotel, and a lot more interesting.

Larry also had Loretta with him, and they also had a room at that Hammond hotel. Loretta had asked me if it was okay for her to hang out with us guys. She was familiar with equipment from her firehouse experience, and she was interested in seeing the tug, barge, and crane. I teased her saying, "As long as you don't stay too close to Larry. I need him to concentrate on the crane, and not on you."

I was very impressed by Loretta. She was a good-looking young woman, but she had a very natural look, which made her very likeable. I noticed that she wore minimal make-up, just like Lois. When Loretta and Lois showed up at the tug on the second morning, both of them were dressed in casual clothes, and Loretta looked like she was there to work. She was carrying a bucket and several bottles and cans of cleaning products. I asked what that was all about.

"I figured if Lois and the babies were going to spend any time here, I didn't want them to catch some weird bugs. Who knows what the last crew was like?"

I wanted to argue with her logic, but I also realized we would not have done any cleaning on that tug for the first few weeks, so I said "I suppose, but don't knock yourself out. I didn't agree for Larry to invite you, to put you to work."

"I really don't mind, Curt. I don't want to be sitting amongst somebody's old cooties, and I don't want your wife and kids getting those cooties either. After I get some initial cleaning done, I'll run to that grocery store by the hotel and get some coffee and some things for sandwiches. I assume the tug has a coffee maker. I will sanitize the darn thig first, however."

"Wow, Loretta. I'm impressed. Do you do this all the time?"

"No, but ask Larry how I've cleaned his place. Once his mom went to the Nursing Home, I don't think Larry ever cleaned, and seldom did the dishes. I am serious about Lois and your kids. They shouldn't be hanging out in a place that was inhabited by unknown crewmen."

"You're probably right. But if you are buying groceries, bring me the receipts and Bill Strauss will be okay if I just charge it to his account. I'll pay you in cash for whatever you spend, and also tell me what you spent on the cleaning supplies. Bill would probably agree with you."

"I didn't buy this stuff expecting to be repaid."

"Well, I'm insisting you get repaid. Okay?"

"If you insist."

I was getting a kick out of Loretta's feisty personality. She was headstrong but in a good way. Larry had said she always spoke her mind and said she also had a lot of snappy responses, which he got a kick out of. I was starting to see what he meant.

I got Lois and Stevie situated in the galley after Loretta wiped down the booth and table with a disinfectant. She was taking her job of protecting my family very seriously. I told Stevie, once we had things safe over on the barge, I would take him over to look around, and he was obviously excited. I just warned him to stay out of the engine room and be careful on the steep stairways up to the pilothouse. I trusted Stevie not to touch the equipment but didn't want him around machinery. Before I left, I took Stevie on a tour of the tug out on deck, then asked him not to go out there alone, because the bulwarks on a tug are low, and I didn't want him falling overboard.

Back on the barge, Mel and Larry had both good news and bad news. Although they found the crane was suitable for our operations, we would need to buy another stone grapple. Larry said the crane was in good mechanical condition, except for some heavily worn bushings on two of the load line winch drum shafts. Larry said they weren't dangerous, but they might not last the whole season, so they should be replaced before we start.

I asked Larry to look at the generator and air compressor, while I called Bill Strauss. Bill said, "I'm sure glad Melvin suggested that Larry go along on this trip. He's right. We don't want to take the chance of stopping in the middle of a project to make repairs. Ask Larry if he can find the parts in Chicago. Walter Payton Crane Company handles Manitowoc cranes, so they may have those parts available. Tell Larry I'm pleased with him being there."

Then I told Bill, "I asked Lois to visit the tug today, and Larry's lady friend, Loretta, came along. She is over on the tug, cleaning out all the old cooties, as she referred to it. She also offered to buy some coffee and groceries for our lunch. Would you mind if I put her purchases on my expense account?"

"Most certainly. That's very thoughtful of her. It is probably saving us money. I wish I could put her on the payroll for her efforts."

"If you got to know her, she'd argue about needing to be paid. I get a kick out of her comebacks. She's a nice person, and fun to have around. I think she's just happy to spend some interesting time with Larry. I know she took some vacation time from her firehouse EMT job to be here, and now that Larry will be spending more time here, maybe even taking the trip up the lake with us, I was wondering what you'd think of offering to let Loretta make the trip with us?"

"I'd have no objections. Sounds like she's a positive influence all the way around. Would she mind giving me a 'hold harmless' declaration so my insurance agent doesn't get upset? Seeing she's not an employee, my insurance won't cover her."

"I'll ask her, but I think she'd be fine with it."

"Let me know what Larry finds out about getting parts for the crane. Otherwise, things look good?"

"So far, that's the only problem with the crane. Larry is checking out the generator and air compressor next."

"Unless Larry and Mel see any big problems, I have the ABS Surveyor lined up for the drydocking tomorrow at Chicago Drydock. If Bob Evers finds the hull okay, we will renew the Load Line, so we are good for five years. And what about the tug?"

"Larry has started all the engines and he found the maintenance records on board. He saw no big problems with the tug. They already have a new Coast Guard Certificate of Inspection, so we should only need to transfer the ownership."

"You guys have been busy the last couple days. It

looks like you have everything under control."

"Thanks for letting me take Mel and Larry on this inspection. Evers and I are okay on the hulls but having those two guys here was important."

"I'm glad you made the request. It's not like it was in the old days, with simple equipment and no Coast Guard certificates needed. I'm glad you're on top of everything."

"Okay, unless Larry finds something else, I'll call Chicago Drydock and see if they want us there tonight or first thing in the morning. I'll talk to Loretta and tell you if she wants to ride with us."

"Sounds good. Stay safe over there."

Larry did not find any more problems and Chicago Drydock asked if we could move the barge into their slip, so it would be there for the next morning

I asked Loretta if Larry might want her to make the trip. She told me we probably had planned to have a bunch of wild women taking the trip anyway, so she'd better come along, just to protect Larry. She saw my eyes open wide in surprise, and Loretta said, "You realize I was just joking, right? Even those wild women wouldn't want to ride on this pigsty."

"Is it really that bad, Loretta?"

"Well, luckily I have a bunch of brothers, and I'm the only woman in our firehose shift, so I don't barf too easily."

Larry heard what Loretta said and interjected, "Just so you know, Curt. You need to take half of what Lorry says with a grain of salt. The tough part is figuring out when she's serious and when she's not."

"Larry, don't tell him that yet. I want to keep Curt guessing."

"So, is the answer, yes? You want to make the trip

with us?"

"Most definitely, yes. I've never had a tugboat ride before. I expect you to give me a good safety briefing, which I will critique, by the way. Then I will send Bill Strauss a hold-harmless, along with a thank-you."

"Be aware, we have no double beds aboard, but the mates' room has two singles."

"I think I found that room, and I sanitized it for Lois and the babies to use, so she could nurse in private. While you're in drydock tomorrow, I'll strip the beds and take everything to the laundry."

"We have new pillows and linens ordered, but if they're delayed, maybe that's a good idea. There are two washers and one dryer aboard, but that would take all day. If you see any bad mattresses, let me know and we'll get new ones as well.

Loretta brought Lois and the babies back to the hotel, then she drove the van to the shipyard, while the rest of us faced up to the barge for a short tow over to Chicago Drydock. We still had to pass through several bridges between our slip and Chicago Drydock, so I was happy to have had my training in Toledo from Captain Stormi. I'd be sure to let her know.

I kept Stevie aboard for the trip to the shipyard, and he sat behind me in the pilothouse. This was the first time he actually rode a tug with me, and I wished I could take him on the trip up the lake. I knew Bill's insurance agent would say, absolutely not, so I didn't even suggest it. Stevie seemed to understand that I had to concentrate, so he was quiet the whole trip, which took about an hour. As soon as the engines were shut down, his questions just poured out, all the way back to the hotel.

"Why did you blow the horn with three lasts at one bridge and two blasts at the next bridge? Who were those guys you talked to on the radio? When that tug was coming up the river, how do you decide which side to pass on, because you passed on his left side, not the right? I think that is Starboard to Starboard, is that right?"

I am always amazed at how perceptive Stevie is, so this shouldn't have surprised me. I was happy to give him detailed answers, and I complimented him on not asking while I was handling the tug.

"I knew it wasn't a good time to talk, Dad. You were busy," Stevie said.

I called Bob Evers and said we were on for the dry-docking the next morning. He said he would call Chicago Drydock and see when they'd be ready for him. I asked Bob if he would mind getting Lois and my three kids to Union Station to catch the train after he was done at the shipyard. I would have Lois and the kids on the tug during the day. He said that would be his pleasure. Then Bob asked me a question I wasn't expecting, "Would I be able to ride up to the Soo with you again? Even with the rough weather last time, I really enjoyed the trip. I guess I should ask about the weather though."

I told him I'd check with Bill, but he certainly wouldn't mind having another set of maritime eyes on board. I was secretly looking forward to more of Bob's cruise ship adventure stories.

That last night at the hotel, Lois and I listened to Stevie, who had not stopped asking questions about the tug, the barge, the crane, and the trip down the river. Lois even said she was learning more about tugs from Stevie's questions than she ever learned on her own.

Lois and Stevie said they were both looking forward to their last day aboard the tug before their train trip home. Stevie had done train trips before, but he was also excited about this trip and getting to spend some time with my folks, whom he had become quite close to after staying with them after Captain Johnny's death when Lois stayed with Johnny's wife.

Our last day in Chicago was busy. Bob Evers showed up at the shipyard with his wife, Jody. Lois hung out on the tug that morning until her train departed Chicago at 12:30. We said our goodbyes and Jody took my family to Union Station. Lois later said that Jody went in with her and got her right down to the waiting area, so she could handle the babies. Even with the double stroller, it is quite a task to carry all the necessary supplies. Stevie is good at pulling the two suitcases, so they made it aboard the train just fine. Lois was worried about getting everything into my parents' car, but when they arrived in Lansing, she told me she was surprised to see, they had borrowed their neighbor's van for the day. My folks had changed for the better once Lois and I were married. I kept telling Lois it was all because of her.

After Jody, Lois, and the family left, I was becoming frazzled with all of the preparations for the trip. On top of the barge drydocking with Bob Evers, I needed to get groceries and pick up some other supplies we had ordered. Larry had to order the parts for the crane, and they were scheduled to arrive the following morning. That meant that Larry and Melvin would need to repair the crane during the trip if the weather was calm enough for me to stay faced up to the barge. I cannot have people working on a barge if it's on the towline.

Loretta seemed to sense my frazzled condition, and when we broke for lunch, she said, "Curt, if we put together a shopping list, I can do the grocery shopping. I don't want to just sit here when you guys are running around like crazy."

"Thanks, but I need to put it on my company credit card, and you don't quite look like a Curt Steiner."

"Is that a racial remark or just a sexist one?"

I started to apologize, but Loretta stopped me, "I guess

I'll need to start my jokes with a warning to you Curt. I wasn't serious."

"Okay, I guess. How long did it take Larry to figure out if you were serious or joking?"

"As soon as I think he's figured it out, I change my tactics, just to keep him on his toes, but with you, I'll try to be more obvious. But unless you think we need more than $800 of groceries, I don't mind putting it on my credit card, and you can have Mr. Strauss pay me when we get home. I'd go more, but I have a fraud alert on my card, which makes me call for purchases over $800. That could be embarrassing in that Hammond grocery store."

"If you don't mind Loretta, that would be a big help."

"Hey, I'm getting a free cruise. Consider this my payment."

Just then, Bill Strauss called. "Curt, I had to do some shuffling with captains. Lonnie Willis needed to be home in Toledo for a few days, and I had planned to have him make the trip with you. Lonnie can work days but needed to run April to some doctor appointments for their baby. So, I hope you don't mind not being the senior captain on this trip, because I'm sending Captain Weaver over tonight to make the trip with you."

"Are you serious? I love working with Stormi. Chicago and Lake Michigan are her old stomping grounds, so I'm sure I'll have things to learn from her. And by the way, I hope little Melissa Willis is going to be okay."

"Lonnie assured me it was nothing critical with Melissa. Phil is on a trip with his new wife, Elsa, and April is not comfortable driving with the baby in the car.

"Okay then. But shall we pick up Stormi at the airport?"

"If you would, please. I got her a flight from Detroit into Midway. She said she'd text you when she had an arrival time. Is everything else going okay over there?"

"Going well. Bob Evers' wife, Jody, took Lois and the family to the train. The crane parts will be delivered in the morning. If I can stay faced up to the barge, Larry and Mel will start those repairs underway. And by the way, Loretta has been great. She's run to the grocery store, washed our old bedding, and cleaned up the tug. Today, she is heading out to buy groceries, and she offered to put them on her credit card, seeing only I can use the company card. She has been a real help."

"That's great. We'll have to do something nice for her after this trip. At least she should be happy to have another woman along for the trip."

"Loretta has quite a sharp wit. I will have to find a funny way to break the news about Stormi making the trip with us."

"Don't be too tough on her, Curt."

"Just the opposite, Bill. This is my chance to get even. She has hit me with zingers ever since she arrived. Even Larry warned me to take everything she says with a grain of salt. This is what several older brothers and working with a bunch of firemen has done to her, apparently."

"Well then. Have fun with her but tell her I really appreciate her doing these things for us."

———◆———

I picked Stormi up at Midway and on the drive back to the shipyard, I updated her on the events, including the crane repairs, and that we had a guest rider aboard. I told her about Loretta's sharp wit, and that I wanted to get even, and I asked Stormi to play along when I Introduced her. Stormi reminded me that she had briefly met Loretta at the Winter Meeting, but they had hardly talked.

Arriving on the tug, we found Loretta in the galley, putting away the groceries she had bought. I walked in with Stormi and said, "See just like I told you. This woman thinks she's running this operation. That's why I called Bill to tell him I wanted another woman on board, to put her back in her place."

I saw Loretta's expression change to one with obvious worry, so I didn't want to wait too long. I gave Loretta a big smile and said, "Gotcha!"

"You dirty devil! You actually did have me worried."

I then said, "Stormi, you remember meeting Loretta at the Winter Meeting. So seriously, I don't know what we would have done without her help this week. She literally sanitized anything that Lois and the babies were near when they came aboard, she has done all the laundry, grocery shopping, and other errands. I told Bill this afternoon, she deserved to be signed on as part of the crew."

"After that scare you gave me, I shouldn't admit this, but I had fun this week. And now I'm glad Stormi is here, so I can tell her what a terrible person you are."

"Darn, you never quit," I said.

"Curt you'll know when our friendship is over if I quit giving you jabs. Life is too short to be serious all the time."

Stormi said, "So, I guess I need to be on my toes when we're talking?"

"Well, give me a day or so. Once I know you better, I'll start treating you the same way."

"Warning duly noted," Stormi replied. "By the way, Bill said that after our two new deckhands arrive this afternoon, we should find a good place to get some carry-out. With the tug in the water and running, we'd have to leave someone aboard if we went ashore, but he said the deckhands will know a good place for some good food. How would that sound to everyone?"

"I think that's a great idea. I know that Mel and Larry will be beat after a long day. I'm not sure if you're aware, but Bob Evers will be riding with us as well. I don't think you've heard any of his stories, but he has some new ones in store for us, he says."

"I've heard about his stories. Everyone is talking about his 'Ship Mice' story, and Lonnie told me about the guys with the young dance teachers. He's met some unusual people in his travels."

Our two deckhands showed up with their bags and we got everyone settled into a room. Bob Evers wanted to stay in the lower berthing again just in case the weather kicked up. One of the errands Loretta had run for me that afternoon, was to pick up our new Weather-Fax from the ship chandler, and it was being installed before we left. It looked like we would have a nice, easy trip op to Sault Ste. Marie.

———

The next morning, our fuel truck arrived early, the barge was back in the water, and last, but certainly not least, the crane parts showed up on schedule. We departed the Calumet River, through the four bridges, and out into the harbor. Stormi wanted to see how the barge was riding before allowing Mel and Larry to work on the crane. We had the two new deckhands and Loretta come to the pilothouse for a safety brief. Even though these two deckhands were quite experienced, Stormi wanted to stress the rules about not being out on deck alone, and always wearing their lifejacket when on any of our barges. She also stressed our non-drinking policy, limiting drinking to one beer or wine the night before we were working. Drug use was cause for immediate dismissal in all maritime activities.

Stormi asked me to show the deckhands and Loretta where the fire equipment was located, and how to start the fire pump, as well as emergency exits from the berthing and engine room. I told Stormi that I would make regular rounds of the engine room until someone else was available, and I would keep her company between my inspection rounds.

I noticed that Loretta was very quiet during the briefing and also during my tour, so I asked her if she was okay.

"I am serious when being serious is required. As soon as we left the dock, I could see that you and Stormi were all business, and I respect that. I can save my craziness for when it's appropriate."

I just smiled, and Loretta smiled back. She was going to be just fine on this trip.

The weather stayed calm and Stormi allowed Mel and Larry to work on the crane. She had them wear lifejackets when crossing out to the barge, but seeing they were working 20-feet from the edge of the barge, she told them they could take them off while working. Stormi had the two deckhands keeping an eye on our facing lines between the tug and barge and also helping the work on the crane when needed. Loretta was spending a lot of time in the wheelhouse with Stormi, asking a lot of good questions. I could see they were bonding well.

About mid-afternoon on that first day, Stormi got on the Loudhailer-PA and asked me and the deckhands to come to the pilothouse. When I got up there, she said she was hearing a lot of radio chatter about a missing fishing boat, somewhere off of Holland, Michigan. We were south of Holland at the time but headed right into the area where the Coast Guard was conducting their search. The Coast Guard was getting a lot of false sightings because there were a lot of commercial charter-fishing boats on the lake, and the Coast Guard was asking for help from all commercial freighters and tugs on the lake to keep their eyes peeled.

Stormi had the two deckhands go forward on the barge to look for boats or debris on the water.

"I've got good observational skills. Is there something

you'd like me to do?" Loretta asked.

Stormi said, "If you can stand the sun glare, Loretta, would you mind standing on the roof of the pilothouse? From up there, you can see both sides for maybe five miles. I'll keep an eye on my radar, but these small fiberglass boats don't show up well on radar. This is reported to be a 28-foot boat, all white, with only a low cabin on her. It sounds like a small cigarette boat. It may be hard to spot. We're about ten miles offshore. The Coast Guard thinks the boat is only five miles off, but keep a lookout in all directions, even an occasional glance behind us.

And Curt, I guess you know, I'd like both of us up here in the pilothouse, so we can keep our visual, radar, radio, and anything else covered. You can run to the engine room occasionally. At that point, Melvin appeared in the pilothouse, asking what was going on. After Stormi gave him a brief synopsis, Mel said he wasn't needed on the crane repairs at this time, so he could make the engine room inspections and keep an eye on anything else that Stormi needed.

I helped Loretta up to the roof of the pilothouse, gave her a pair of binoculars, and told her to stomp her foot on the roof if she saw something suspicious, or just needed a break.

An hour later, Loretta stomped several times, and I figured she might need a potty break. As I climbed the ladder up to the roof, Loretta said, I don't want to take my eyes off of this but look west at about ten o'clock. There is a boat out there, just drifting, and I don't see anyone outside. Maybe they're in the cabin making whoopee, but I've seen no movement for the last couple minutes.

I told Loretta to keep her eyes on the boat, and that I would tell Stormi to head in that direction, and call the Coast Guard."

Stormi changed course and told the deckhands what was happening. As we got closer, Loretta stomped again. I went up to the roof and she said as we started heading toward the boat, she saw a woman on deck, waving like she needed help.

I gave Stormi the update and she continued heading toward them. I called the Coast Guard, and they said their helicopter had returned to base for refueling, and they would send one of their small boats toward our position, which they were tracking from our AIS signal. Once Stormi had the boat in sight, she told me to get Loretta off the roof.

"Great job Loretta. They were certainly further out than the Coast Guard estimated. They're darn near in the middle of the lake. I'm not sure what we will do with them, seeing the Coast Guard is a good thirty minutes away."

"Stormi, you realize I'm an EMT, right? Let me go down on the barge as you get to them. I'll find out if someone is hurt, or maybe it's just a mechanical problem. Can you have one of the deckhands bring all the First Aid supplies down there, just in case? I think I saw an AED in that little office while I was cleaning the other day. Have them bring that too."

"I didn't realize you were an EMT. I thought you just worked in a firehouse. Yes! Please go down there and I'll get everyone down there to assist you."

Minutes later, we pulled up alongside the boat. The woman looked like she was in shock. Loretta jumped on the boat and started talking to the lady, then the lady pointed over the side of their boat. Loretta looked over and saw the woman had tied the man to the side of the boat.

The woman whimpered, "I told him not to go over, but he was trying to un-foul our propeller. I wasn't strong enough to pull him back in after he hurt his shoulder."

Loretta motioned for Larry and me to come aboard. The three of us could barely pull the man back onto the boat, and we finally had him up on deck. The man was turning blue from the cold water. Loretta said we needed to get him over to the tug fast and asked the deckhands to pull the boat to the side of the tug. A few minutes later, the man was in a main deck cabin, covered with several layers of blankets, and Loretta was massaging his arms and legs. After about thirty minutes, Loretta said he was stabilized, but severely hypothermic.

The man's wife had calmed down by this time and told us what happened. Apparently, the boat's twin propellers had become entangled in some discarded mooring line, and her husband had tried to free the props by repeatedly starting the engines and reversing the gears. Each time he did this, the battery became weaker until the engines would no longer start. When he realized he needed help, his radio also had no power, He tried to look over the stern to see the ropes, and he decided to jump into the water, hurting his shoulder as he went over. With only one of his arms useable, his wife couldn't get him back aboard. Being an older man, spending over an hour in 55-degree water, he became dangerously hypothermic. The wife luckily was able to tie a rope under his arms to keep him from slipping under the water, because he was barely conscious when the tug and barge arrived.

The Coast Guard finally showed up, but Loretta said it would be dangerous to move the man to another boat. Stormi asked the Coast Guard if they could find a safe mooring for her in Holland, where an ambulance could get to the dock. The Coast Guard said it would be easier in Grand Haven, and it was the same distance from our position, so they led us into Grand Haven for the transfer.

On the way to Grand Haven, I figured I'd better call Bill Strauss to tell him what was happening. Bill said,

"It turned out to be great all-around that Loretta made this trip. She sounds like a real trooper."

"Looks like we've found another good member of our Tugboater family," I said. "I hope you get the opportunity to meet her."

"I'll make a point of it," Bill said.

Bill suggested we stay in Grand Haven overnight in case the Coast Guard or the hospital needed any input from Loretta. I watched Loretta talking with the man's wife and with the EMTs in the ambulance. She was very serious and did a great job to calm the wife down. When she was in her working mode, she did not talk the same way she did during our friendly conversations. That evening, I called Lois to tell her about our little adventure, and I told her how impressed I was with her friend.

"Yup. That's Loretta. She was always the one to act goofy and she started all our crazy nicknames, like sauerkraut for me, and Taco Bell for her. She loved seeing people's shocked reactions to her wise cracks. But I teamed with her in our emergency room rotation during nursing school, and she had a total personality change as soon as a patient came into the ER. Her foolishness stopped immediately until the crisis was over. Yet she did seem to know when the patients could use a little levity, particularly when the kids were in the ER. If she saw the child was terrified, she found a way to ease the tension. I remember one time a little girl was holding her doll, and the doctor was trying to take it away from her, so he could do his examination. Loretta saw the girl tighten her hold on the doll, so Loretta dabbed a drop of blood on the doll's arm. Loretta asked for the name of the doll and then told the little girl she would work on the doll's 'owie' while the doctor looked at hers. I was happy to see that the doctor thanked Loretta afterwards, saying 'I guess you made up for my poor bedside manner. Thanks.' I'm sorry to say, a lot of doctors are not as considerate toward their nurses."

"It took me a while to understand her little jabs and snide remarks, but once I started finding some good come-backs, and she knew I caught on to her style, we had a good time. Then she spent a lot of time with Stormi in the pilothouse, and I was afraid she'd act foolish with Stormi, but she was serious."

"Again, that's how Loretta acts. When she is in a place where people are being serious, for good reason, she acts the same. And you got to see her when she had to act professionally herself, and I'm sure you were impressed."

"We all were. She even calmed down the man's wife, who felt responsible for the man's hypothermia, because she hadn't convinced him not to jump over the side. These people take these boats out into the lake without proper training, no tools, and limited experience. If we hadn't been in the right place when they got in trouble, I think that man would have died."

"I'm glad Loretta was along on that trip. She's a real pro. So, you'll leave in the morning? Who is staying in the Soo with that new equipment?"

"Stormi was about to take her time off, and Lonnie is back in Toledo to help April with their baby, so I think I'll be staying in the Soo for a while. As soon as Bill gives us our marching orders, I'll let you know."

"The reason I ask is because I feel good enough to drive again. I've rigged up a safe place for the babies in the back seat, and Steve can ride up front with me. If you're staying up there for any length of time, I'd like to drive up and spend a week with you. Last year, Steve didn't want to miss his Summer Day-camp sessions. But this year, he keeps asking if we can spend more time with Dad. That little trip on the tug, going to the shipyard in Chicago, really impressed him. I heard him describing the trip, blow by blow, to his computer gaming friends. Even Becky was asking him for more details."

"I think that would be wonderful. We can stay at the Longships Motel, so Stevie will be right across from the Locks. It's also a nice, comfortable place for you, with the babies. As soon as I know my schedule, I'll call you. I know that Bill is one captain short right now, so if I offer to stay on the job a little longer, I think he'd appreciate it."

"Okay, lover. Call me when you get up to the Soo. I hope you don't have any more delays, but I'm glad you were in the right place to help that stranded couple."

"Me too. Love you, Babe. Say hi to Stevie for me."

———

That evening, we decided to order pizza from a local restaurant in Grand Haven. We were all sitting around the table in the mess deck when Stormi said to Bob, "I keep hearing about your sea stories, Bob. I haven't heard any of them yet. Are you in the mood to give us one?"

"Well, first of all, my stories are not sea stories. As you know, sea stories keep getting embellished, to the point nobody can remember how much of it is true. My stories were written down soon after I experienced them, and some were crazy enough on their own. They didn't need embellishment."

"Okay, I stand corrected. What story are you going to give us tonight?"

"Well, Stormi, you didn't get to meet my wife, Jody. I don't think she'll mind me telling this story about her, which occurred during our cruise ship audits. Both Jody and I were going through some tough times with our previous spouses at the time, and we were confiding in one another, still hoping we could work things out. So, here is what happened to Jody on that cruise. I call this story *The Cruise Ship Doctor*. I think Loretta may like this one as well. I bet she has seen some doctors like this with the work she does.

"Once Jody and I became serious with our relationship, we wanted to be honest with each other about everything that might affect our relationship. Jody had sought my counsel about a potential relationship during one of our first cruises together, and I needed her to know about my tryst. So, one evening while both of us were at home in Oak Park, I told Jody about Sylvia… you remember…the lady over in Nelson, New Zealand. Well, I had continued to communicate occasionally with Sylvia as friends, now that I knew she had finally found a good guy in Wellington. I didn't want Jody to think that I was thinking romantically about Sylvia.

"After telling Jody the story, including the reason for my two unusual questions about bundling and oral sex, when Jody and I first got together, Jody reminded me about a doctor she had met and her feelings of being cheated by not taking him up on his offer. I wanted both Jody and myself to be aware of anything which could affect our trust in one another."

THE CRUISE SHIP DOCTOR

*W*E *ALWAYS STARTED our audits on the cruise ships with a ship's tour of the main areas of environmental concern, including the bridge, engine room, garbage room, pools, and so forth. Some of the areas, such as the ship's infirmary and photo lab, were not open on embarkation day, so visits to those facilities were usually delayed until later in the week.*

Jody and Sam had visited some different places during this second day of the audit, and they wanted to tell the rest of us about some unusual experiences.

Jody said, "Sam, do you want to tell them our interesting news, or shall I?"

Sam said, "Oh, please, let me tell them! I'm sure this is not news to Olaf and Hans. While we were in the Medical Facility, which was quite interesting, including the doctor, we were about to leave, and the nurse asked us if we needed to inspect the morgue? I think we all thought we hadn't heard her correctly, but Jody asked, 'Did you say morgue?'"

Then Jody continued, saying, "The nurse said, "of course," and I told her yes, we needed to see the morgue. She then led us to a small cargo hold, near the stern of the ship, where we saw a small, walk-in freezer. It was empty, and not running, but she told us they've had as many as five passengers a year die during cruises, and unless the family decided to send the body home from one of the ports of call, they'd wrap the body and place it in the freezer, until they get back to the home port. They help the family decide, because the cost of flying a body home from a foreign country can be very expensive, and complicated unless the passenger has a very good travel insurance policy."

Hans then added, "When you realize we have over 3000 people on board, including crew, and the average age of the 2400 passengers is quite high, compare it to a small city of 3000 people, and how many people die in a year."

"I guess that never occurred to me," I said. "But Jody, you mentioned the doctor. Tell us why he was so interesting."

"First off, he's a very nice guy, and very talkative. I asked where he was from, and he said, 'Well, born in Sweden, but now live in Istanbul,' and when I seemed surprised by the answer, he came right out and said, 'I'm hiding from my ex-wife.'"

Sam jumped in with, "We were all pretty surprised with his answer, and I think Bob was the one to start asking questions."

So, I then chimed in, "Seeing the doctor was being so matter of fact with his statement, I figured he wouldn't mind a few questions, so I asked why he was hiding from his wife? He quickly corrected me, saying, 'Ex-Wife!' so, I then corrected myself and asked, 'What happened with your ex-wife?'"

Hans looked surprised, saying, "I know you think this ship is getting more interesting every day. But what was his answer to that?"

I continued, "Well, I'll paraphrase because I can't remember his exact words. The good doctor apparently has always had an eye for the ladies, and his wife, at that time, suspected as much. She hired an investiga-

tor to follow him, and he was filmed with his nurse at a hotel one time, and with one of his patients during another rendezvous. The court judgment was very hard for him to swallow, apparently taking a good percentage of his future earnings, so he just ran away. At least in his mind, it was a simple solution."

Jody then said, "We all thought he may have been exaggerating, so when the nurse took us to see the morgue, I asked her if she believed all he'd told us. She said it was all true, and the doctor still had a good reputation with the women on board."

"Well, it's time for me to head for the brig," I said with a laugh. "The brig has been a great place for my engine room meetings. We never get disturbed."

"Just be sure it's empty," said Sam.

Hans added, "Remember, tonight is Formal Night. If you don't want to dress for dinner, there's also the option to go up to the buffet. At night, they serve steak, sushi, and a great seafood buffet, for those who are not interested in going to the dining room."

Jody spoke before anyone else could answer, "I'd like to experience Formal Night. I packed a nice dress, and I want a chance to wear it. Maybe we can try that buffet for dinner another night. Okay with everyone?"

Everyone nodded in agreement and planned to meet in the bar before dinner. They all split up and headed back to work.

JODY AND THE DOCTOR

———

I SHOWERED AND DRESSED in my business casual attire for dinner. I looked in the mirror, and like my wife had told me when we shopped for it, the dark blue jacket went well with my quickly graying hair.

Everyone was nicely dressed for the Formal Night dinner. None of us had ever taken a cruise, so we didn't know what to expect, other than what we'd heard from friends who were cruise veterans.

Jody told the team to order wine this evening, and she would get Stolton to pay for it. "Hey, it's our first Formal Night. Right?" she said.

The waiters then took everyone's dinner orders.

After talking over the plan for the next day, Jody asked if anyone had gone shopping aboard the ship. They had all been so busy working, they had forgotten about the great gift shops aboard.

I had promised to send e-mails to the family and had not done that all week, so I declined the chance to look for souvenirs, saying, "I plan on buying some gifts on the next cruise, so I don't have to haul them around all week."

"Well, I guess I'll spend money alone, or at least see what's worth buying," said Jody.

Jody was walking through the gift shops after dinner, when a familiar, heavily accented voice behind her said,

"Well, Miss Jody, are you spending all your money on board?"

Jody turned to see the Ship's Doctor behind her. He was in civilian clothes, which surprised her. "Doctor Mogensson, you surprised me. I almost didn't recognize you without your uniform. I thought the crew always wore their uniforms on board."

"Technically, the medical staff are not crew members. We are contractors, similar to these shopkeepers here, the entertainers, and a few others. We wear uniforms during the work day, but it is not required after hours."

"Very interesting. So, you're free to do as you please after hours?"

"The nurse and I carry a ship's telephone, so we can be summoned 24-hours, in case we are needed, but otherwise, we are on our own. It's a good gig, and our life aboard is quite pleasant. That is if we don't have a virus problem on the ship."

"We only discussed environmental issues during our visit to the Infirmary, so I guess I was unaware of your non-crew status."

"Even many of the crew are unaware of our contractor status. The officers understand, of course. So, are you buying souvenirs tonight?"

"I saw some good ideas for souvenirs. But our auditor, Bob, whom you met briefly, said at dinner tonight, he was going to save his buying until next week, before we head home from the next ship. The more I think of it, that makes more sense than dragging the gifts around another week."

"If you are done shopping, can I buy you a drink? We can discuss your role on board, and I can better explain how this contractor thing works," Doctor Mogensson offered.

"It's early, and a drink sounds great," said Jody. "Are we heading to the crew's bar?"

*"If you don't mind, the booze is cheaper in my cabin,"
said the doctor.*

"I thought the crew was not allowed to have passengers in their rooms," Jody said, with some surprise in her voice.

"Remember, I am not a crew member. And besides, you are not a passenger."

"Well Doctor, just so you know, I am a married woman," Jody quickly added.

"No hanky-panky intended, Miss Jody. And please call me Bjorn. This doctor thing is much too formal."

The pair left the shopping mall and went to the hallway, near the infirmary, where the doctor's cabin was located. The cabin was not any larger than those of the other officers' cabins but was furnished and decorated to a higher level.

"Nice digs" Jody exclaimed. "How did you get this one?"

"Our other relief doctor on this ship also likes nice things, so we shared expenses to buy some extras. If we happen not to come back to the same ship, the next doctors will just have a nice surprise. By the way, I have scotch, brandy, and vodka right now, and can offer most mixes."

"Brandy on the rocks would be nice. How long have you been on this ship?" Jody asked.

"This is my fourth contract, so nearly three years; four months on, and four months off."

"Is that unusual, to be on the same ship for so long?"

"It would be for an officer or crew member, but I like this ship, and have asked to return each time. The cruise line hates finding new doctors, so they have always cooperated."

"Why do you like this ship?" Jody then asked.

"It's smaller than the newer ships, with 5000 passengers. Those ships have two doctors and some even have

three nurses, but here, we run our department with just the two of us, and that's nice. I have been lucky to have good nurses, and we always get along well."

Jody had been waiting for a chance to ask the nagging question, after the doctor's earlier admission of hiding from his wife, and the nurse saying he was a ladies-man. So, Jody then said, "We were surprised by your statement about your marital problems. Can I ask, what happened?"

"It is long, complicated, and a little shameful, I suppose. My wife and I had been married for just two years when she made it clear that she only married me because I was a doctor, not for my companionship. I was young and wanted a full love life, so I had a couple of affairs. I should have expected it, but was naïve, I guess. My wife's father hired a detective, and they filmed me with those two women. I had no chance to fight the charges because the charges were true. Because my wife held no job, the Swedish judge gave her half of my income, so I found myself in a tough situation."

"I must say, this is not quite as salacious a story as I expected. That is if you are telling the whole truth," Jody said, with a questioning tone.

"Well, I said the charges were true, and it was quite awkward. I don't think I left much out. My only defense is that my wife married me under false pretenses. Before she started to ignore me sexually, I was a true-blue husband."

"And what about now?" Jody asked.

"I think I am a good, caring person. I occasionally invite a pretty woman to my room, but I never attack them, nor do I force myself upon them. Nothing happens unless the feeling is mutual."

"So, Bjorn, am I one of those potential conquests?" Jody then asked.

"I'm not that bold," said the doctor. "But you are very

pretty, and I invited you to my room. I guess the rest is up to you."

Jody looked very bewildered. She had always loved her husband and had never strayed in their marriage. She was reasonably sure that Les had a couple short affairs, but now she was hoping to repair their marriage. She did not believe in one-night stands, and there was no possibility of any long-term relationship with Bjorn. However, she had never heard someone so straightforward about his sexual relationships, and for some reason, this attracted her to this man.

Jody finally responded, "Bjorn, I'm actually tempted. You're a very interesting man, and your honesty makes you appealing, in some strange way. You are catching me at a very vulnerable time in my life, which is why I will probably have to say no. My husband and I are having a rough period in our marriage, and if I stayed here tonight, I would not be able to go home and try to work things out."

"Jody, I certainly understand. If I led a normal life, I might suggest this could end up as a serious relationship. I was very attracted to you during your visit to the infirmary. You have a real authoritative strength, which I like. I don't want to be a bad story in your life, and I hope you can mend your relationship with your husband."

"Wow, you really know how to hurt a girl," Jody said, with a smile on her face. "I expected the opposite reaction, trying to convince me to stay."

"I told you I was a nice guy'" Bjorn said. "We can have another drink, but then I will send you on your way."

"That sounds great. And I also want to hear more about your life in Istanbul. I've heard other officers mention they live there, so I want to know what attracts you guys."

Jody and Bjorn spent another hour talking as friends, then she gave Bjorn a hug and a kiss on the cheek and left. She learned a lot from Bjorn and had a strange respect for him after that evening.

FEELING CHEATED

——◆——

*J*ODY WAS WALKING *through the Casino on her way back to her cabin when she spotted me at one of the Nickel-Machines near the door. "I didn't know you were a gambling man, Bob," she walked over to me and said.*

I turned upon hearing her voice, "Nah, I always feel guilty if I actually gamble. With three kids at home, and one on the way to college, I know they can use the money, so I never put more than twenty bucks in nickel slots, if I really get bored. I heard a suggestion from a riverboat casino manager one time, to use the nickel machines by the doors. The casino wants those machines making noise, to attract the people passing by."

"So, how is that theory working tonight?

"Well, I've been here twenty minutes and still have ten bucks left in the machine. Better than losing all twenty in five minutes, which is more typical."

"Hey, Bob, can I talk to you? Got time to catch a drink?"

"Sure, Jody. Something wrong?"

"It's personal. Can we go to that Sky Bar up front? It usually seems deserted this time of night."

Arriving at the Sky Bar, Jody related her experience with the ship's doctor. I had only met Bjorn briefly, so Jody probably thought I would be a good sounding board to discuss what happened.

I was immediately concerned, thinking the doctor had tried to force the liaison, but Jody explained further, "No, he was a perfect gentleman. He made it clear, he was attracted to me, but when I told him about my shaky relationship with Les right now and said this was a bad time in my life, he backed right off."

"He sure doesn't sound like a lecherous old man, that's for sure. Why did you go to his room in the first place?" I asked.

"That's the strange part of the story. I was attracted to the guy. Not his looks so much, though he is decent looking, and not that old, by the way. It was his straight-forward approach to his sexual life. He admits to having a lot of flings, but he does not seduce women that do not want to be seduced. He sure doesn't fit the mold, does he?"

"And obviously, you were not tempted?" I asked.

"That's what worries me. I was tempted to stay the night. Life at home has been shaky the last couple of years, and I miss having a man hold me. I know Bjorn would not have started anything serious or long-term, but he was honest and charming, and I was nearly ready to say okay. It really scared me, thinking that way."

"I think you made the right decision," I said. "What more would you like me to say? I'm confused, I guess."

"I think your situation at home, and your efforts to solve your problems with Chris, has made me respect your opinion. I'm glad you said I made the right decision, but then why am I feeling cheated right now?"

"I think we all need sexual companionship in our life, Jody. And it sounds like you haven't been fulfilled for a while. I know the feeling, seeing Chris has been in such turmoil, our sex life has been lacking. What else can I say?"

"Just tell me I'm not a slutty bitch for thinking this way. I almost spent the night with a guy who told me it

would be a one-night stand."

"Jody, you are a beautiful woman with natural needs. You are not a bitch, and certainly not a slut. You are at a tough spot in your personal life, and maybe a bit vulnerable."

"Thanks, Bob. My life is confusing, and I'm frazzled. I hope you don't mind I told you about this."

"I'm honored you trust me that much Jody. Anytime you want to talk, just ask."

"I will. I'd better let you go. Thanks for the great counsel session," Jody said, with a big smile on her face.

I was heading to my cabin, feeling something was wrong, and I couldn't put it into words. I was upset by what she had told me, and I knew I couldn't sleep. I went back to the bar instead, ordered a Mojito, and sat in a deserted corner booth. What was it I was feeling?

Then it came to me because I had not felt this way in years. I was jealous! I was upset that the doctor had tempted Jody, but I was jealous because she said she felt cheated. I had kept telling myself that Jody and I were just friends, but with things falling apart at home, my emotions were changing. My attraction to Jody was evolving.

———

"I have known a couple of doctors like that, though I think the majority are good guys," Loretta said. "I think it has something to do with the power they must feel when they know that they hold people's lives in your hands. Most people take that responsibility seriously, but some people let their egos take over. It surely happens with people in government and a few doctors."

I said, "I saw that happen with some captains I served under in the Coast Guard. Most of my captains were good guys, and they treated the crew with respect. We did have a couple of egomaniacs who put the crew in

danger, just to make them look important. We called it
the God-complex. That's why I got out. I must say, all
of the commercial vessel captains I've met so far have
been great people."

Stormi added, "Well, I've served with a couple-a bad
captains, but they don't seem to last very long. Headstrong captains tend to make mistakes, even causing
bad accidents, which ends their careers. We just hope
that they aren't serious accidents, like the Italian captain
who ran his cruise ship aground over in the Mediterranean. His ego actually killed some passengers."

Bob then said, "If you remember, it was the unlicensed
crewmembers who saved the day on that ship. When
the captain and some other officers left the ship, supposedly to supervise the rescue from their lifeboat, the
crew, most of whom were Filipino deckhands, galley
staff, cleaners, and engine crew, stayed at their emergency stations and launched the lifeboats. If it hadn't
been for those guys, doing their assigned duties, many
more would have died. I always complemented those
people when I was working on the cruise ships"

"Yes, those guys were great. Just like today, our deckhands stood on the bow of our barge, even missed eating
lunch, to keep a look-out. And with all the excitement,
I never thanked you guys. Sorry, fellas! Thank you for
doing what needed to be done, without complaints."
The two deckhands smiled and nodded at Stormi for her
recognition.

Bob then said, "I have another story about one of the
few captains we didn't respect during our cruises. Is
anyone in the mood to hear another one?"

We all said we wanted more, so Bob started his next
story.

———

Bob Evers had other stories to tell about those eight

years he spent auditing the cruise ships. In Bob's own words, "Not everyone we met on the cruise ships was wonderful. Generally, the unlicensed crew were very friendly and cooperative, once they recovered from their nervousness and understood we wanted to help them wherever we could. Some officers were a little aloof, but still nice people. However, we met one captain who reminded me of the obnoxious, Type-A, or even narcissist ones we see on the news when their ship goes aground or catches fire, and they are the first ones in the lifeboats. I don't think this one would leave his ship in flames, but he certainly treated the opposite sex with disdain."

THE CAPTAIN

OUR FIRST EVENT on every audit is to arrange an opening meeting, to lay out the plan for the week, but also to meet and learn about the senior officers aboard the ship. Seeing the officers' reactions to the audit process not only helps the auditors understand the officers' personalities, but it many times explains, even points to, potential problems on board, which are called findings.

Olaf, the company's East Coast Operations Manager, guided us to the captain's Conference Room, where seven men were waiting, in addition to Olaf. Introductions were made, and the group included the captain, staff captain, safety officer, hotel manager, chief engineer, and environmental officer, all in uniform. In addition, another man, Hans Nilsen, the Stellaris Fleet environmental officer, was also attending. He was from the Long Beach Operations Center. Olaf also remained for the meeting.

The captain, Oleg Romanov, was in his late 50's and looked like a captain should. He had a well-trimmed beard and wore his uniform well. He spoke with a Russian accent, and introduced his officers, "As you can see, we have a very international team at Stellaris. We have Norwegians, Swedes, Danes, and a Croatian environmental officer on this ship, in addition to this

Russian captain you see in front of you. We have 34 nationalities on board, with 583 crew members. I have seen as many as 45 nations represented on one ship, several years ago."

The captain continued, "I know you are here to investigate possible violations of United States Law. I can assure you; this ship complies with MARPOL in all respects. We do not pollute! Now, please tell me how we can cooperate to make your job easier."

Jody started to speak, and it was noticeable, the captain expected one of the two men to take the lead for the audit team. It was also noticeable, Olaf Thorsen and Hans Nilsen were not surprised, as they smiled when Jody began.

"Thank you very much, Captain, for your introductions, and your offer to help with our work. We'll need a secure room, away from the passengers, which we will use for meetings, and also where we can spread out documents for review. We'll also need to interview the officers and various crew members. But first, we would appreciate a quick tour of the operational areas of the ship, preferably today, before you depart. We don't want to interfere with ship operations, so it's best to make the tour while you are in port. If we need to return to any of the operational areas, we will only do so when you are moored at one of the ports during the cruise."

The captain spoke again, "I'm happy you understand our operations would not allow outsiders on the bridge or, in the engine spaces while at sea. As for a room to review records, and speak to crew members, you are welcome to use my conference room, where we are now."

Jody responded, "Thank you, this room should work fine for record reviews. We may need something more private on some occasions, I'm sure you understand. Also, Bob is a very experienced marine surveyor, so we were hoping he could spend most of his time in the engine control room. He will need to review Oil Record Books and verify the operation and calibration of many of the ship's pollution equipment items. Lastly, we will hold a closing meeting the evening before we reach Miami, at the end of the cruise. I believe that would be our night in Nassau."

It was obvious the captain was a bit irritated by Jody's comments, and he was not used to having his suggestions being countered, particularly by a woman.

The captain then suggested the ship's tour could start, right after a quick lunch. He suggested they have lunch in the crew's mess hall, rather than the main passenger buffet, to avoid the curiosity of the passengers, who were already boarding.

Everyone agreed with the captain's suggested course of action, and they headed for the crew's mess hall. The crew also ate buffet-style, with many of the same offerings as the passengers ate. However, the crew also had several ethnic entrees on their buffets, such as nasi goreng and vindaloo. This ship happened to have a lot of Indonesian and Indian crew members, so the cruise line hired an assistant chef from that region, to satisfy the tastes of the crew. The captain also said the Chinese laundrymen had a small galley to prepare dishes for them. Jody, Sam, and Bob tried some of the ethnic dishes and agreed that eating in the crew's mess would occasionally be a nice change. The captain ate quickly and excused himself.

———◆———

The next evening, we met in the bar before dinner. I was explaining my findings in the engine room, particularly the poorly written Oil Record Book entries.

"Well, I hope you find a way to solve that problem, Bob. It could be why they're in trouble. So, let's head into dinner, and I can give you my weird news," Jody said. The others could see the smile on her face, so it must be something important.

The team sat at their assigned table, and all were happy to see the table nearest them was empty. Those passengers must have decided to eat elsewhere this evening. In fact, there were several empty tables, and their waiter solved the mystery, when he asked, "Not going to the pool-side barbecue tonight?"

Jody answered for all, saying, "We don't like crowds much. And besides, we didn't want you to be lonely."

The waiter smiled at her remark.

We were all waiting to hear what Jody had to tell us.

Jody began, "When we left breakfast this morning, Olaf was leading me to the captain's conference room. You two had gone to the Bridge office to gather record books, and Bob went to the engine room. If you remember, we had to pass through the captain's office to get into the conference room. Olaf knocked, and the captain said we should enter. Sitting in the large armchair, in front of the captain's desk, was this young, pretty woman, maybe twenty-five or so. She was dressed, but obviously in some kind of negligee, like a lacy wrap. I could tell she was humiliated, and she did not like being there. However, the captain had a smile on his face. I think he was flaunting the situation, to either impress me or upset me. As soon as we went into the conference room, I heard the captain tell her to leave."

"Oh my God!" said Sam. "Maybe he forgot you were coming?"

"No, because Olaf called him before we started up from breakfast. Olaf apologized to me after he closed the conference room door. He said this was improper behavior. He said he wanted to report this event, but he knew someone in Operations would defend the captain, saying we'd misunderstood the situation. But there was nothing to misunderstand. Olaf told me not to think this was acceptable behavior, and not every captain in the Stellaris fleet would act like this. Olaf was obviously upset!"

"Remember what Niko said to us yesterday," Sam said. "Ship-mice were treated with respect, by most of the officers. He emphasized the word, most. Maybe Niko is aware of the captain's treatment."

"There is more to the story," Jody went on. "After lunch, we returned to the conference room, and at around 2 o'clock, the same girl came into the conference room. I could see she was embarrassed. It turns out, her part-time job is Ship's Social Director, working for the captain, in addition to her other duties. The Social Director is not a full-time job, but I'm not sure where else she works, other than in the captain's bedroom."

"Oh, how terrible for her," I said. "Why did she come back this afternoon?"

"So now, the rest of the story!" Jody replied. "She came to tell me the four of us were invited to the captain's table for dinner tomorrow."

"I'm not sure we should go," Sam said. "It would be like approving his actions!"

"That's exactly what I said to Olaf, but Olaf said the captain would then know how upset we were if we declined his invitation. That was his intention; to disturb me by showing off his woman. We should not let him see it upset us, or he will think he won the contest."

"I'm still not sure we should go," Sam said.

"Olaf also said that dinner at the captain's table, on any night other than Formal Night, is not a big deal. The captain fills his table several times each cruise with various VIPs, like the couple with the most Stellaris cruises, or even people celebrating a significant wedding anniversary. Olaf was sure the request for us to sit at his table, actually came from the Long Beach office, and not from the captain himself."

"Changing the subject, I've been invited to the crew's bar for a drink tonight. Would anyone else want to go?" Sam asked.

Everyone declined, wanting to get a good night's sleep.

———

Loretta said, "Wow! That captain was a real ass..., I mean jerk! Was this a common occurrence to find guys like that on those cruise ships?"

"Actually, Loretta, it was very unusual. You haven't heard some of the other stories I've told, but the officers and crew typically act more like family, looking out for one another. They do have romances aboard. They are human after all. But it seems like there is an unwritten code of conduct between them, which does not allow them to take advantage of seniority when a romantic liaison is involved. This captain was obviously an exception to that rule."

"That's good to hear," said Stormi.

BOB Evers also explained to the new members of the crew that the auditors occasionally witnessed some very unusual behavior, or at least were informed of the behavior when they asked questions. One such occurrence had occurred late at night when the ship made a refueling stop at an island where the passengers were not allowed off the ship. Some of the crewmen were supposedly leaving for dance lessons. In fact, those crew members had girlfriends ashore, and they were caring for the woman and her children, because they did not have a good man in their lives. Even in this case, there was mutual respect between them, which was hard for an American to understand, using typical Western values.

———◆———

Each new ship was a learning experience, Bob told us. Not only the differences in crew members but the changes in cultures. Bob had learned from his previous travels to be careful about saying and doing things that are very American. Most Americans believe the entire world thinks like Americans. But Bob has found that most people are friendly and are good-natured, but in some middle east countries, you must ask permission to take pictures of people, particularly if a woman is in the shot. Therefore, Bob said he was proud of his team members for being sensitive to various cultural differences during their audits. This became more obvious during their audits of a subsidiary of this company's ships, Delphinus Cruise Line.

However, each ship Bob audited had new experiences to find and customs to learn, due to the changes of nationalities amongst the crew. So, Bob offered another story to explain what his audit team had learned.

NEW CULTURES

—————

WE MET OUR next ship in Curacao, and this ship was part of the Delphinus Cruise Line, which was a Stellaris subsidiary. Delphinus was based out of Singapore, and most of the marine officers were from various Asian countries.

We arrived in Willemstad the evening before the ship arrived and stayed at a beautiful beachfront hotel. We had our normal pre-audit meeting at the hotel that evening.

The team met in the hotel lobby after breakfast, checked out, and met the Delphinus Agent outside. The agent's van was loaded with our luggage, and we headed to the Port. Willemstad has three cruise ship docks. The outer harbor is reserved for the large, 5000 passenger ships. Smaller ships enter the harbor through the historic Floating Bridge, and one dock is located along the channel, opposite the colorful Dutch shops. The third dock is further into the harbor, generally reserved for the smaller ships, such as the Delphinus Empress, our next ship.

The Agent introduced the team members to the ship's security staff who were all dressed in uniforms resembling Asian policemen. They looked very sharp; indeed, much flashier than their Stellaris counterparts.

As I was about to head toward the gangway, a man

approached me, holding two large iguanas on his shoulders. The man said, "Pictures? Just five dollars."

I yelled to Jody, "Can you come and take my picture? My kids will love this," I asked her.

The man put the two iguanas on my shoulders, and Jody snapped several photos. I paid the man his five, plus an extra couple for helping to pose the iguanas just right. I was delighted, knowing my girls would get a kick out of these pictures, and Jody teased me, saying I was as bad as a kid myself.

Boarding was certainly easier in a port without the turnaround mess, and we all appreciated the ease of getting into our cabins, with no waiting for luggage. Otherwise, there was just a simple passport check at the Service Desk.

Olaf had contacted the ship and arranged for the officers to be ready for a ten o'clock opening meeting, and had told Jody, the environmental officer would meet us at the Service Desk when we arrived on the ship. We had a name, Aadesh Patel, but weren't sure if that was a man or woman until we met.

Aadesh was a man; Indian, not Asian as expected. We met him at the front desk, and he said, "We have time for a coffee. Shall we go and talk before the official meeting?"

Aadesh led the way to the back corner of the buffet, which was now deserted. Nearly every passenger was ashore because Curacao was a popular port for shopping and excursions. Aadesh had coffee and tea pots already waiting, so it was obviously his intention to have this pre-meeting.

"I'm sure you are curious about me," said Aadesh. "You were probably expecting an Asian environmental officer. Most of the Delphinus environmental officers are from India, but we do have two Greek ladies in this position as well. As soon as these environmental issues

arose several years ago, Delphinus realized they needed good English-speaking EOs. You know I mean environmental officers, right?"

"Yes, EO is fine," said Sam.

"Delphinus Management was very concerned, wanting to avoid misunderstandings, and their original EOs, who were Asian, did not communicate well with the authorities. Because we Indians work so closely with the U.K. and the United States, and we speak good English, they decided to hire many of us as EOs. I mentioned we have two Greek ladies, and you will meet one of them tomorrow. She will meet us in St. Maarten. We overlap for one week at contract change-over, and she will start her overlap. You will like Anna Kaklamanis. She has a degree in environmental science and has been an EO with a Greek cruise line before coming to Delphinus."

"I must say, I'm impressed, Aadesh. We were not sure what to expect," said Jody.

"Oh, and I should have told you, the crew just calls me Addie. You can use either name. I like both."

"Can you tell us what to expect from the officers and crew, Addie?" asked Jody.

"Our captain is a very experienced, older gentleman. He is very polite and proper, and his English is very good. He has been with this cruise line for eight years but was a captain for over 20 years. He comes from a seafaring family."

"Is he unhappy with us auditing his ship?" Jody continued.

"The captain understands, but he is aware that Delphinus management is unhappy. Delphinus thinks this is their mother company's problem, not theirs. The captain wants to cooperate with you and wants to know if anything is wrong."

"What about the chief engineer?" I asked.

"The Chief is a good man and honest, but very

old-fashioned in his way of thinking. He is having trouble with records, and he has tried to remedy them. He has not been able to find good English writers among his engineers to fix the problems. Even I have problems reviewing their records, so we may find problems there."

"Anything else we should know, before the meeting?" asked Bill.

"Only to ask, do you all like Asian food? Our crew mess has excellent dishes. You are welcome for lunch, but I think the officers are expecting you to eat with them for dinner. They have an Officer's Dining Room, and they eat there except on days they must be in the Main Dining Room."

"That could be interesting," Sam said. "With this cruise being two days shorter, spending more time with the officers may be good."

"Will you organize our ship tour this afternoon, Addie? And tomorrow, we will want to start some crew interviews, so please show us a list of the crew, with their job descriptions, after the Opening Meeting," Jody added.

"I already have those organized. The list is on my desk for you. But now, we should head up to the captain's office."

The Delphinus Empress was slightly smaller than the Stellaris Prince but arranged very similarly. Other than a few changes in elevator locations, the four auditors generally felt at home on this ship.

The captain's office was just beneath the Pilot House, and it seemed much larger than what the captain had on the Prince. Then the reason was clear; there was no separate conference room next to the office.

The officers had already gathered, and extra chairs had been provided. The introductions were made by the captain, very formally. He was much more welcoming than Captain Romanov had been, on the Stellaris

Prince. Except for Addie, and a British hotel manager, all of the officers were Asian, and everyone was having trouble with names.

The captain spoke up, saying, "You will never remember all our names, so please just address us by our job title: captain, staff, safety, EO, chief, first, second, hotel. We may confuse your names too, so all is okay."

The captain had a pleasant smile on his face, and it was obvious he wanted everyone to be comfortable with the cultural difference.

Jody thanked the captain, introduced her team, explained the main focus of the four auditors.

The captain then asked, "Can we invite your team to dine with us in the Officer's Dining Room this evening? Tomorrow I must be in the Main Dining Room with the passengers, but I will have our officers all meet us for dinner this evening if you agree. I should ask, does everyone enjoy Asian food? That is the majority of our menu in the Officer's Dining Room, as well as the crew's mess."

"Captain, we would love to join you this evening. We were discussing food with Addie, and we all enjoy good Asian food. If you would be kind enough to explain any foods that we may not be familiar with, we are looking forward to it."

"Agreed," said the captain. "We will dine at 1900. Addie will direct you to the dining room."

Addie suggested a quick lunch before the ship tour, but also said this might be a good opportunity to eat in the buffet, seeing most of the passengers were ashore.

"The crew really loves Aruba and Curacao," Addie said. "They have very few passengers left onboard to deal with on these two days. But because we anchor and use tenders in St. Maarten, some passengers stay aboard for lunch. Here, they have many opportunities ashore, and they don't have to deal with the tendering

boats, which can be a problem for some of the older passengers."

When the tour was complete, Addie asked, "Is there anything else you wish to do today? We are refueling and landing garbage today. I could use some time to finish that, and get my reports done."

"Please go ahead, Addie. Just give us that crew list before you go. Shall we meet you at the Officer's Dining Room a little early?" Jody responded.

"Thank you, this is one of my busy ports. Just five minutes before dinner is fine. I will see you there. You remember the location I showed you?"

———◆———

Anna Kaklamanis arrived in St. Maarten on Monday. The ship was at anchor in the harbor, so passengers were being shuttled ashore using the ship's tenders. Addie suggested we meet with Anna for an early lunch in the crew's mess, as soon as she was settled in her cabin.

We arrived in the mess and found Anna greeting many of the crew. She was obviously well-liked. In addition to her beautiful, black, Greek hair, hanging midway down her back, she had bleached a portion on just one side, with totally blond highlights. At first, it seemed shocking, but it made her face shine. She had a bubbly personality that fit the unusual hairdo.

Anna saw Addie enter the room and skipped over to him, hugging him. Addie appreciated the hug and smiled, but he was very reserved and did not cooperate by hugging back. But his smile showed he was happy to see Anna.

Addie introduced the audit team, giving her a brief description of what we were doing aboard. Then Anna suggested everyone sit down and look at the menu. There were many things on the menu which were not common to American tastes. Even if they liked Asian food, Anna needed to give practical explanations of the lesser-known foods.

"Unless you are brave, you may want to avoid that one," she advised, pointing to an unusual item. "I understand it is some type of white worm, which the Koreans on board really love. I never tried it, but just so you know."

"Oh, I've heard of those," I said. "Glad you warned us. I eat almost anything, but I won't try those."

Then Anna described her favorites and advised on the spice levels. They all ordered, and after eating, everyone raved about how good their meal had been.

"Addie, did you see my plane land this morning? We were coming in low, and all those nutty tourists were lined up on the beach. I looked out my window and saw about ten of them fall on the sand. I know we were maybe 100 feet high, but it must look like the plane will hit the ground, if you are standing under it. That has become a cult event here, with bragging rights if you get blown over. That's just on take-off, of course."

Addie said, "I was making my morning rounds, and the airport is too far away to see the landing anyway."

"I know, Addie. I was just kidding about you seeing me land. You Indian guys take everything literally."

Then Sam spoke up, curious about this landing, "So, Anna, what's the big deal about the plane landing?"

"Oh, if you've never seen it, search online. This runway in St. Maarten is very short, and except for a very low fence, the runway is right next to a public beach. On landings, the wheels are not that far over the heads of those tourists on the beach. When the winds require a take-off, starting at the beach, people stand there, and the thrust of the plane blows some of those crazies into the water. You've got to search for it and watch. Those people are nuts!"

"I'd never heard about it," Sam said. *"I'll have to look for it online."*

"I'd heard about it too," I said, *"But I'd forgotten that it was here, on St. Maarten."*

Anna was not only a lot of fun, but she also turned out to be another great environmental officer. It appeared that both Stellaris and Delphinus had realized the importance of hiring good EOs.

During a long coffee break one afternoon, Jody and Sam had a chance to talk to Anna alone. They confided with her, telling her about what they were learning of the love life on the Stellaris ships, and they wondered what it was like at Delphinus. Jody and Sam gave her a brief run-down of their own problems, which they blamed on their nomadic working life.

"So, we aren't just being nosy, you see. We're learning how the ship crews deal with similar trouble," said Jody. *"We're actually starting to think the ships are better off than those of us ashore.*

Anna responded, chuckling, *"Well, it certainly is not as out in the open here. I didn't realize the people at Stellaris would talk so freely about what goes on, but most of them are either Scandinavian or Eastern European, so I guess their culture is more open about sexual matters. At least the senior officers at Delphinus are much more private when it comes to their sexual dealings on board. But I do occasionally see a young lady sneaking out of an officer's room at night. I don't think the ship mouse thing goes on over here. I really like that description, by the way."*

"Why do you think there are no ship mice over here, Anna?" Sam asked.

"I think it is the Asian pride, which is obvious amongst the officers. They don't want it publicly known that they have sexual needs. They prefer to keep that side of their life very private. They'll have a girl sneak in and out of

their room in the middle of the night, but God forbid, they don't want the rest of the crew to know they have sexual urges."

"That's funny. But what about the non-licensed crew?" asked Jody.

"Publicly they appear very proper. No flirting between men and women. But from what I see in the infirmary, there are a lot of STD problems amongst the crew. The doctor gives out free condoms, but apparently, they aren't using them."

"Oh my. Terrible," said Sam. "I'm learning a lot on these ships. I notice you have not mentioned Addie. What about him?"

"Oh, yes. Addie. He seems to be a big exception to the rule. Addie is married to a lady back home. They have a bunch of kids, and as far as I can tell, they are happy, and he is very loyal. His room is plastered with photos of his wife and kids, so I don't think he is inviting any young girls to his room."

"Well, isn't that a nice thing to hear? Pretty uncommon; not just on the ships, but in the world in general," said Jody.

"I notice you haven't asked about me," said Anna.

"Well, maybe we're nosy, but we're not that impolite," said Sam. "But seeing you brought it up...."

"I think my life is pretty dull, particularly onboard. I'm the only European in the crew, other than the hotel manager, so even if I wanted something on the side, it would be difficult. I'm not married, but I have a band back home, with four guys and another woman. She and I are the singers. We work in nightclubs, and occasionally at some weddings. We don't play Greek music, so that limits the requests for wedding gigs. One of the guys is my steady squeeze, but we haven't made any commitments."

"By the way, Anna. Some of the guys have similar

problems. It's not just us girls. Bob is loyal, but having a tough time at home," Jody added. "And with that, I suppose we need to get back to work."

———◆———

"Wow! I'm glad I got a chance to hear some of your famous stories, Bob" Loretta said. "It does make me realize that our way of life is not the only way to be happy. Looking at how messed up a lot of American relationships are these days, we sure cannot judge others."

"I think that's the conclusion our auditors came to as well," Bob responded. "I was personally on around 165 cruises over eight years, and we all learned a lot. With all the people we met on those ships, very few did not earn our respect. They lead a tough life, being away from home for as much as eight months at a time, and they have found a way to support one another. We probably see worse inter-relationships in our hometowns."

"Well, I hate to interrupt," Curt said, looking around the group of coworkers who had quickly become close friends and more like family, "but we are back on the lake early tomorrow morning."

"You're right, Curt. I'm just along for the ride," Bob said. "I'm probably out of stories that some of you haven't already heard. I'll let you go about your duties. Let me know if I can be of any help along the way, but I'll be leaving from Sault Ste. Marie when we arrive."

"It's been great to have you with us, Bob. I'm sure we'll see you again as Bill seems to keep buying new equipment," Stormi said.

CURT

STEVIE AT THE SOO LOCKS

———

IWAS BACK AT the shipyard in Sault Ste. Marie, babysitting our new tug and barges when Lois called to see if I could fit her and the three kids into my busy schedule. I was also filling in as needed on the two shore-protection projects our company was working on in the area

"I might find a few minutes every few days, if you want to come up here," I told her.

"Hey, mister! That had better be a joke. I think I've taught you too many of my tricks."

"Yah, you know I miss you and the kiddos. When can you head up?"

"I was thinking about starting up tomorrow morning, maybe leaving around nine? How long of a drive is it up to the Soo?"

"It's about three and a half hours if you drove straight through, but I assume you'll need to stop to nurse the little ones. Take your time; it's a nice drive. Lots for Stevie to look at along the way."

"Speaking of Stevie, he is so excited about going up there. He'd love to get on a tug again, but I warned him you cannot take him out on a working project."

"I spoke with Bill about that. He said I could keep him

with me in the pilothouse if I am just shifting around the shipyard, but insurance would never accept him being on a tug while working on a project. I hope he'll understand."

"I think he'll be happy with the shipyard idea. He so enjoyed that short move down in Chicago. He never stops talking about it."

"Okay, Babe. I need to run. You be careful on the drive up. You have some precious cargo along."

"I'll take my time. Stevie likes those roadside historical monuments, and we'll certainly stop at the park before crossing the Mackinac Bridge. He can watch the ships going through the Straits. Can't wait to see you tomorrow. Will we have any privacy, if you catch my drift?"

"I've arranged that. I'll surprise you. Love you. Be careful."

"Love you too. Have a good day. Bye."

———

I had explained to the rest of the crew that Lois and the kids were coming to spend a few days, so I was changing hotels during the time they were in Sault Ste. Marie. The other guys liked Lois and Stevie, but they had not yet met the babies, Robert, and Ellen, so I promised to have dinner with them a couple nights while the family was here.

I wanted Stevie to be near the Soo Locks, so he could watch the ore carriers locking through, and there was a beautiful park with restrooms and a small museum, where Lois could get inside with the babies. I had gone to the Lock Visitor Center and explained the situation, and the ladies seemed happy to let Lois use one of their small cubicles if she wished to nurse the babies in private. I told them that Stevie was a very responsible, almost 12-year-old and he would not be a problem. The

Long Ships Motel was right across the street from the Locks, so it was perfect. They had only a few adjoining rooms, but I was able to book one, to satisfy Lois's request for some privacy.

I worked at the shipyard all day on Tuesday and found Lois had already checked in at the Long Ships. The owner told me that Lois and our "sweet little tribe" were over at the Locks because Stevie had heard one of the ships blowing its horn. She said Stevie was so excited, he could hardly contain himself. He had told Lois he would help her get things into the room, so they could hurry over to the Locks.

I went to the Locks and looked up and down the railing, trying to find Stevie. Then I heard his voice, explaining the locking system to a family of tourists, up on the raised, observation platform. I went up on the platform and Stevie stopped talking just long enough to run over and give me a big bear hug. I noticed that Stevie had a big growth spurt this summer, and I didn't need to lean down as far to get my hug.

I then went back to the family to whom Stevie had been talking, and said, "I hope Stevie hasn't been talking too much? He can be a wealth of knowledge sometimes."

The man replied, "On the contrary. Your son has been great. We knew nothing about this locking procedure, and Steve has been quoting the Corps of Engineers website for us, adding interesting things he's seen while watching. He has been a great tour guide."

"That's my boy! He teaches me things all the time."

"He told us you are a tugboat captain. Do you work at the Locks?"

"No. My company bought some new equipment to do some construction work along the waterfront up here. I delivered the new tug and a crane barge from Chicago, and now I'm overseeing some repairs at the local shipyard up here."

"That sounds like an interesting job. That now makes sense because Steve told us you had rescued some boaters in Lake Michigan."

"It sounds like Stevie is learning to tell Sea Stories. I guess he learned that talent from me."

I saw Stevie smile, and I smiled back, patting him on the back.

"I was on the tug, handling the radio communications with the Coast Guard, but the other captain and a passenger, who both happen to be women, really were the heroes in that rescue. Luckily, the passenger was an EMT, the lady friend of our crane mechanic, and she probably saved the man's life. He had been in the cold Lake Michigan water for over an hour, and he had become severely hypothermic. He was lucky we found him in time and lucky we happened to have a knowledgeable EMT with us."

"That's an amazing story. I'm an attorney in Chicago, and my wife is an accountant, so we lead very sedentary lives. Our children here, Brad and Emmy, have enjoyed listening to Steve. We've all learned a lot from him. My name is Taylor Jennings, and this is my wife, Sarah."

"I'm Curt. Curt Steiner. And that reminds me, Stevie. Where is Mom?"

"She went into the Visitor Center to feed the babies. That was just before these people came up to the observation platform. She told me to stay here until she came back."

"I think I should go find Lois. I can have her come up to meet you. She is nursing our twins, just four months old, so she was probably looking for some privacy."

"Why don't we come down to the Visitor Center as well. We wanted to see the displays down there. Then we can meet your wife and the babies."

"If you don't mind. That'd be nice. Where are you staying?"

"Right across the street, at the Long Ships Motel."

"Really! So are we! If you'll be staying a while, maybe we can catch lunch or dinner."

"We leave the day after tomorrow. Let's see what your wife thinks, and maybe we could do that. I know our two kids would love to keep talking with Stevie, and I have a lot of questions for you about this maritime business. It's something I've never thought about."

We all went down to the Visitor Center, and I didn't see Lois. The lady I had spoken with the day before, saw me and waved, motioning to the cubicle behind her. "I think we delayed Lois on the babies' feeding time. We all had to take turns holding them and then they started crying. Lois is back there nursing, so you can go check on her."

Lois was just finishing, and the second one was about to fall asleep, with the first zonked out in her other arm. I took the sleeping one from her and I leaned down to kiss Lois. "Is this Bob or Ellie? I still can't tell them apart."

"That's Robert. So, you've decided on nicknames already?"

"I like nicknames. Don't you?"

"I do, but you hadn't called them that before."

"Maybe because I have seen so little of them. I'm so glad you can travel again, so we can be together more often. By the way, there is a family outside, who had been talking to Stevie outside. They'd like to meet you three."

"Sure. Let me make myself presentable. Could you take Ellie too? I'll be out in just a couple of minutes."

I nestled one baby in each arm and went out to the Jennings family. The babies were gaining weight, and I wondered how Lois could hold both of them for double nursing. I now realized why she was so happy when only one would wake up before the other, so she could handle them one at a time. Sarah Jennings gently took baby Ellen from me. Taylor seemed happy just to look.

Sarah said, "With Brad at fourteen and Emmy twelve, it's been a while since I've held a baby. We don't have many young families around us, and my sisters are older, so we don't have much contact with little ones. It's nice to hold one again."

"Where do you live in Chicago?" I asked.

"We live in River Forest, a close suburb on the West Side," Sarah answered.

"That's amazing. One professional who helps us lives in Oak Park. I think he had lived in River Forest, before downsizing. His name is Bob Evers."

"I don't think we've met the parents, but I think Emmy or Brad may know one of their children. We share the high school with Oak Park, and I believe Brad may have one of the girls in some of his classes this fall. We can quiz him later, but I see the three kids sharing E-Mail addresses over there, so I think we are connected forever."

Just then, Lois emerged after putting herself back together. She came to us and offered her hand to Taylor and Sarah, "Hello there. I'm Lois Steiner. I guess you've met the rest of the family."

Sarah said, "Yes. Steve had us captivated with locking details up on the observation platform, and then Curt found Steve. And now we've met these two precious little ones. I think I heard Robert and Ellen?"

"That's their given names, but Curt just called them Bob and Ellie for the first time today. It appears they now have nicknames."

"That's the same with us. That's Bradley and Emily over there with Steve. But they soon became Brad and Emmy. They sure have bonded to Steve this afternoon."

"Steve does have a way of making friends quickly. I hope he isn't dominating the conversation."

"I've been listening, and he seems to be asking them a lot of questions and has been very interested in their answers," Taylor said.

I interjected, "The Jennings live in River Forest, next to Oak Park. They think that Brad or Emmy may know one or both of Bob Evers' daughters."

"That's amazing," Lois said. "That small world thing again."

"The Jennings are staying at the Long Ships as well. I asked if we could meet for dinner one of the next nights, or lunch tomorrow. They leave the day after tomorrow. They wanted you to decide, seeing the babies might factor into the decision."

"I think you had planned for us to meet your crew at The Antlers tomorrow night. I think tonight would be better."

Taylor spoke up, "We ate at The Antlers last night, so maybe we can pick a place close by. That would make logistics with the babies much easier."

"That would be nice," Lois said. "I saw a nice restaurant about a block away from the motel, so if the babies get fussy, I could take them back to nurse them. I can't wait until I can tide them over on baby food, but their doctor says, 6-months-old. He told me that even mild baby foods can cause problems before that. I nursed Steve for a while and thought that was tough. But two hungry ones are tough to keep satisfied."

"I can imagine," said Sarah. "I didn't nurse Brad, and he was allergic to cow's milk in the standard formulas. I tried soy, and that was worse. My doctor said it was too late to start nursing, so we used a special formula until he was old enough for solids. Therefore, I nursed Emmy and had no problems. You're doing the smart thing."

"Well, maybe we should get back to the motel," I said. "I understand Stevie wouldn't even let you unpack, because of the ships he heard at the Locks."

"Yes. Once he heard that ship's horn and saw the ship coming, he was quick to get the luggage in the room, so I didn't want to upset him with unpacking. I think he can wait until tomorrow for another session over here."

"Shall we meet in the motel parking lot around six? Or is that too early?" I asked.

"Six is fine. I know Lois won't want to have dinner too late because of the babies."

On the walk back to the motel, Lois said, "Steve, it looked like you made some good friends. Do you like the Jennings kids?"

"I was telling them about our two trips to Chicago, and what we did. Bradley is okay, but I really liked Emily. She's neat!"

Lois looked up at me and smiled, with a weird look on her face. She mouthed, "Later!"

———————

We had a nice dinner with the Jennings family and the babies cooperated, being content for nearly two hours. Stevie was in deep conversations with Brad and Emmy, but I didn't overhear much because Taylor and Sarah were great conversationalists. We were asking questions about Chicago, and they wanted to hear more about the maritime business and Lois's school nurse job. We recommended they take the Carferry *Badger* across Lake Michigan on the way home, and then drive from Wisconsin to Chicago, for a pleasant change, and a memorable experience. They seemed convinced to try it, seeing they were in no hurry to get home.

We said goodbye to the Jennings and promised we'd contact them before our next trip to Chicago. I told them it seemed to be our major source of new equipment, so it could easily happen again.

After getting Stevie settled in his room, he was asleep within minutes. Lois said he'd had a rough day, packing for the trip at home, unpacking at the hotel, and all the excitement at the Locks.

I asked Lois, "So, what was that smile you gave me, and the 'later'?"

"I wondered if you noticed Steve's comment about Emily? He said 'I really liked Emily. She's neat,' but Brad was 'okay'?"

"Maybe Brad isn't as likeable. He's going into high school, and Stevie is too young."

"Maybe. But here's the rest of the story. Steve has another girl admirer lately. She has been hanging out near Steve at the park. Steve has never been a park person, spending more time at the library. I noticed lately, he spends more time at the park than usual, and he even missed a couple sessions with his library friends. One day last week, little Becky, the other admirer, showed up at the house. Steve and Becky had arranged for one of their computer and math sessions at our house. I told Becky that Steve wasn't home, and he may have forgotten. I told her he was at the park, just down the street."

"Oh boy! I see a problem coming!"

"I realized later, I shouldn't have told Becky about the park, because she went there and she saw the new girl, Lindsey, who goes by Linney, talking to Steve. Steve told me he greeted Becky, but Linney kept talking, and Steve thinks Becky got mad. Becky has skipped two library meetings since then. It upset Steve and he asked me what he did wrong. I told him I'd talk to you, so you could give him some advice. Then today, I see the same thing with this Emily, very attracted to Steve. Do we have a problem on our hands?"

"Like we've discussed in the past, I think girls are attracted to boys before boys are attracted to them. Because Stevie is so social, which is unusual for boys that age, I think the girls are perceiving that as him also showing interest in return. I don't want Stevie to think he should stop being social with people. I was really proud of him today, explaining things to the Jennings family at the Locks. Maybe I just need to explain to him that these girls are seeing that as being interested or liking them beyond friendship. I'm thinking we should do this together because I don't want to get into a sex talk for at least another year, just before high school."

"Well, at least Emily lives in Chicago, so the two girls in Cadillac won't see them together. I don't remember life being this complicated when I was twelve or thirteen. Then I went into high school, and there you were. I've never really had another serious love interest in my life. Don't you feel lucky?"

"I actually do feel lucky. Do we have time for a shower before the babies wake up to be fed?"

"I thought you'd never ask. Get your butt undressed ad let's head for the shower. The shower is quite small, so this may get interesting."

After our shower, the twins started to stir some, so Lois said she'd nurse them before we got "down to serious business." Those were Lois's words. I was enjoying our serious conversations during these times when Lois was nursing, and I lay next to her. She was relaxed and I really enjoyed watching her with the babies. It's not a sexual thing. Instead, I just feel very close to her on these occasions. It's hard to explain, but I just respect her for being such a great woman and a caring mother.

Once the babies were asleep, we continued talking. Finally, Lois said, "You'd better start making the moves on me before we just fall asleep. Not interested tonight?"

"I'm interested. It's just that when I see you being a mother, it's hard for me to think about sex. It's like I would be intruding, by making sexual advances on someone I just watched nursing my children. Does that sound weird?"

Lois started to tear up and said, "That's one of the

sweetest things you could ever say to me, and I love you for thinking that way about me. But this mother is also worried about her mental health, and she is giving you permission to start thinking about her sexually right now. Okay?"

Darn. I love this woman!

The next day, I told Lois I had forgotten to mention that Loretta Sanchez was coming up to Sault Ste. Marie to spend a few days with Larry, who was working on the various Strauss equipment working the projects around the area. Loretta had gone home after making that trip on the tug from Chicago.

"Oh, fantastic. I can't wait to hear her details about the man you guys pulled from the lake. I understand the man's wife has sent her a bouquet and a very heartfelt thank you note. It's so lucky for them that Loretta was with you on that trip."

"She was a real pro that day, and she seemed very shy about the praise she was receiving."

"I've seen that side of her too. For someone who is so demonstrative in normal interactions with people, she has a hard time with being the center of attention."

"That's why she seemed to fit in so well with the crew. She enjoys complimenting others for their contributions, to turn attention away from herself.

"I seldom got to visit with Loretta before, but now that she's smitten with Larry, I never get to see her. While you guys are working, I hope we can have some quality time together."

"I think this is one of her longer scheduled breaks. I have a hard time understanding her schedule at the firehouse. I think she swapped some days with another EMT, to stay here until Larry gets his time off."

———

Loretta showed up in Sault Ste. Marie that evening,

and had convinced Larry to change hotels, so she could be with Lois every day. She asked where the Steiner family was staying, and the desk clerk called their room to say they had a friend checking in. Lois told the lady to send her over.

Loretta lightly tapped on the door, suspecting the babies could be sleeping, and I came to the door to let her in. Hugging her, I ushered Loretta to the bedside where Lois was nursing the babies.

Loretta said quietly, "Well, isn't this the picture of motherhood if you had to describe it. It's one heck of a way to expand your boob size, Sauerkraut."

Lois laughed and replied, "As much as these guys are nursing, you'd think they'd be shrinking, but you're right. I've had to increase the size of my nursing bras."

Loretta bent down and gave Lois a quick squeeze, with a light pat on each of the babies' heads, and said, "I'll get a better hug when you've finished. Where's Steve, by the way?"

Lois chuckled, "Even though Steve now understands what nursing is all about, he takes off for another room whenever it happens. His little girlfriend had to explain nursing to him and showed him pictures on the Internet. Steve was mortified. Becky explained the incident to me. She was so cute about it but very concerned that I needed to explain the process to Steve."

"Oh my. So, is Steve in the adjoining room?"

"Yes, he's over there on his iPad. Drop over and say hi."

Loretta came back after seeing Steve, and Lois had finished nursing. They both enjoyed a long hug. Then Loretta said, "I haven't even told Larry I've arrived, so I'd better get going. He's going to move over here from the crew's hotel. Can we spend the day together tomorrow, while the guys are working?"

"Tomorrow would be perfect. Curt is taking Steve to

the shipyard tomorrow, which Steve is excited about. So, it will just be you and the three of us. These guys are my constant companions until they start crawling and walking. Our doctor won't let me start baby food until six months. I hope I can last that long."

"I can imagine it's tough, but the doctor is correct. Hard to beat Mom's natural food. They'll be much healthier later. And you must be doing well, they have really grown."

"Okay, I won't go to breakfast with Curt and Steve. Maybe send Larry with them, and we can go to breakfast together. How does eight o'clock sound? It's after the workers are gone and before the tourists hit the restaurants. There's a nice restaurant in the next block."

"Perfect. I'll knock on your door about eight."

The next morning, Lois nursed the babies and laid them in the crib the motel had provided. She was showering but had the door open to listen for them, in case they started to cry. She was halfway through lathering herself with soap when she heard one of the babies choking. Not bothering to rinse, Lois jumped out of the shower. It was Robert. She picked him up, but the choking continued. Lois could tell that the baby was having difficulty breathing and she began to panic.

She called Loretta's room. Loretta picked up the phone and could immediately hear the choking sounds and the panic in Lois's voice, and she dropped the phone and ran to Lois's room. Lois already had the door open and was holding the baby, crying.

Loretta said nothing, grabbed the baby from Lois's arms, sat on the edge of the bed, and placed Robert on her knee, face down. She started doing back strikes and told Lois, "Run to the office and have her dial '911'."

Lois hesitated and Loretta said sternly, "Now, Lois! I've got this!"

Lois ran to the motel office and told the lady clerk to

call '911'. The lady saw the tears in Lois's eyes and the fear on her face and didn't question the request.

Lois returned to her room and saw Loretta continuing with back strikes, then alternating with chest strikes. She watched Loretta working and realized how her own nursing skills had disappeared when it was her own child.

"He's breathing again, Loretta said. I'll see if he will breathe on his own now, but I'll ask the EMTs if I can stay with him on the ride to the hospital. You grab Ellen and grab a taxi to the hospital. You might want to put some clothes on first though."

Finally, Lois calmed down and even smiled at the last remark.

The ambulance arrived within minutes. Loretta explained to the crew that she was a certified EMT, and what had happened. She asked if she could accompany them to the hospital, and the mother would follow shortly, with the baby's twin sister. The EMTs could see that Loretta had handled the situation well, and they agreed to let her hold the baby on the ride.

Lois arrived at the hospital about ten minutes after the ambulance, and she found Loretta waiting for her at the ER admitting desk. "Lois, Robert's okay. Just give them your ID and insurance info, and we can go back. The doctor is with Robert, and he wants to talk to you."

As Lois entered the room, seeing her baby laying on the large gurney, her face was a combination of dread and relief, seeing that Robert was breathing restfully and drifting off to sleep. She said, "What exactly happened? He was fine one minute, and when I got in the shower, I heard him coughing, and then he started to choke."

The doctor smiled and said, "First of all, you are lucky to have had your friend nearby. She recognized the problem. Can I ask, have you had any problems producing enough milk for these two? It doesn't look like it, judging from their size at four months."

"None at all. I joked with Loretta last night that I've had to upgrade the size of my nursing bras."

"Well," the doctor continued, "you apparently have what is called 'Overactive Letdown'. I understand you are a nurse as well. Do you remember that term?"

"Like a lot of unusual terms, I remember it being mentioned, but with few details."

"Most women complain about not producing enough milk for one child. However, you are producing so much, Robert couldn't get it all swallowed. Your friend told me that when she started performing the Heimlich, a substantial amount of mother's milk was ejected. It seldom happens, but the quick response avoided any real damage to the baby. I'm suspecting the mother may have suffered from the shock more than the baby, but otherwise, I see no reason to keep your baby here. However, I suggest you see your pediatrician back home and tell them what happened. I think they will suggest that you pump and then bottle feed your own milk, to better control the rate at which the babies feed."

"I feel like a failure as a nurse and a mother. I just panicked."

"No, just feel lucky to have an EMT as a friend. They see these things more often than a nurse, or even a doctor. She did all the right things."

"Thank you, doctor, and Loretta, I owe you big time!"

"Nonsense. You found Larry for me. I owe you. Now we're even."

(WO)MAN OVERBOARD

WE HAD JUST bought another tugboat from a company in Duluth. Bill Strauss, my boss, was always looking to upgrade our fleet. I now had my 600-ton Master's license and was training a new guy, actually, a young woman, Ashley, who was about ready to sit for her 100-ton master's license exam.

We had already departed Duluth when the boss, Bill Strauss, called. Bill had found a couple of old stone scows in Ashland, Wisconsin, and Bill had a purchase pending on those barges. Bill told us to stop in Ashland, and I was to inspect the two scows.

After inspecting the scows, I called Bill, asking him if he realized how old these two scows were.

"I know they're old, Curt. But the guy will sell them to me for almost nothing. Are they worth rebuilding? If so, I want you to drop them at the shipyard at the Soo, on your way home.

"The owner said they passed the last Load Line renewal on drydock and the bottoms were still sound. He sent me the last hull thickness gauging report, which looked pretty good. However, both of the decks are now badly indented in some areas, and the internal truss structures need a lot of repairs. He knew that ABS would require those decks and trusses to be repaired on the upcoming drydocking, and he doesn't have enough business up there for these barges to justify that expense.

"New deck scows that size run more than two million dollars these days, Curt. If we can repair these for a couple hundred thousand, and get ten or fifteen years out of them, it's a good deal for us."

"Then I think they're worth taking, Bill. When will you know that you own them?"

"Spend the night in Ashland. I should have the deal done by morning. How are the two deckhands you picked up in Duluth?"

"Young and inexperienced, but they have potential. They seem eager to learn and ask a lot of questions. I'm glad the tug owner offered to let them come along for the ride, but now that you are buying these barges, I'm worried about them. They have no towing experience."

"Is the weather okay up on Superior?"

"A little snarky, but nothing over three feet. I'll have to be careful while towing these two scows, with no cargo on deck. I'll have to keep it slow to avoid them pounding in any high waves."

Bill called the next morning and said we now owned the two scows. We hadn't planned on making this trip with barges in tow, so we pulled out the extra hawsers which were in the tug's lazarette. They looked pretty ratty, so I asked the scow owner if he had any extra rigging we could buy. His gear didn't look any better than what we had aboard, so we rigged one scow about 300 feet aft of the other using soft-line, and then rigged our towing bridle to the lead barge, with the cable from our large towing winch on the stern of our tug. We departed Ashland in decent weather, with nothing over two feet.

I called Captain Stormi, who was filling in for Captain Wright on the tug *Samantha B*. I had just passed Ontonagon, and I didn't have a good Weather-Fax on this new tug. I wanted to have Stormi fill me in on the weather once I would round the top of the Keweenaw

Peninsula. If I was to hit an East or Northeasterly wind in that area, I could be in trouble, towing these two light barges.

Stormi said, "I think you may need to get into the Waterway at Keweenaw. It's currently running four feet, east of the peninsula, and it looks like it's building. You should be okay to proceed in about thirty-six hours."

"Darn it. I have a couple new guys aboard on this trip, and I hoped not to handle the tow lines again until we got to the Soo. Then I could have called the shipyard to send some help out to us. I guess we'll have to shorten up to enter the Keweenaw Waterway at Houghton-Hancock. I wasn't going to tow through there with two scows behind me, but once we're there, we may as well take the shortcut when we leave."

"So, Curt, how is your new 'captain in training' doing?"

"She's standing right here, so I can't be entirely honest, but she treats me better than the last woman captain I worked with."

"Ashley, don't let Curt push you around. Keep reminding him that it was a woman captain that got him the training he needed to get to his 600-ton license," Stormi said.

"Well, enough chit-chat, Cap. We need to get to work over here," I said.

"Okay, Curt. But Ashley, keep watching that guy. Despite him being a man, he's a good captain."

"Did I hear a compliment? Thanks, Stormi!"

———

"Okay, guys. Nothing like learning under real-life conditions. We can't continue into Eastern Lake Superior until this weather subsides, so we need to shorten these tow lines and get into the Keweenaw Waterway. Ashley has been working with us for two years and she is very experienced with towing, so you guys follow her instructions on deck. I know neither of you has had Lake towing experience. I'll be handling the tug from that after control console, overlooking the aft towing winch. Everyone understand?"

As I started to shorten up the towing cable, using the aft winch controls, I saw Ashley grab one of the new deckhands by the arm, as he was about to walk across the after deck. It looked like Ashley was trying to warn him he was walking into the Danger Zone: too close to the towing cable. Towing lines can snap, or just jump across the Dutch Bar when changing directions, and people are easily killed when this occurs.

The deckhand swung his arm as if he objected to Ashley grabbing him, and Ashley fell backward against the bulwark, then falling overboard. Ashley had her life-jacket on, and I could see she was unhurt, but she was quickly moving away from the tug, with the easterly winds. I threw the life ring towards her from the upper deck, but it came up short. She motioned to me that she was okay, but I knew that Lake Superior water is cold, so we needed to retrieve her quickly. I stopped the propellers and went down on the aft deck. I glared at the deckhand who had caused this to happen, but this was not the time to deal with him. I had to drop these barges and get to Ashley fast.

There was no time to waste, pulling in the barges, so I grabbed the ax which was stored adjacent to the towing winch, and I hacked the cable-free where it crossed the Dutch Bar. The barges started to drift west, away from the peninsula. At least they wouldn't drift aground if we could retrieve them quickly.

I went back to the control station, used the loudhailer to contact my engineer, the only other experienced man aboard, telling him to come up on deck. I then engaged the propeller again and was able to position myself downwind of Ashley, so she would drift up to us. The Engineer, Adam, appeared on deck, and he quickly appraised the situation. Adam grabbed another life ring from the main deck, and when close enough, Adam threw the life ring to Ashley, and I declutched the propellers again. Ashley was able to grab the ring, and Adam pulled her to the side of the tug. Adam is a big guy, so he was able to pull Ashley aboard by himself. He gave her a huge hug, then quickly walked to the other side of the deck.

Ashley is a tiny little lady, just five feet two, and probably weighs under a hundred pounds. Her shoulder-length hair is brown but tends to get naturally lightened by the summer sun. She has a healthy tan from all her time working out on deck, where she pulls her weight, keeping up with the crew. She is muscular for her size and worked as a deckhand on the construction crew until one day, she was needed to fill a slot on one of the small tugs when their deckhand had emergency surgery. The captain thought Ashley had potential as a captain, so she worked the small tug for a few months, then worked with Captain Stormi on the Samantha B, until I was given the responsibility to get her ready for her licensing exam. Everyone she has worked with liked her, and she handles the crew well, which is why this incident was so upsetting.

I went down on deck, also hugging Ashley, and asked how she felt.

"Just cold. Let me go down and change clothes. Then I can come up to help retrieve the barges."

"I'll keep Adam up here to help with that. Use my cabin and take a warm shower. I think we can handle this. You may be more chilled than you think, so stay inside and drink some coffee. If you don't feel right, maybe we should send you to the hospital."

"Okay, but as soon as I warm up, I'll come out to help.

I really do feel fine. I don't need to go to the hospital."

Once Ashley left, I looked over to the deckhand that had caused this mess. I didn't want to deal with him until after we had the barges secured. We now had our towing cable cut and had a real mess on our hands, and I didn't want him around to mess up again. I told him to sit in the galley and stay out of my sight!

It took over two hours for the three of us to get the barges on a short towline and to get the severed towing cable up on the deck of the lead barge. We entered the Keweenaw Waterway and moored near the old Coast Guard Station near the west entrance. Ashley came out on deck as we were mooring, and she looked to be recovered, but she admitted she was pretty drained, due to the tension of the incident.

I gave Ashley another hug and told her I was sorry I let this happen.

"What do you mean? This wasn't your fault," Ashley responded.

"I should have waited another day in Ashland to train these new guys."

"It wasn't the training that went wrong, Curt. The second new man, Allen, worked out just fine with the training we gave them. I think Teddy just didn't like having a woman tell him what to do, or in this case, what not to do."

"Whatever the reason, he'll be gone, after I talk to Bill about what happened. I put you in charge out there on deck, and he ignored that very important instruction."

"I know, I saw him start walking into the Danger Zone, as you always call it, and I tried to stop him. I could feel him tense up, taking offense. I didn't have time to explain before he hit me."

"You did the right thing, Ashley. If he takes offense at a woman giving orders, he won't work well in our company. If he'd have done that to Stormi, she would have cold-cocked him when she got back aboard."

"You're probably right. Stormi doesn't put up with any sexist crap."

"Now that things are under control, let's go up to the pilothouse and call Bill. I'd better cool down a little more before I talk to this Teddy guy."

Bill told us to send Teddy home. Even if he was apologetic, Bill said his abrasive attitude may surface again under stress, and that was not a trait we could accept in our employees. Bill had a friend in Houghton who would help us find a deckhand for the remainder of this trip. Then Bill would arrange with the supply house in the Soo, to have a new towing cable waiting for us at the shipyard, but for now, he would buy a manilla towline in Duluth, delivered to Houghton, for us to complete the rest of the trip.

Bill then said, "Why don't you take Ashley out for a nice dinner in Houghton tonight. You've both had a rough day. Let the Engineer mind the tug while you're gone."

"No way, Bill. Adam came through for us today. He's the one who got Ashley back aboard. I like your idea, but it will be Adam and Ashley going to dinner if that's okay with you? I want to stay aboard until this Teddy guy is gone."

"I understand, and fully agree. You're the captain, and I'm just riding a desk these days."

"Thanks, Bill," Ashley said. "We'll bring back a nice dinner for Curt, as carry-out." Ashley shot me a smirky smile.

"Well, it looks like you'll have a couple days in the Keweenaw to get things back together. I'll talk to you both, tomorrow. And Ashley, I'm sorry you had this happen, and I'm so happy you are alright."

"Thanks, Bill. It is scary, but nice to see my crew-mates' concern for me. I'm just sorry we had to cut that towline."

"Towlines are cheap, Ashley. Lives are irreplaceable."

When Bill hung up, Ashley said, "Are you sure you're okay with Adam and me going off to dinner?"

"Of course. I didn't do much, other than cut that cable."

"Well, the reason I ask, is that I saw tears in Adam's eyes as he was pulling me aboard. I want to find out what that was about. The tears looked like real concern. When I noticed, he turned away."

"I know Adam likes you, but maybe that liking is deeper than I thought. Am I hearing that you share the feeling?"

"I guess I hadn't given it much thought. Adam and I worked together when I was training with Stormi on the *Samantha B*, and I thought he was just being polite, but today made me wonder if he was just too shy to show that he liked me. I had a bad breakup a couple years back before I came to work over here. So, until now, I was avoiding relationships. I must admit, I like Adam's shyness. Can I go ask him about dinner? If he refuses, then maybe I was wrong."

"By all means, you handle it. Tell him dinner is on the company, so find the most expensive place in town."

"Are you sure? I don't want to take advantage."

"Hey, we darn near drowned you today. I think a nice dinner is not nearly enough to make up for that."

PLAYING MATCHMAKER

A DAM SEEMED KEEN on going out to dinner with Ashley, and I called a taxi to come and take them into town. Ashley had Googled a nice seafood restaurant for them to try. I told Ashley I was in the mood for a huge, juicy hamburger, so they could bring one back for me. I gave her my company debit card and PIN, so they could pay for dinner.

Then I had to deal with Teddy. I had cooled down so decided not to make a scene. He seemed apologetic, but I told him his reaction was unacceptable, and he was terminated and should arrange for his return to Duluth. I told the guy, our company had two licensed women captains, plus Ashley and another woman training to be captains, so not taking orders from a woman was not acceptable in our company. I think Teddy learned a big lesson this day. He didn't argue, made a phone call home, and said someone would pick him up first thing in the morning.

I went to my cabin, called my wife, Lois, and discussed the events of the day. "So, Babe, what do you think so far?" I asked Lois.

"You left Duluth with two inexperienced deckhands. Do I see a problem coming?"

"I thought you might see that. I think that was my mistake. When Bill said he was buying those two barges, I should have reminded him it was just Ashley, me, and our Engineer who I could depend on. I never should have assumed good weather would prevail."

"So, I saw the problem. Now tell me what happened that has you worried."

I described the incident with the deckhand knocking Ashley over the side, cutting the towing cable, and Ashley's rescue.

"Was Ashley hurt?" Lois asked.

"Not physically, but very chilled. I had her take a long, warm shower and she seems fine, other than a bit shaken by the experience."

"Well, that's good. What did you do with the deckhand?"

"Just before I called you, I told him we were letting him go. He didn't argue. I hope he learned a big lesson."

"Did you ever figure out why he struck out at Ashley?"

"It looks like he didn't like a woman giving him orders. Ashley was just trying to warn him he was walking into the Danger Zone around the towline, and when she grabbed his arm to stop him, he lashed out. It says something about his core personality, which neither Bill nor I can tolerate. So enough about my problems, how are the kids doing?"

"Just get your butt home. I'm sick of being alone. I need some lovin', my man! Understand?"

"Understood. As soon as I deliver this tug to the Soo. We need to replace the towing cable at the Soo, and I'll ask Bill to find a replacement for me, so I can head home for a while."

"And you're sure Ashley is okay? I really like her."

"Yes. She wasn't injured and we had her back aboard in about twelve minutes. We really hustled. A nice side story though. Bill suggested I take Ashley out for a nice dinner tonight, but I recommended our Engineer,

Adam, accompany Ashley. She seemed pleased with the suggestion because I think she might be sweet on the guy. Adam was the one to pull Ashley aboard after the incident, and she told me she thought she saw tears in Adam's eyes. She felt the tears were of real concern for her, and when she noticed, Adam walked away. She said Adam is quite shy, so if she finds out he also has feelings for her, we may have a budding romance going here. I'll have to lay down the law about no cohabitation aboard."

"I guess that could be bad, huh?"

"Knowing Ashley, I think she knows better than to have a heated relationship aboard, but let's see what happens. I'll keep you informed."

"I'd better let you go. Any idea when you'll be home?"

"If the storm is short-lived, we only have thirty hours to the Soo. Allowing for problems, I should be home on Monday. Four days away."

"Okay lover, I'm feeling awfully horny lately."

"I'd laugh, but I guess it's not really funny. Tell the kids I'll see them soon. Love you all."

"Love you too big guy. Stay safe out there."

———————

Ashley and Adam came back aboard about eleven o'clock. They had left at six, so I was quite curious. I was making the rounds of the engine room when Adam came down.

"Sorry we were gone so long, Curt. I can take the watch, now that I'm back."

"That's okay Adam. I'm not sleepy, so why don't you get some sleep. I'll roust you around five in the morning. Okay with you?"

"Sure. That works. Are we leaving tomorrow?"

"I doubt it. We have a manila line coming from the ship chandler in Duluth. We're also getting a new deckhand from a local operator, who is a friend of Bill Strauss.

So, we need to get rigged again tomorrow, and probably leave the following day."

"Then you got rid of that Teddy guy?"

"Yeah. He was a poor fit for our organization. I hate picking up strangers like this on our delivery trips, but the other guy, Allen, seems to be a good one."

"Yep. I think Allen works well, and he respects Ashley."

"That's good to hear. If he works out on this trip, we could use another steady deckhand. Head down and get some sleep, Adam. I'll wake you at five, and then I'll catch a few hours of shut-eye."

I didn't miss the statement by Adam, about Allen, the other deckhand, respecting Ashley. I'm no relationship expert, but that sure sounded like more than normal crew respect for one another. I was drinking coffee in the mess deck about fifteen minutes later, and Ashley walked in, dressed in work clothes.

"What are you still doing up, Ash? I figured you'd be sawing logs by now."

"I'd never get to sleep right now. I figured you'd have a busy day tomorrow with the new towline coming and finding another deckhand. I saw Teddy's bags packed in the berthing area, so I figured he was leaving tomorrow. And I'm sorry, but we forgot your hamburger."

"I'll get my burger tomorrow. But after your stressful day, I thought you'd need the sleep."

"I'm okay, really. You guys got me out quick. I hope I remembered to thank you for that."

"I know you'd have done the same for me. As Bill keeps telling us, we are family here, and we watch out for each other."

"It sure feels like family, so much better than anywhere else I've worked. But I have a lot of thinking to do, so I may as well take the watch and let you get some sleep."

"If you're sure you're okay, that's great. I told Adam I'd wake him at five, and then asked him to wake me at seven. The ship chandler's truck is due here around eight. Is your thinking about anything serious? I don't want to be nosy, just worried about you."

"It's actually about this evening with Adam. Thank you for sending us out together. We talked about our screwed-up lives and started to realize we both think the same on most serious subjects, including relationships. We danced around the gorilla in the room, but I know I want to get to know Adam better, and I think he feels the same. Neither one of us was brave enough to say so, but I'm sure it became obvious to Adam, just like it did to me. At least five times tonight, Adam said he was so afraid that I could have died today, and each time, I saw tears come to his eyes."

"I understand screwed-up lives. Someday I'll have to tell you about Lois and me. Adam is one of those great guys, from what I can tell. He is serious and caring, and I would suspect he's very loyal. He's probably afraid of being rejected. I think you need to tell him how you feel and ask him if he feels the same. I know there's not much privacy on a tug for those conversations, but I was going to have you stand watch on the bridge tomorrow, while I work with the deckhands. I'll ask Adam to spend the time between his engine room rounds, keeping an eye on you up on the bridge."

"I told you, Curt. I'm really okay."

"I believe you, but let me get you two some private time, so you can talk. Okay?"

"You'd do that? You don't have to. You're my boss on this tug."

"Remember, it's family here. Let's just say I'm a concerned older brother right now. I just hope it works out well, or the rest of this trip will be really tense if you two don't work this out."

"Thanks, Curt. You go hit the sack, so I can start thinking about how I can get into that conversation. I'll keep an eye on the generator in the engine room, wake up Adam at five, and tell him to wake you up at seven. Anything else?"

"Just try to get some sleep after Adam takes the watch. I'll wake you up when I need to be out on deck, rigging the new towline. You need to be sharp for this conversation you're planning."

Ashley laughed at me, and playfully slapped me on my arm, saying, "Get up to your cabin, big brother."

———

The following day went as planned. I told Adam I was still concerned that Ashley could suffer some residual effects from her being chilled by that cold Lake Superior water, and would he mind spending his free time in the wheelhouse with Ashley, between rounds through the engine room. He seemed to buy into that idea quickly.

Our new deckhand, Tim, showed up around seven-thirty, and I was glad to see he was an experienced tugboater, about age-45, with most of his time spent on the Lakes, towing barges. With his help, three of us had the barges rigged to the tow in a few hours, and the weather looked like it would be ready for us to depart the next morning. Tim saw my hesitancy about towing out through the Waterway, but he assured me, he could help with the transit, having done it over a hundred times.

I went back aboard the tug and found Adam in the galley, cooking up a batch of chili.

"I didn't know you were a chef. When did you start cooking?" I asked him.

"Ashley only had some toast and coffee for breakfast, so I told her she needed a good meal. I made enough for all of us. I hope you don't mind," Adam replied.

"On the contrary, I was just going to slap together a

sandwich," I told him. "When will it be ready?"

"It's ready now. I was just about to take a bowl up to Ashley. Help yourself."

I walked over to the pot and dished a spoonful of chili into one of the bowls. "So, Adam, does Ashley seem to be okay after her experience yesterday?" I asked.

Adam smiled faintly. "She says she's fine. But if it's alright with you, I'll continue to keep an eye on her."

"I think that's a good idea. I'm worried about her as well. I'm glad you don't mind looking out for her."

Adam took the bowl of chili and headed to the wheelhouse. I saw the pleasant smile on his face as he walked away, and I knew their conversation had gone well. Later that day, when Ashley came through the galley, I saw a similar smile on her face as she nodded at me. I was darn curious, but it was none of my business.

AUTHOR'S NOTE

As stated at the end of my other novels, "Romance Novels" always seem to be written about the rich boss seducing his innocent yet willing secretary, or the college sports hero seducing the cheerleader. Even Navy Seals or lonesome cowboys seem to be popular these days. If you have read my previous novels, <u>A Tugboater's Life</u>, and <u>The Tugboater Family</u>, maybe I have now convinced you that *real* people are not only worth reading about, but they have fantastic love lives as well.

Real people survive tragedies in their lives and struggle to find meaningful love. They experience dangerous situations and support those around them.

While my stories are fiction, many of the characters are based on the lives of my real friends and acquaintances (both good and bad), as well as many personal experiences from my maritime career.

I have more stories that need telling, and they are already in process. I hope my readers will continue to enjoy my *real* people in my *Blue-Collar Romances*.

ABOUT THE AUTHOR

Bob Ojala earned a BSE in Naval Architecture and Marine Engineering from the University of Michigan, longer ago than he wishes to admit. He spent four years in the U.S. Coast Guard, seventeen years with the American Bureau of Shipping, and seven and a half years with the U.S. Army Corps of Engineers. He also worked in his own business (including the time while with the USACE) for over thirty years and is still active in marine surveying.

Bob's father was a merchant mariner for thirty-two years, which is where Bob gained his interest in the maritime industry. Although Bob always found life in the maritime industry exciting, he never wanted to become a sailor. Instead, he worked as a Naval Architect, designing small passenger vessels, tugs, and barges after graduation from college. With time, he found that he enjoyed working in the shipyard with the workers better than sitting in the design office, so when the opportunity came to join the American Bureau of Shipping, working as a field surveyor, inspecting ships, and the materials and equipment going into shipbuilding, Bob jumped at the opportunity.

Eventually, Bob started his own marine surveying and consulting business. Because Great Lakes clients were slow in changing loyalties, he traveled the world, surveying cruise ships, tankers, dry docks, and even some warships. He also investigated accidents, pollution incidents, and several accidental deaths.

Bob has written several non-fiction books about Marine Surveying, including *Sweetwater Sailors,* a pictorial history book with first-hand stories from sailors, describing the lives of the various kinds of Great Lakes sailors. Bob has worked with many men and women in the maritime business, whom he respected for their serious lifestyle. Writing about them in fiction, changing names where appropriate, was his way of honoring them.

With his background, Bob feels that he can describe the life of these merchant mariners and show the reader how exciting and dangerous their careers are, and also how important these people are for the country. He hopes readers enjoy the stories, many based upon actual events. More stories are on the way, including more Bob Evers stories about the crew members on those ocean cruise ships, where Bob (the author) worked during 165 cruises (Really! It was tough and eye opening!).

Bob and his wife of 35-years had six children together, and lived in Oak Park, Illinois. Bob is a Wisconsin native with Finnish roots.

Made in United States
North Haven, CT
07 November 2023

43713378R00150